The Duesenberg Caper

A vacation in Sicily turns deadly when young schoolteachers Andrew and his wife Ada find themselves commissioned to solve one of the oldest mysteries in the car world. The whereabouts of the priceless 1935 Duesenberg SJ Emmanuel owned by King Victor Emmanuel of Italy has been concealed for decades. Hot on its trail, Andrew and Ada are drawn into a world of high-stakes intrigue. Following the clues along a path of potential landmines in a desperate attempt to survive against overwhelming odds, they become immersed in the dangerous landscape of Sicily's mafia.

In a land of high rollers where the money flows, Andrew and the feisty Ada must contend with a series of riddles, perilous complications, and the most notorious crime boss in Sicily.

Classic car enthusiasts rejoice—*The Duesenberg Caper* is lush with the rarest and costliest cars money can't buy. Roger Corea delves into a wealth of loving detail only a true aficionado could deliver. Following in an opulent parade of the world's most valuable cars, Corea's riveting page-turner speeds by, reaching a spellbinding climax at the Autodromo di Pergusa with a vintage car race, Concours d'Elegance, and a classic car auction that will change the face of organized crime in Sicily.

Shrouded in enigma, the intoxicating Sicilian countryside is a catalyst for this electrifying thriller to unfold. As the hair-raising plot untwists, *The Duesenberg Caper* turns a one-eighty, revealing a momentous conclusion.

Advance Praise for The Duesenberg Caper

"Take Duesenbergs, Ferraris, Jaguars, Mercers, Alfa Romeos and more. Mix them into a thrill-driven tale that includes high-stake auctions, races, and elegant concours. The result is a book that you'll need to buckle your seatbelt before you start to read, and you won't be able to unbuckle until you've finished."

Keith Martin, Publisher, Sports Car Market Magazine

D1359436

Roger Corea has authored an exciting novel of adventure and intrigue featuring some of the greatest classic cars every made set in one of the most beautiful countries of the world. This exciting story lives up to the saying, "IT'S A REAL DUESEY."

Joel E. Givner, 2015 President, Auburn Cord Duesenberg Club

"There is nothing that suits my heart more than a story about a lost Duesenberg!"

Randy Ema, Duesenberg Restoration Specialist

"What a thrill to read! Hilarious yet scary enough to keep you reading—and the ending will knock you on your butt."

Vivian Probst, author of *Death by Roses*

"I was impressed with the accurate descriptions of the automobiles. The SJ Duesenberg specs were accurate as were the specs on the other autos described in the 'dream collection.'"

Skip Marketti, Chief Curator, The Nethercutt Collection

"These automobiles are the epitome of beauty, design, class and craftsmanship. Bringing them together in a tale of mystery and intrigue brings them to life!"

Laura Brinkman, Executive Director/CEO, Auburn Cord Duesenberg Museum

"The Duesenberg Caper is a riveting thriller. With classic cars as a life long passion, I became completely immersed in the drama as two young schoolteachers search the Sicilian countryside for King Victor Emmanuel's lost Duesenberg SJ and become targets of the Sicilian mob. Believe me! You will love the characters and you will love the story!"

Robert Pass, avid classic car collector

"I've been a collector car enthusiast for over 25 years. I cannot remember when I've read a more exciting novel as well as learning so much about the most valuable cars in the world. I guarantee it—you will be rocked by this novel!"

Frank Mazzarella, avid classic car collector

"A thrilling provocative novel which captured my fascination from start to finish and I was caught completely off guard by the incredible ending. Having been an antiques collector for several years, I am now a vintage automobile aficionado— thanks to this novel!"

Richard Rice, avid classic car collector

"I found *The Duesenberg Caper* to be so thoroughly enjoyable that I finished the nearly 300-page pre-release copy of the book in less than 24 hours. It was a journey, away from the crazy world in which we currently live, to a place where the 'good guys' let me close the cover after reading the last page, with a smile on my face.

Robert Tobin, avid classic car collector

The Duesenberg Caper

A Novel by

R O G E R   C O R E A

SelectBooks, Inc.
New York

By the Same Author
Scarback: There Is So Much More to Fishing Than Catching Fish

This edition published by SelectBooks, Inc.
For information address SelectBooks, Inc., New York, New York.

First Edition

ISBN 978-1-59079-310-7

Library of Congress Cataloging-in-Publication Data

Corea, Roger.
  The Duesenberg caper : a novel / Roger Corea. – First edition.
      pages cm
  Summary: "A vacation in beautiful Sicily turns deadly when young
schoolteachers Andrew Robinson and his wife, Ada, find themselves
commissioned to solve one of the oldest mysteries in the classic car
world–the whereabouts of the priceless 1935 Duesenberg SJ Emmanuel,
formerly owned by King Victor Emmanuel of Italy, that has been missing for
decades"– Provided by publisher.
  ISBN 978-1-59079-310-7 (pbk. book : alk. paper) 1.
Vacations–Italy–Fiction. 2. Antique and classic cars–Fiction. 3.
Duesenberg automobile–Fiction. I. Title.
  PS3603.O73428D84 2015
  813'.6–dc23

                              2015004386

Frontispiece illustration of Duesenberg Model J car: Carolyn Swan, © Unlisted Images/
Fotosearch.com

Manufactured in the United States of America

10 9 8 7 6 5 4 3 2 1

Acknowledgments

This book would not be possible without the support and encouragement of my family: my wife, Mary Ann, and Christopher and Janine, Katie and Frank, Marc and Sarah, and my grandchildren Nicholas, Christina, and Luca. I am grateful to my sister, Janice, her partner Joe, my brothers-in-law, Mike DelPlato and Jim Austin, and my sisters-in-law, Kathy Austin and Ann DelPlato. I am grateful to Sarah and Marc Corea, Kathy and Jim Austin, Joyce Austin, Mike DelPlato, Dave and Nina Corea, and Bob and Jo Tobin for reading the early manuscript and providing valuable feedback and encouragement; and I'm grateful to Dorie Jennings and Dick Rice for spending countless hours on the later manuscript. Thank you also to my godson, Andrew Ward, for his interesting observations during his two-year stay in Italy, and Frank Mezzatesta for his assistance with the Italian language.

My words of gratitude extend to Kenzi Sugihara, publisher and founder of SelectBooks, Inc. of New York, for his willingness to publish *The Duesenberg Caper*; Kenichi Sugihara for his marketing work on the book, and Nancy Sugihara for her insightful final edits and outstanding teamwork. Thank you to Tom Cotter, best-selling author and fellow classic-car collector aficionado, for writing the foreword and Kevin Simonson, a truly gifted illustrator, for his creative cover design.

One of my most meaningful experiences has been to spend time with Steve Eisner and Jon Reisfeld at *When Words Count Retreat* in Vermont. Thank you both for your wise counsel, encouragement, and increasing my motivation to write.

Finally, I want to recognize and thank all my car guy buddies, past and present: Marc Corea of Motorcartrader.com, Mike DelPlato, Jim Austin, Dave Corea, Frank Mazzarella, the late great John Alexanderson, Craig Everhart, Jerry Mayo, Howard Sharp, Richard Cina, Paul Gluck, Jerry Condello, Mark Gibson, Warren and Scott Riter, and Clark Rittersbach I and II, the Duesenberg experts from Macedon, New York. —Thanks for all the wonderful memories!

I dedicate this novel to my wife,

Mary Ann

Hours fly,
Flowers die
New days,
New ways,
Pass by.
Love stays.

Henry Van Dyke

Contents

Strive for perfection in everything.
Take the best that exists and make it better.
If it doesn't exist, create it.
Accept nothing nearly right or good enough.

Sir Henry Royce
Co-Founder of Rolls Royce

Foreword

By Tom Cotter

As baby boomers see their children graduate from college, their mortgages discharged, and their discretionary incomes escalate, the thought of owning the cars of their dreams becomes realistic. Thus, in recent years, the classic car hobby has grown exponentially, spawning vintage car races, classic car auctions, and Concours d'Elegance events all over the world. Yet, prior to all these activities, the cars must be tracked down. I call it automotive archaeology: the art of finding and refurbishing long-forgotten automotive treasures. Discovering unusual and desirable cars all over the world—from barns to junkyards to old warehouses—has been the theme of seven of my books, so obviously I find the subject extremely fascinating.

This is also why I find Roger Corea's novel, *The Duesenberg Caper,* so engaging. A thriller for sure, it is about the unexpected discovery of the long lost and priceless 1935 Duesenberg SJ Emmanuel owned by King Victor Emmanuel of Italy, and the high-stakes intrigue that ensues with its unearthing. Roger's narrative is descriptive; I too could imagine myself being on vacation in Taormina, Sicily, and (much to my wife's chagrin) receiving a lead to the whereabouts of the most valuable car in the world. I could imagine myself with the book's characters, young schoolteachers—Andrew P. "Punt"

Robinson III and his new wife Ada—pursuing the lead as they become unwittingly involved in the Italian government's scheme to locate and seize the car.

While I loved the adventure Roger wove into his story, thirty-two legendary classic cars played a role in the action as well, including a 1910 Mercer Raceabout, a 1933 Alfa Romeo Spider, a 1957 Ferrari Testa Rossa, and a 1956 Jaguar XKSS similar to actor Steve McQueen's "Green Rat." As opposed to Clive Cussler's Dirk Pitt novels, where interesting cars are mentioned and sprinkled into the storyline, Roger makes these automobiles the stars! Add the beautiful Sicilian countryside as the setting, and you have a most exciting novel.

I should note that many fiction books have been written about classic cars, often unsuccessfully. This is the first fiction automotive book since the Henry Gregor Felsen books of my youth where non-fiction facts are woven into Roger's intriguing prose.

Forget about reading *The Duesenberg Caper* one chapter each night; you'll be up until sunrise to finish it!

A former contributor to Road & Track *and* The New York Times, *Tom Cotter is the author of twelve bestselling automotive books, including seven about automotive archeology, such as* The Cobra in the Barn *and* The Corvette in the Barn. *His most recent book,* 50 Shades of Rust: Barn Finds You Wish You'd Discovered, *is already a best seller. He also is the co-author of an award-winning history of the legendary race team Holman-Moody. Before focusing on writing, Cotter built one of the most successful PR agencies in motorsports with clients in NASCAR, Formula One, Indycar, road racing, drag racing, and motorcycle racing. He formerly served as co-chairman of the Amelia Island Concours d'Elegance and lives in Davidson, North Carolina.*

The 1910 Mercer Raceabout

The thirty-foot-high overhead booms swivel like gantry cranes over the broad assemblage of wealthy car collectors. Their intrusive television cameras ascend, descend, and circle the amphitheater as if they are systematically slicing and dicing a large ham. At first, they focus on the glistening objects lined up on the floor near the stage, then on bidders struggling to obtain front row seats. Now their giant, unforgiving lenses converge on me, and I've never been a fan of the spotlight.

Then the announcer booms: "Andrew Robinson, owner of one of the most famous motorcars in the world, and son of the celebrated Supreme Court Justice by the same name, will record here today, at the world famous Noble-Dean Auction, the highest price ever paid for a pre-war brass racecar!" At least the announcer calls me by my correct name. For years he has referred to me as Eben Cruise, a moniker I shed decades ago.

It is October of 2006. Classic car collectors from all over the world gather here at the Hershey Park Giant Center. They come prepared to spend millions, even if the price of the car on which they are bidding exceeds its market value. They are predominantly middle-aged men and women, successful entrepreneurs, who now can afford the cars they once longed for in their youth. They are people well known for their astute business judgment, people the *Wall Street Journal* and *Barron's* write about. Yet these icons of American business become weak-kneed and wide-eyed when bidding on classic cars. Somehow, at classic car auctions, the acuity that enabled them to build Fortune 500 companies from the ground up plummets like the price of an over-inflated penny stock. For them, the true market value of a classic car is irrelevant. What truly matters is the conquest. What matters most is winning!

Amid the servers plying bidders with a vast selection of cocktails, men in black tuxedos tender trays of hors d'oeuvres to the anxious crowd. I prefer the old-fashioned method: leaning on a bar to the left of the stage, stealing olives from the trays, and kibitzing with the bartender. Chivas Regal, or *courage on the rocks* as I call it, is my special nutriment during classic car auctions.

On the rocks has another unintended connotation for some overzealous bidders, the ones having neither the bankroll nor the credit line to participate legitimately. I call it blind passion or asset infatuation. This is the other side of the "car collector coin." It is easy to get caught up in a bidding frenzy, even if one doesn't have the financial wherewithal to play the game. And, make no mistake. This *is* a game.

I watch my yellow 1910 Type-35R Mercer Raceabout Speedster move stubbornly up the auction ramp. Her new 32-inch white tires give her a spiffy appearance, like she is dressed for the Pebble Beach Concours d'Elegance instead of the hard-hearted auction block. Her white spare tires, tied together by a black leather belt, are slanted behind her 25-gallon gas tank. Two prominent shiny brass filler caps rest on top of the tank, adding to the brass flavor of the era. Rakish fenders connected by short running boards provide a fast, streamlined appearance, even though the flat brass radiator is anything but streamlined. It is simply an exquisite automobile that became popular in the early 1900s, when America first started to flex its racing muscle.

Then she ruins everything and backfires. *Old gas*, I think. I haven't driven her in several months. I should have drained the tank. I just hated to poison her with unleaded gas even with the special additives. Now she is just being sassy, knowing this will be our last day together.

The frustrated driver waves me over. "Take her, will you please?" he asks. "I'm nervous as hell!"

I position myself on her low mounted driver's side-bucket seat, so low I have to stretch to reach the stirring wheel. How many times have I sat in this position, looking through her bolt-on monocle windshield and seeing her large Rushmore kerosene-fired brass headlamp on top of the hood? *What an unusual place for a headlamp.* I have to tilt my head to the right or left just to see the road ahead. It is crazy, yet all part of the car's special mystique.

By all measures, the Raceabout is a functionally rugged machine. I used to drive her to the high school where I taught English, and on every Labor Day weekend I raced her at the Vintage Races at Watkins Glen, the well-known racetrack in the heart of the Finger Lakes. Ada, my wife of thirty-three years, a history teacher at the same school, finally moved my first-place trophies to my back garage, or as my friends call it, my man-cave. Spending time there with my car buddies, working on our cars together, is just about the closest thing to Nirvana I could ever hope to achieve on this Earth.

We also loved to compete with the Raceabout. While my buddies would serve as my pit crew, Ada would sit in the passenger seat shouting out directions. Most of the time I couldn't hear her. The unmuffled three-inch exhaust pipe would have made an effective elephant call, had we been on a safari instead of a racetrack. With the wind rushing down our throats and up our nostrils, with the ground slipping under us at an incredible pace, and with the 58-horsepower engine catapulting us around the track at more than 70 miles per hour, it was truly an exhilarating experience!

The Raceabout's provenance is impeccable. She is the third Raceabout built by Washington Roebling, the builder of the Brooklyn Bridge. Sadly, he perished on the Titanic in 1912. My grandfather purchased the Raceabout from the Roebling family when I was fifteen years old. He willed the car to me when he died, knowing how much I enjoyed taking care of her. She was a perennial Best of Show winner at all the local car events around Fairchester, a small upstate New York community where we have lived and raised our three daughters. Last year at the Amelia Island Concours d'Elegance, the Raceabout won Best of Class, an honor that will surely add value to its already respectable price tag.

So why am I selling her? Ada and I are both sixty-three and will retire from our teaching positions next year. I don't want to sell her, but our goal has always been to purchase a vacation home in Taormina, Sicily, where, thirty years ago, we experienced the adventure of our lives. We were on a mission to locate the most valuable classic car in the world, a 1935 Duesenberg SJ formerly owned by King Victor Emmanuel of Italy. It had been missing since the end of World War II.

Although small-town high school teachers like Ada and me were not your typical soldiers of fortune, we became deeply involved in a high-stakes contest to locate the car they called the Midnight Ghost. We are fortunate, after our harrowing escapades in Sicily, to be alive today to tell the story.

An auction official motions to move the Raceabout to center stage. With delicate precision, I press down on the accelerator pedal. Her engine moans with delight, as she rolls forward. She is being brave, but I know, deep down, thoughts of betrayal unsettle her proud spirit.

Behind the red-velvet-draped podium, a haughty auctioneer, in a perfectly tailored black tuxedo with shiny lapels and a bright-red silken bow tie, looks more like a groomsman than a car salesman. Malcolm Carlisle, the renowned British auctioneer, full of himself as usual, is ready to inveigle fortunes from overanxious buyers.

Once the auction begins, the intoxicating fervor will make even the most ardent non-buyer collapse into a buying frenzy. After it's over, Carlisle will ceremoniously donate his bright-red boutonniere to one of his favorite mega-rich female bidders. That act alone, for her, will be worth the price she will pay for a car. I used to laugh at him, accepting his extravagance with a grain of salt. Today, I hate his pomposity. I loathe the awful finality of his words, and I detest this auction process. The fate of my Raceabout has come down to a five-dollar wooden gavel in the hands of some fast-talking auctioneer. I feel sick to my stomach.

The auditorium clatter recedes to a quiet drone. All eyes focus on the stage, as two thousand of the world's most affluent classic car collectors erupt into thunderous applause. Carlisle's posh British accent fills the room. You'd swear he was getting ready to announce the grand entrance of the Queen of England. "Here, ladies and gentlemen, we have a 1910 Type-35R Mercer Raceabout Speedster, arguably the first American sports car, and one of the most extraordinary and most coveted motorcars in the world!"

With the adrenalin surging through my veins, I feel like my blood is on fire. Filled with anxiety and doubt, I realize I have violated a sacred trust. *Maybe I should call the whole thing off. I could easily drive down the exit ramp, be on the highway in a matter of minutes, and be home in a few hours, where I could pamper and polish her every day. What could be nobler than dedicating the rest of my life to caring for one of the most legendary automobiles in the world?*

It doesn't matter. At this point, second-guessing is foolish. Carlisle is in control now. In five minutes, the Raceabout will belong to someone else. I begin to wonder how much the new owner will have to pay. And, of course, we still have the Silver Arrow, the 1937 Mercedes W 125. We can always race that car at the Glen. It has 600 horsepower! We would *never* sell it, even though it is a replica, not after it saved our lives when we were searching for the king's Duesenberg. Gradually, my uneasiness dissipates. My conscience clears, and I no longer feel sick to my stomach. I look at Carlisle, hesitate for a moment, and nod.

"Let the auction begin!" Chalk up another victory for pragmatism!

From the front row, my misty-eyed wife smiles. I knew selling the car would make her very happy, especially if it would get us back to Taormina. I am grateful she could be with me.

"C'mon now, ladies and gentlemen, don't be shy. Do I hear five-hundred thousand dollars?"

ONE

The 1949 Green Latrine

My fascination with the automobile began at age seven in 1950, when a new Nash Ambassador graced the Robinson household. The large bulbous "super Bertha" look, as my father called it, received a lukewarm reception by the automotive public. Made by the Kelvinator Corporation, the same company that made refrigerators, it shared many similar features. But for me, it was an object of beauty—rolling exhilaration, perfection on wheels. Why not? It fulfilled all my requirements for automotive idolatry: a motor, four tires, and a steering wheel.

Still, this car was innovative. Not only did the seats turn into beds. The blinking red light on the turn signal lever was so bright that in the evening the car looked like a rolling bordello, certainly not the outcome intended by Kelvinator. The next year they retained the beds, even adding pillows, but thankfully eliminated the red light.

As a teenager I was obsessed with cars, unable to wait until I was old enough to drive and earn money to own one. That day arrived sooner than I expected. It was 1958. At fifteen, amid the odor of cigar and cigarette smoke, stale beer, and a group of misguided teenage boys; I was playing a hot game of eight ball at Eli's Pool Emporium. Nino "Torpedo" Fidanza just ran the rack on me.

"Hey, Punt," he said. "One more, okay?"

Everyone called me "Punt" in high school, and concession was my typical reaction. I hated that nickname, but never found a way to completely get rid of it. It sounded like retreat to me, and bothered me the way certain things rattle self-conscious teenagers who are afraid of being bullied. I almost asked the football coach to change my position, but that would have been detrimental to the team because I really was a good punter. And since the fullback's "handle" was "Fumbles," I figured I shouldn't complain.

When I thought about it, at 5′8″, standing on my toes with my sneakers on, and 130 pounds, I was lucky to be on the team at all. What's more, my birth certificate read Andrew P. Robinson III and my family called me "Three Sticks." I got to wondering one day— what was so terribly wrong with the name Andrew or Andy?

"Okay, Torpedo, rack 'em up," I said mildly.

"What are we playin' for, *Punter*?" Torpedo asked.

"One dime. Cost of the rack?" I was looking for consensus. There was none.

"Hey Eli," Torpedo yelled, "Anyone here who ain't chicken? The Punter here—he's wimpin' out on me again. Some rich kid with no guts!"

"I'm no chicken," I said with the resolve of a wet sponge. It was a feeble remark, one that I couldn't substantiate until later in life. Most of the time, I sat in the corner and watched everyone else bet, wishing I had the backbone to participate.

Eli Palimeri, owner of the pool hall, watched dimes being flipped on tables like white chips in a poker game. A tall, thin seventy-year-old man, Eli wore white shirts with red sleeve garters, dark suspenders, and a black visor that came down over his glasses, making him appear more like a bean counter than a pool shark. His generous crop of shiny jet-black hair, combed back with liberal portions of hair tonic, and mostly concealed by the black visor, was too perfect to be real.

Several years later, at Eli's funeral, as I prayed over his open casket, I could see where the glue from his hairpiece was attached to his forehead. *Too bad,* I thought. After all those years of skillful concealment, his secret had to be revealed by some inept mortician who couldn't care less about Eli's enduring secret.

The pool tables were deceptive. The regulars knew they were tilted with matchbooks, rigged with the famous "Eli slant." Few people understood the roll off. Eli taught me how to read the tables. He felt sorry for me and knew I needed an advantage. He was right.

"Punt," Eli said, "let me give you a couple pointers on the fine art of shooting pool."

Just about everyone in the place gathered around us. When Eli spoke, he drew a crowd. He liked to brag about beating Willie Mosconi at a USO tournament in Philadelphia during the war. In his day, Eli was one of the best.

"Go ahead, Eli," Torpedo taunted, "even show 'n tell ain't gonna get rid of *his* yellow streak! Why do you think we call 'em Punt?"

"Lay your hand flat then raise it a little to build a bridge for the cue stick," Eli instructed. "Get eye level with the table. I told you before—you're always too damn high! You can't see the line when you look down on everything. Keep your feet flat on the floor and don't use any of that fancy English stuff unless you have to. Always think at least two shots ahead for position. And, one more thing: Remember what I taught you about the roll."

Torpedo's face blistered with impatience as he stood with his legs crossed and his elbow propped on top of his cue stick. "Now that you had a free lesson from the master, how 'bout we play for that there Benrus on your wrist? That thing would look great on my wrist!" Torpedo smirked.

That was all I needed: losing the watch given to me by my grandfather as a Confirmation present to some guy named Torpedo in a pool game. That would be tantamount to the kiss of death. On second thought, forget the "kiss" part. My butt would get kicked all over Fairchester.

"C'mon, Punt!" someone yelled. "Show 'em your stuff!"

"Yeah, Punt, grow a couple!" someone else prodded.

"Tell you what," Torpedo said. "Your Benrus against my Green Latrine."

My eyebrows rose a couple inches. When I looked at Eli, he gave me a few quick affirmative nods and a tentative thumbs up sign. The Green Latrine? The 1949 Ford he "restored" with a paintbrush and roller had the most disgusting shade of olive-green house paint I had ever seen. Warped with rust, the fenders shook so much on the road, the car looked like a fluttering goose being chased by a hungry fox. But, oh those dual Hollywood mufflers! That sweetheart flathead V-8! It was a symphony of the most beautiful sounds in the world! Then again, what the hell would I do with the Green Latrine? I was only fifteen.

"Okay, who breaks?" I asked politely.

"Eli, flip a damn quarter!" Torpedo's sharp tongue annoyed me.

"Heads," I said.

"Tails!" Torpedo yelled.

"It's your break, Torpedo," Eli said.

Boy, did I ever get lucky. Torpedo sunk the eight ball on the opening break. The next day, he grudgingly delivered the car to Cosmo's Service Station, where I pumped gas during the summers. Fortunately, Cosmo allowed me to keep it there until old man Furman rented me his garage on West Avenue for five bucks a month.

My parents didn't know about the car until old man Furman called Officer Kryer. I was driving up and down the driveway too fast.

Not only did I destroy Furman's tomato plants, but also the neighbors called the police and complained about me disturbing the peace. My father had The Green Latrine picked up and delivered to the crusher at Sebastian Brother's junkyard. As inauspicious as it was, that was my official entry into the classic automobile market. There have been occasions, as an adult, when I wished I still had The Green Latrine.

People took great pleasure in telling me I was fortunate. The affluence in my family came the old-fashioned way; my parents earned every penny. My grandfather, Andrew P. Robinson I—the original "One Stick"—bought thousands of shares of Eastman Kodak stock in the early 1920s, making him very wealthy. Then he bought heavily on margin until he was wiped out on Black Tuesday. Yet, he was a survivor.

His investment wheel again churned prolifically in the 1930s, until he was able to build a fine classic car collection. The collection even outperformed the stock market during the 1950s, although it still didn't make up for the assets he lost during the Depression. He introduced me to my first classic car auction in Greenwich, Connecticut, just after I became a licensed driver. It was held at the Ferrari dealership owned by Luigi Chinetti, the famous Ferrari race-car driver. It was this auction, along with meeting Mr. Chinetti, that ignited my passion for European sports cars.

My grandfather, employed by Eastman Kodak his entire life, was responsible for the distribution of the T13 Beano Hand Grenade, manufactured by the company before World War II. Shaped like a baseball, the Beano was supposed to be easier to throw. His job, prior to the advent of World War II, was to sell the grenade to friendly governments around the world.

My father told me the story of how he miscalculated and sold them to the Italian government, believing they would be our allies if war broke out. My grandfather made several trips to Italy, mingling with the high command, only to be later ostracized by the military when many Italian soldiers were killed because of the Beano's propensity for premature detonation. "Better them than us," he would say, attempting to explain away his embarrassing gaffe.

For some unknown reason, despite my mother's vehement opposition, every Fourth of July, my grandfather would explode a few Beanos in the woods behind our house. She worried about their malfunction, fearing he might loose an arm, leg, or worse.

After his first two marriages failed, my grandfather vowed he would be a bachelor for the remainder of his life, attributing his matrimonial woes to extensive travel. Most people who knew him would contest that notion, preferring instead to ascribe his marital problems to a wandering eye and an overactive libido. My father, Andrew P. Robinson II, was his only child and never mentioned anything to me about his mother. I don't believe my father ever knew her true identity.

When I think of my grandfather, what stands out most is how he allowed me to take care of his classic cars at the storage facility where they resided. I polished them, checked their fluids, rearranged their positions in the garage, and pretended they belonged to me. I would sometimes take a spin around the block in one, always taking the long way back to the garage. The car I most admired was a 1910 Type-35R Mercer Raceabout Speedster. The Mercer Company was owned by Washington Roebling, the engineer who gained fame and fortune building the Brooklyn Bridge.

My grandfather's Mercer raced in the first Indianapolis 500. It went on to win several races, including the American Grand Prize held at Santa Monica, California. Its documented racing history made it extremely valuable.

One day Officer Kryer caught up with me—for the second time. This time, he turned out to be a reasonable man. As long as I allowed him to drive the Mercer, he promised not to tell my parents. How I wished he had wanted to drive the Green Latrine, too!

Until I was eighteen, we lived in the upscale community of Dansforth, in upstate New York. As the son of Andrew and Jennifer, I enjoyed all the benefits of being an only child with few deprivations. I attended the prestigious Dansforth High School but my parents never knew I spent most of my teenage years carousing in the pool halls and bars of Fairchester, a predominantly blue-collar railroad town. Newport Road, a busy four-lane highway, divided the two towns.

I became a member of one of those fraternities or "gangs," as my mother called them, whose members wore black and red jackets with nicknames sewn into the back collars. Collars up meant we were ready to rumble. With the gang, I was fearless, even heroic. When alone, I kept my collar down.

My ultimate claim to high-school fame rested on an athletic scholarship offer to play football at the University of Buffalo. One day, when we scrimmaged a high school from Pennsylvania, a hard-charging linebacker named Jack Ham hit me so hard he crushed my dream of college football glory. I suppose it was a blessing since that knee injury allowed me to focus on my studies.

My parents? Well, my father became a famous judge. He breezed through law school with honors and garnered national attention as president of the Harvard Law Review.

It was often mentioned that he opposed the War Powers Act of 1941, passed after the attack on Pearl Harbor to give greater power to the executive branch of our government to execute World Ward II, believing that neither President Roosevelt nor any other president should have unilateral power over the military.

After his own military service in World War II, my father practiced law in Dansforth, even though he yearned to return to the Harvard classroom. During this period in his life, he wrote several books on constitutional law.

When I was a freshman in college, he applied for and received a professorship at Harvard. Later, as one of the premier authorities in the country on constitutional law, he was appointed to the Permanent Subcommittee on Investigations (PSI), chaired by Senator John McClellan, and worked with the committee that changed the face of organized crime in America.

Before we moved to Cambridge and later to Washington, DC, my mother was an English professor at the University of Dansforth. She was a popular and effective teacher and a good wife and mother.

In June 1968, after my undergraduate study, I entered the University of Buffalo Law School, a feat downplayed by my father, who preferred the more elite law schools of the northeast. Although our relationship was never disagreeable, I knew Andrew P. Robinson II was disappointed.

While he was never one to express his opinions, I learned to read his body language, which frequently signaled his displeasure with me. I wish my father had asserted himself more directly. His unexpressed wants were obvious to me, especially as I became older. They created a distance between us and adversely affected my self-confidence, especially when I held him in such high esteem.

I dropped out of law school after the Kent State shootings in 1970. My parents were livid, but I felt angry and betrayed by President Nixon. As a popular figure in Nixon's administration, my father was embarrassed and disappointed. It was about the time he was lauded by Senator McClellan for his work on the Racketeer

Influenced and Corrupt Organizations Act (RICO). Crime syndicate bosses could now be tried for crimes they ordered others to commit. It closed loopholes that crime bosses used to evade prosecution, and it was the most devastating legislation against organized crime ever enacted.

The most controversial element of RICO was that it gave law enforcement agencies the power to seize assets, even before a conviction was rendered. In many instances, the FBI confiscated land, homes, and businesses. This, of course, greatly angered Mafia chieftains, as it shut down their operations.

An unfortunate outcome of my father's success was his near-celebrity status, especially after *Time* magazine did a cover story on him. I had nightmares he would be killed, loathed as he was by crime families.

During this period in my life, I was busy protesting the Kent State Shootings and President Nixon's incursion into Cambodia and was one of 100,000 dissidents who converged on Washington in May of 1970. Ironically, I was a member of the delegation that met with Nixon at the Lincoln Memorial. He knew who I was and called me by name, which angered many of my fellow protestors. After subsequently reading excerpts from the Pentagon Papers, I wondered how my father could have been part of his administration.

Eventually, my father's stand on the War Powers Act of 1941 was reflected in the War Powers Act of 1973. I was proud of my father. I wished he could have said the same thing about me. But by this time, I was my own man and was living life on my terms.

TWO

Carpe Diem

In September of 1971, after a year of innocuous rebellion, I buckled down and secured a job at Fairchester High School as an English teacher. One of my college professors had urged me to select one of two career paths: teacher or author. I decided to teach. It was much safer, as I had little confidence in my command of the written word. I wanted to influence the younger generation and believed that teaching high school kids was a good way to accomplish this. I felt eager to pursue my objective and grateful that I had decided not to become a lawyer like my father. Soon I experienced a dramatic change in the direction of my life.

During orientation week I became attracted to Ada Rossi, the new history teacher. As we sat in the Curriculum Room, listening to the principal enlighten us on school policy, I could tell she was from the tough side of town.

"Could you explain the procedure when I'm forced to kick someone out of my class?" she asked.

The principal would always begin his answer with, "Our policy is . . ."

"What if my policy is inconsistent with your policy?" she asked. "Who wins?" The principal did a good job of sidestepping her question, but I'm sure he realized that crossing swords with her would be something to avoid in the future. When we reached the subject of lunchroom duty, Ada became more assertive. "I get paid to teach, not watch kids eat."

"All the teachers in the building share lunchroom duty," the principal responded. "It's school policy."

"How can I get the policy changed?" she asked.

"The school board and the administration approve or disapprove policy change recommendations by teacher committees."

"Oh, God! Death by committee!" she exclaimed. Everyone in the room cracked up, and Ada made her point. "I'd like to volunteer for that committee."

"I will be glad to submit your name for consideration," the principal said as he laughed.

Over the next few days, I was surprised how easy it was to get to know this spunky woman from Newark, New Jersey, especially considering our very different personalities and vastly different upbringing. I was completely taken by her vitality and zest for life. She seemed to be trying to make up for lost time, trying to recover something that had been stolen from her, and I wanted to learn all about her—her childhood, adolescence, and young adult years.

At 5′6″ and rather slender, Ada walked with a graceful stride. Her vibrant hazel eyes locked on mine like magnets when she spoke, and that was the extent of any control I had over her. Her short auburn hair was in a pixie cut, a popular hairstyle at the time. As I got to know her, the notion of the word "pixie" was completely out of character. She brushed her hair back, so she had an understated, sassy look. She could attract attention if she wanted to, but like so many other things about her, her beauty was subtle yet not aloof.

I loved her reaction when we were first introduced. I explained how my high school and college friends referred to me as "Punt" but that I preferred "Andrew" or "Andy." "I don't blame you," she said. It isn't at all flattering is it? Okay, then I'll call you, 'Andy.'

"Perfect." I said, grateful that at least from Ada, I wouldn't be hearing that annoying tag and all it inferred.

Despite being a beautiful woman, I was attracted to Ada Rossi for other reasons. There was mental telepathy between us—an unspoken understanding that we would find each other in a crowd, no matter where we were. From the beginning, our relationship moved forward swiftly. When not in the classroom, we were together. Not long after the school year began, we went out for dinner. I decided to probe more deeply into her upbringing.

"We never had money," she admitted. "My father emigrated from Taranto, Italy. His father pulled him out of grade school when he was in the fourth grade and made him work in a steel mill where the environmental contamination was the worst in Europe. I remember my father coughing and wheezing all the time. When he came to America, at first things were good. He worked as a stevedore at Port Newark. Have you ever heard of the First Ward in Newark, Andy?"

"Used to be Little Italy, right?"

"That's right, Little Italy. After I was born, we had a reasonably good life there for a number of years . . . until we had to move into a small apartment on 17th Avenue. Among my father's many addictions was an obsession with the horses. He would leave work early, take the subway to Aqueduct, and gamble away his paychecks, then come home inebriated and fight with my mother. I can still hear their vicious arguments.

And Andy, I cannot believe how destitute we were, always accepting handouts, hand-me-downs, and money from family and friends. There was never enough food. My clothes were always tattered and torn. We lived in a ghetto, one of the most impoverished neighborhoods in the country and definitely one of the most violent. The riots broke out shortly after we moved there. Three of the people killed were close friends of mine. I was with them when they died." She hesitated. "It's still tough to talk about."

"Sorry," I said.

"We set up a triage center at a school gymnasium. I worked there for five days. That changed me."

"How?" I asked.

"I've thought about that. I knew I wasn't the same person, but for years I couldn't put it into words. Even though so many people were killed and injured, the riots were really about the living, about the people trying to define their lives. It was a desperate cry for help. To me, it was the saddest thing I had ever seen." Ada paused a few moments. "We should look at the menu." She placed her hand against her forehead and rubbed it back and forth as if she needed to snap out of a stupor. "I'm staying with the basics: turkey, mashed potatoes, and gravy." I reached across the table, gently placing my hand over hers. "I think I'll have a small salad, too," she said.

"Whatever your heart desires," I said obligingly. "Another Chardonnay?"

"Sure." She smiled warmly.

"The pasta puttanesca without the capers looks pretty good to me. Ada, do you want to tell me the rest of the story?" I asked.

"I don't want to bore you with the details. My childhood wasn't pretty."

"I'd like to know more, if you feel comfortable telling me." I treaded cautiously.

"When I was a teenager, my father was killed when a full cargo net fell on him. I still struggle with the memories. I was devastated." She dabbed her eyes with a tissue. "Even though he was irresponsible, I loved him very much. After he died, my life was empty for a long time." She was lost in her thoughts and it became obvious she didn't care to elaborate. "Can we change the subject, Andy? I'll tell you the rest another time, okay? It upsets me too much, and I'll ruin both of our dinners if I keep talking."

"That's fine, Ada," I said. My hand was still on hers, as she gently turned it and squeezed.

"Thanks for understanding," she said. "I don't like to talk about these things."

On the drive home, Ada was uneasy and preoccupied. I sensed she wanted to finish her story, but was reluctant to burden me with her family tragedies.

"What's wrong, Ada? Is there something you want to tell me?"

"My father wasn't really killed by a full cargo net. That was the official version—you know, the convenient version, the one you don't have to explain. He owed money. It seemed like he was always borrowing money from someone. This time, he borrowed from the wrong people. They ganged up on him and beat him to death.

The day after his death, four men came to our house demanding money from my mother. She eventually paid back the debt, working fourteen-hour days as a waitress. She worked in a grungy, dirty little hamburger place. My younger sister, Rina, quit school and went to work in an Atlantic City casino when she was fourteen years old. I lost track of her years ago. After my mother remarried and moved to California, I went to live with my aunt and uncle in Newark. I was sixteen when I got a job at Master Kiyoshi's Gym as a custodial assistant."

"That's the self-defense guru, right?"

"Yes, he was very good to me. I jumped at the chance to get into one of his Taekwondo self-defense programs. After I earned my Black Belt, guess what?

"You took on Bruce Lee?"

"Not quite. But I did become an instructor."

"Ada, that's impressive. I tried Taekwondo once and dropped out."

"It was a way to earn money for college," she continued. "I had six years to complete my undergraduate education. I had to work between semesters to earn enough money."

"I'll bet you graduated with honors."

"I learned, Punt, that bad things happen in life. I'm still petrified about being poor. Actually, it isn't the poverty that scares me so much. It's more about what people do to cope with their poverty. I had plenty of opportunities, or I should say, temptations. I chose hard work and college, but it wasn't easy."

☆　☆　☆

We spent Thanksgiving with Ada's aunt and uncle in Newark and Christmas with my family. On spring break, we hit the beach at Lauderdale, and then traveled up to Pensacola to visit a friend in flight school. We enjoyed being with other couples, although I enjoyed being alone with Ada much more.

But my constant need for reassurance that our romance was real was starting to annoy her. It seemed like a classic case of things appearing to be too good to be true. I began to understand it was her complete lack of dependence on me that made me feel insecure. While I knew Ada wanted to be with me, I also knew she didn't need me. And, even though I admired her independence and realized it was the reason for her survival in the ghetto, it bothered me that I couldn't be strong for her.

Just before the school year ended, Ada decided to change my appearance.

"I was looking at a picture of your father the other day," she said, "and you have the exact same receding hairline as he does."

"Exact? I doubt it," I said. "First of all, he has much less hair than me."

"He also has a few more wrinkles, but your resemblance to each other is pretty amazing." Ada grinned. "Admit it. You're getting a little sparse on top and on the sides, too. It looks like one side is racing the other side to your crown. Can you move some hair around? You know—a little camouflage, maybe?"

"I tried a 'comb-over' strategy."

"I know. It failed miserably," she said. "Time for a new look!"

I don't know why, but on June 17, 1972, the day of the Watergate break-in, I allowed Ada to work on my appearance with sharp scissors and a new Gillette Techmatic razor. "Just don't make me look like Nixon," I pleaded.

"'The times, they are a changin,'" she sang, as she clipped. "Now I won't mind being seen in public with you!"

Thanks to Ada's barbering, or should I say, barbaric skills, a clean, well-defined part on the right side with short sideburns replaced my chin curtain beard. A pair of bug-eye glasses that I didn't need magnified my dark brown eyes. Then, presto! Before I could say *The Love Song of J. Alfred Prufrock,* I was transformed into T.S. Eliot.

"Now you look erudite, the way an English teacher *should* look!" she said.

When I looked into a mirror, all I could see was my father glaring back at me. He was obviously much older, yet he had an incredibly young look. People were hard pressed to tell us apart, which presented a whole new list of challenges neither one of us needed.

One evening reporters mobbed us in a hotel lobby after Ada and I returned from a Broadway play in Manhattan. We escaped to our room, but the next day they were waiting by the elevators. Once they realized who I was, they still wanted to interview me, a request

I eventually learned how to evade. Ada enjoyed the spotlight, always encouraging me to lighten up and have fun with it. I'd play along for a while, and then I'd try to recapture my former identity when she wasn't looking. It didn't work. The scissors and the razor were always close at hand.

☆　　☆　　☆

The day the 1973 school year ended, as we walked to the parking lot, Ada asked, "So, tell me, what are you doing with yourself this summer?" It was a strange question. She was well aware of my summer plans.

"Painting houses," I said with minimal enthusiasm. "You have any better offers?"

"I'm going to Italy. I always wanted to tour the castles in Sicily," she replied. "I saved money this year and it's burning a hole in my purse."

"Thought you were teaching summer school."

"Changed my mind, Punter. Is that okay with you?"

"Well—sure . . . sounds like a good time. May I ask if you are going with someone?" I was just playing along with what I thought was idle chatter.

"Yes. You!" She smiled broadly. Caught completely off guard by her lightning answer, I had the good sense to provide a lightning response.

"When do we leave?" I asked.

"Tomorrow," she said. "I already purchased two plane tickets."

"You're kidding!"

"You can stay here and climb ladders all summer if you want, or you can be the man who accompanied Ada Rossi to Europe."

"Sicily, huh?" I pondered as I leaned on the top of the door.

"I remember you said your dad and grandfather spent time in Sicily during the war, so I thought you'd say yes rather easily." Of course Ada thought I would say yes. That's why she ordered the tickets without telling me. I would have said yes to a camel ride to Kabul just to be with her.

"I can already taste the *Prosecco*!" I said joyfully. She hopped in the front seat, and we drove off, eagerly anticipating our new adventure together. We left the next morning from JFK on Alitalia Airlines.

☆　　☆　　☆

Ada had a roguish grin on her face all the way to Italy. I could tell something was up. While I thought we were headed for Rome, and then south to Sicily, we suddenly landed at Marco Polo Airport in Venice. Before I could say "Casanova," she had me on the Grand Canal happily ensconced in the back of a gondola drinking fine *Veneto Bardolino* as the gondolier sang everything from "That's Amore" to "La Solitudine."

"You can keese her under the Breedge of Sighs," the gondolier said with a happy face. "I inseest! Keese-a you *bella signora!* C'mon! Keese her now!"

"Why do you *insist?*" Ada asked, always the contrarian.

"You Americani—I teach-a you everyting! Leesen to Peepee! You keese on a gondola at a sun-a-set under the Breedge of Sighs, and you be in a love fereve!"

"In love fereve? Oh, that sounds like fun!"

I couldn't tell if Ada was being romantic or just her pedantic self. I liked Peepee's instructions so much, I really didn't care! By now, a cloudy orange sunset saturated St. Mark's Basilica with a warm pinkish glow. Finally, we kissed. At first, it was abbreviated.

Then it became more passionate, more heartfelt, like one of those "fereve a keeses" that comes with a bear hug and soft whispers. When Peepee broke out in "Al Di la," I was on a different planet. I buried my face in her shoulder, feeling elevated to a new level of euphoria.

Suddenly she pulled away. "Hey, Andrew Robinson," she asked, "How the hell do we explain this to the kids?"

"I was waiting for an 'I love you' and not thinking about our students!"

She hesitated then giggled. "No, Andy. *Our kids.* How are we going to explain to *our kids* that *you* proposed to *me* on some canal in Italy." As usual, Ada was way ahead of me, putting words into my mouth and life into my words. Actually, I had intended to propose on this trip. Was she doing the job for me?

"Marry *you*? I assume that is what you are asking. Am I correct in that assumption?"

"Yes," she said, "your assumption would be accurate."

"Now, why would I want to do such a thing?"

"Because you love me to death. You can't live without me. You idolize me. You . . . I could keep going; I'm sure you've got the picture by now."

I squeezed her, kissing every inch of her face until she dropped her head backward to catch her breath. "I adore you," I said softly.

"Well of course you do," she laughed. "Why else would you be in this silly boat with me and Peepee?"

It was naïve of me to expect a reciprocal response. Despite her banter, Ada made me feel strong. With most women, my guard was always up, but with Ada, I was comfortable with my vulnerability. For the first time in my life, I liked myself for who I really was, and not someone I thought I needed to be. Although suspense was a large part of our relationship, I knew she loved me.

After our gondola adventure, Ada commandeered a waterbus to Cantinone Storico, a canal side ristorante in Dorsoduro, the quieter section of Venice. We were immediately seated on the terrace side overlooking the canal. I remember the shiny ribbons of red, white, and blue light reflecting on the canal surface in the darkness, a gentle breeze, and most of all, our uninhibited closeness. We were completely at ease, the two of us, suddenly entwined in a common destiny.

"Best *Prosecco* I've ever had," she said.

"It's the bubbles," I said. "They jump right out at you."

She started to read the menu.

"What are we having for dinner?" she asked.

"Dinner? Oh, yes. We are here for dinner, aren't we?"

"You know, she replied, it really is a beautiful night. I really love the atmosphere of this place."

She leaned over and kissed me, softly and tenderly, without pressing too hard. It was a special moment, like some powerful narcotic invaded my body. *Was it really possible this wonderful woman wanted to spend her life with me?*

"Andy," she said, "you have to promise me something."

"Oh yes. I *will* love you tomorrow," I said with a reassuring smile, as I sipped the rest of my *Prosecco*. Then I realized this was one of those rare instances when Ada *was* actually serious. "Sorry," I said. "Promise what?"

"Let's never lose the sense of adventure in our lives."

"You mean like having carpe diem as your motto?" I asked.

"That's right," she said. "Here's a longer version: *Life is short, art is long, opportunity fleeting, experience deceptive, judgment difficult.* I want to experience everything, travel everywhere, and I want to do it all with *you*."

"Do we ever settle down, stay home, and have children?" I asked. "That's what husbands and wives usually do, you know."

"Sure. But not right away. Just think how much we can teach our students, and eventually our own children, by traveling all over the world the next few summers. What a fabulous opportunity! Did you know there are over 138 pyramids in Egypt?"

"And you want to visit every one of them, right?" I chuckled.

"Yes, every single one—with you!"

"What about those castles in Sicily you baited me with?"

"Hey. Remember, you're *my* guest on this trip and I'm still calling the shots!"

That evening, we stayed at the Palazzo Stern in Dorsoduro. We became officially engaged and were married in June of 1974 in Dansforth. It was a wonderful wedding. Our wedding cake was shaped like a castle, even though we never made it to see the castles in Sicily. Nevertheless, that's what Ada wanted, and I wasn't ready to dismiss the idea of a trip to Sicily in our near future.

THREE

The Blackhawk Auction

Ada radiated a unique blend of audacity and affability. Always smartly dressed, whether formally or informally, she was, without exception, the most attractive woman in the room. Nothing interfered with her strict diet and exercise regimen. Her use of make-up diminished neither the sparkle in her eyes, nor the warmth of her smile. Her charm, when she wanted it to be, was as percipient as it was appealing. There was quickness to her wit, crispness to her words, and an attentive gaze when she listened, as if she understood everything spoken to her.

Sometimes, appearing to understand more than she actually did, she would continue to nod encouragingly, only to be embarrassed when she was asked a question. Yet, as she did with so many other things, she managed to convert any potentially embarrassing moment into tasteful humor. It was a remarkable quality and Ada was truly gifted.

We attended many local car shows together and, like me, she developed a deep affinity for classic cars and the hobby itself. Sometimes we'd talk until the wee hours about price trends. She had an amazing capacity to predict which cars would increase in value and which ones would tank. I offered to take her to a classic auction during spring break. I couldn't believe how much fun we had.

It was the summer of 1975. The auction was the famous Noble-Dean Classic Car Auction held in Monterey, California at the posh Blackhawk Inn on Fisherman's Wharf. For three days, we observed one classic car after another cross the auction block.

"I love watching rich people bid," Ada observed. "I like it when they compete with other rich people and bid up the cars. Some are determined to own them at *any* price."

I always had difficulty comprehending that sort of behavior. Paying well above market value for a classic car seemed like throwing money away. However, I realized that sometimes there's a big difference between being rich and being smart. Then, again, if you're rich, it probably doesn't matter.

"Egos prevail over common sense here, Ada. It's great fun to watch."

"It's probably great fun to bid, too!" she said.

"Don't get any ideas. We're not in the same league."

When we arrived at the auction, we checked out the auction brochure and read about car number 128, the 1963 Aston Martin DB5 used in the James Bond movies *Goldfinger* and *Thunderball*.

"Are you kidding?" Ada laughed. "This thing has more gadgets than an Edsel!" It had revolving license plates, which could change to British, French, and Swiss plates, a passenger ejector seat, radar, hidden car phone, smoke and oil blaster, an anti-bullet vertical screen system, bumper extensions, and a tire-shredder. "What do you think it will sell for?"

"I'd say half a million, at least. Let's check out the scuttlebutt, but this car is a hot ticket!"

"No way!" Ada's reaction turned twenty heads.

"Careful, I said softly, "or these people will think I just propositioned you!"

Ada smiled. "Now if you were 007, you might get lucky!"

"You *could* speak a little more quietly, you know," I said. "We're going to get thrown out of the place!"

The featured auction car was a 1931 Duesenberg Long Wheelbase Model J Whittell Coupe. I read the auction brochure aloud: *"This is America's most elegant automobile and was originally designed by Murphy Coach Builders under the direction of one of America's outlandish Roaring Twenties bad boys, Captain George Whittell. Beautifully restored and boasting just 12,000 original miles, the automotive masterpiece captivates admirers with its striking and glamorous black and chrome livery. The Whittell Coupe is now considered to be one of the most extraordinary and valuable Duesenbergs in existence."*

"Look at this!" Ada exclaimed. "We have to buy this car!"

"With what? It's a seven-figure car!"

We began walking through the auction preview tent where about 200 cars were neatly parked and professionally polished by attending detailers. A cluster of European roadsters—Ferraris, Mercedes, Alfa Romeos, and Jaguars—were parked in the far corner of the tent.

"Oh my God!" Ada exclaimed. "I've never seen such beautiful sports cars!"

"Ada, these are my favorites, especially the Ferrari 250 Testa Rossa sitting right in the middle. Too bad it's a display car and not for sale. It's one of only twenty-two produced from 1957 and 1958. The car is known for its V12 Colombo engine, the prominent pontoon fenders, and the 'headrest' bump behind the driver. The Testa Rossas were very successful racers. My goal is to drive one someday, but I really don't think that will ever happen."

For the next couple of hours, we perused an impressive array of pre-and post-war auction cars. Ada loved the early 1900 cars, the Ford Model T Runabouts, and the Stanley Steamers.

By the time we got to see the 1931 Whittell Duesenberg Coupe, the auction was about to begin. Four less-than-friendly security guards surrounded it. They reminded me of the stoic Old Guard assigned to the Tomb of the Unknown Soldier. They never blinked or moved a muscle.

"Ada," I said, "some people live their whole lives without seeing a Duesenberg. Only wealthy people could afford them. Their heyday was during the Depression when they sold for an astronomical $8,500 and that was just the chassis! Some cars, after their coachwork was completed, went for more than $20,000! Wait until you see how much this one sells for today!" We quietly admired Whittell's stunning black paint and her low profile brushed-aluminum roof that appeared to be a folding convertible top. "Look at the waterfall effect on the rear deck, Ada. The chrome strips are perfectly placed."

"I would call the interior an art deco masterpiece!" Ada said. "It looks like black patent leather upholstery, too. And that polished aluminum trim on the doors and the dash is simply exquisite!"

"The chrome work alone must have cost a small fortune," I noted. "The bumpers, wheels, front grille, and front headlight housing—they are all striking."

"This is what they call automotive art, isn't it?"

"That's what it is exactly, Ada."

"Andy, what does your price guide say?"

"It says $380,000 in number one, perfect condition," I replied. "Don't believe it! I heard the reserve price is $1,000,000. Price guides are meaningless for cars of this caliber. I'm surprised it's even listed in the guide."

"So, if it doesn't get bid up to at least $1,000,000, it won't be sold, right?"

"That's right, they'll take her home."

"In previous auctions," I said, "the highest price paid for a Duesenberg was $230,000. That was just last year."

"What a God-awful amount of money to pay for a car!" Ada said.

"Listen to this." I read from the program. *"This car was purchased at Tubby's Used Car Palace in Brooklyn, NY twenty years ago. The current owner paid $1,500 for it.* How's that for an ROI?"

"What's an ROI?"

"It's an acronym for Return On Investment," I answered.

"That certainly says a great deal about the current owner's ability to forecast a winner, doesn't it?"

"Sure does! But he probably invested at least $100,000 in the restoration."

"Oh, how tragic! That means the poor guy will only clear about $900K!"

After we took our reserved seats in the front row, we anxiously waited for the Whittell Duesenberg to arrive on the auction block.

"Here she comes, Ada! Look how gorgeous she is! What I wouldn't give to own a car like that!"

Malcolm Carlisle, the flamboyant auctioneer, moved to the podium, his bifocals draped over his chest with a thin red strap. His black tuxedo was accessorized with a purple cummerbund and matching bow tie. With one hand on each side of the podium, and his shoulders arched forward, he looked down at an audience of about one thousand people. It seemed like he was ready to deliver the Gettysburg Address.

"In the illustrious world of classic car collecting," he said, "one and only one auction company stands out. That company is the Noble-Dean Classic Car Auction Company. We are the Mercedes Benz, Rolls Royce, and Bentley of auction houses all rolled into one! Welcome, ladies and gentlemen!" Carlisle's distinctive British accent echoed through the auditorium like he was singing at the London Palladium. "It is altogether fitting and proper that we should do this here today."

"What a crock!" Ada laughed.

"Sometimes he thinks he's Aristophanes," I said.

"But he's British," Ada said. "The nerve of that man!"

"But the automotive world has been waiting for this moment," Carlisle said. "The moment when one of the most treasured automotive jewels in existence will be sold, and it will be sold right here at the Noble-Dean Classic Car Auction! Look at her lines, ladies and gentlemen! Tell me she isn't the most beautiful automobile you've ever seen. Don't—I repeat—don't let this one get away!"

"Ladies and Gentlemen, do I hear $200,000? C'mon now, don't be shy."

Suddenly, our bidder paddle shot straight up into the air.

"Ada!" I said. "What the hell are you doing?"

"The auctioneer said not to let this one get away!" she answered with a high-spirited tone, as if I was a fool to ask such a stupid question.

"Exactly where the hell are we going to get $200,000?" Then it occurred to me that owning the Whittell Duesenberg would take much more than $200,000. I let it pass, so Ada could have some fun.

"I have $200,000 from the beautiful lady in front of me. Do I hear $300,000? Someone step up before it's too late!"

The man right next to Ada raised his paddle.

"I have $300,000 from the charming man in the front row. Now $400,000. Do I hear $400,000?"

Someone in the back jumped in. The crowd was abuzz with anticipation.

"Okay. I have $400,000! Do I hear $500?"

"What do you think, Andy? Is it a good deal?"

"Stop fooling around before we get stuck with this thing!" I was seriously starting to question my wife's sanity.

Ada reached for the sky.

"Okay, I have it—again from the delightful lady in the front row."

I whispered hoarsely, "My God! That's half a million bucks! Have you gone completely mad? If you don't stop, I'm going to have a stroke—right here and now!"

"$600,000?" Carlisle asked. Ada's paddle went straight up again.

"Ada! You just bid against yourself! C'mon! You already placed a bid for $500,000!"

"Okay! We have someone here that wants this car so badly she just trumped her own bid." Carlisle sounded cavalier and patronizing. The audience laughed. "I don't blame her," he said. "See how crazy people get over this car? Ladies and gentlemen, we are now up to $600,000! Right now, I need $700,000!"

"$700,000 it is! Thank you, Marc, our good customer from Charlotte."

"$800,000?"

"This is it," Ada said. "Last time." She was becoming quite proficient; instead of raising her paddle, she merely nodded once. In a few more minutes, I figured, all she would have to do was raise an eyebrow!

"Okay, lovely lady. You have $800,000 in this ballgame!"

"Stop, Ada! If you win this thing, we're both going to jail! Do you understand that?"

"She smiled, "I'm just buying some transportation for my wonderful husband, someone I love very much."

"Do I hear $900,000?"

The audience was deathly still. The only sounds I could hear were cocktail servers collecting empty glasses. I grabbed Ada's hands as she struggled to release them.

"Oh my God. No more bidding!" Ada was going to end up with a million-dollar car and I was headed for a dark cubicle at Attica!

"Going once!" Carlisle said. He surveyed the audience for another paddle in the air. "$800,000 going twice! Fair warning, now!"

"Looks good, Andrew P. Robinson. Looks real good!"

"Don't you dare!" I asserted. "I mean it!"

"Yes!" Carlisle shouted. "I have $1,000,000 from our old friend sitting behind the lovely lady!"

"Thank God! Now, keep your hands down!"

"Going once! Going twice!" He paused a few moments. "The famous Whittell Duesenberg is going to be sold for $1,000,000!" he said and paused again. The crowd anxiously waited. "SOLD! SOLD! SOLD! to the nice-looking man with the red sport jacket sitting behind the lovely lady!"

After five minutes of thunderous applause, the man behind Ada extended his hand and said, "Hello, fellow bidder. My name is Maxwell Riter. Call me Max."

"I'm Ada. Ada Robinson. This is my husband, Andrew."

"Sorry to have outbid you on the Duesie. I could tell your husband was getting pretty nervous, so I thought I'd jump in and rescue you."

Ada laughed. "He was the one that needed to be rescued. I was doing just fine."

I *wasn't* laughing, although I was pretty amazed at Ada's audacity.

I turned toward him and extended my hand. "Congratulations and thank you. You purchased an incredibly fabulous car. My wife didn't want the car anyway."

He nodded politely with an engaging smile.

"Thanks," he said. "I understand. It would be my pleasure if you and your charming wife would join me for dinner this evening. You

know, as my token of appreciation for your not bidding any higher."
He smiled broadly.

"How wonderful," Ada said, without a second thought.

"Ada, I thought you wanted to rest tonight?"

"Oh, I'm all charged up now!" she said.

I started to worry. First, she bid hundreds of thousands of dollars on a car she didn't want and couldn't afford. Now she was accepting a dinner invitation from a total stranger.

"I checked the menu at Calista's Restaurant right here in the hotel," Maxwell said. "It looks excellent. I would be honored if you accept my invitation. We can make it an early evening."

"That's perfect," Ada said.

"Shall we meet at . . . say 7:00?"

She looked at me for agreement. "That'll give us some time to relax and freshen up a bit. What do you think, Andy?"

I smiled politely. "Sure, Sweetheart. That sounds like fun."

"Great. It was a pleasure meeting you both."

"Same here," I said.

We walked to the elevator. My head was spinning.

"Ada, please tell me exactly what you were doing bidding on that car. Do you really have $800,000 buried in our backyard someplace?"

"Andy! You know we don't have that kind of money."

"Then why were you bidding on it?"

"Didn't you say the reserve was $1,000,000? Just thought I'd have some fun, that's all."

I just about lost it.

"Ada, do you realize that if the owner had lifted his reserve or if Maxwell Riter had not bid, *you* would now be the proud new owner of the 1931 Whittell Duesenberg Coupe?"

"Now," she giggled, "wasn't that your name they put on the bidder's paddle?"

"Ada, you are impossible!" We both laughed hysterically as we rode the elevator up to our room.

Calista's Restaurant was crowded with classic car hobbyists from all over the world. Japan, Australia, Russia, you name it—the world loves American and European classic cars. Fortunately, Max Riter had reserved a table outside on the covered garden terrace, away from the rest of the crowd. It was a beautiful evening, with a light breeze blowing softly across an adjacent cove. Brass candle lanterns on the table and eight-foot-high stainless steel torches provided the only light—and that was more than enough for all of us to enjoy a cozy evening atmosphere.

I was curious. When someone dropped a million bucks on a car, I always wondered, *where did the money come from? What kind of business did the person run,* and so on. In his mid-fifties, Maxwell was a tall, thin man—about 6′2″ with a George Hamilton look. His long, dark brown, wavy hair was parted on the right side and combed to perfection. He wore a plain gray suit, with a white shirt and black tie. A light gray silk handkerchief was tucked neatly in his suit pocket.

When I looked closer, I noticed what he didn't have: no aggressive plaids, no *I'm the man in the pinstripes,* and no four-button jacket. Instead, his message was smart, confident, and thorough. He made a statement by not making one. He was simple and streamlined, the quintessential man's man.

I was still suspicious. A multi-million dollar car collector inviting us to dinner was, to say the least, an uncommon event. I wanted to know all about this man, yet I resisted the temptation to interrogate him. As it turned out, that wasn't at all necessary.

"So what did you think of the day's auction activities?" he asked.

"Well . . . " I started to answer.

Ada answered for me. "It makes me feel vibrant and alive, like I would do anything to own one of these cars."

"I know," Maxwell agreed. "It's a real adrenaline rush. My senses are dramatically heightened at these auctions. In fact, sometimes I worry about my heart rate and blood pressure." He laughed.

"Do you attend many?" Ada asked.

"Usually every month I'm somewhere with a paddle in my hand. I travel all over the world to these auctions. Sometimes it gets old fast and I . . . "

"You must have quite a car collection," I interjected, before he had a chance to finish his thought. "I'm sorry; I cut you off."

"Not at all. I never get tired of the thrill of buying or selling a classic. It's just the travel. And, yes, I do have a car collection."

"Well, now you have another one for your collection—a magnificent one at that," Ada said.

He folded his arms over his chest and sat back in his chair. "No, that car isn't for me. Wish it were, though. I'm a classic car broker. I have five very wealthy clients: three in America, two in Europe. They put me in charge of their classic car portfolios. It's a full-time job, believe me."

"That's about the most exciting occupation a person could have. How did you get started?"

"Connections," he said quietly.

"Can you disclose the collectors you represent?" I asked.

"No. Sorry. They're private collectors who prefer to remain anonymous."

"What kind of cars do you have in your collection?" I asked.

"Mostly vintage race cars, the most original examples I can find."

"Any Mercedes or Alfas?"

"Yeah, some Ferraris, too."

"Hey, Andy, maybe someday Mr. Riter could buy us a Ferrari Testa Rossa."

"Ah, now there's a car," he said. "I actually prefer the two-seat European sports cars—especially those from the 1930s. Nothing is prettier than the early Mercedes and Alfas."

"You would not believe what I saw when I was in Sicily a few months ago. My client lives in Enna—you know where that is?"

"In the central part, isn't it?" I asked.

"He has a huge car collection. I understand Italy has been working on a project to recover classic cars hidden in caves during the war years. Allied bombs destroyed many of them. I know my client is very interested in that project."

"Yes. I remember reading about that in *Autoweek*," I said.

"I believe, as do many knowledgeable collectors, that when they complete the project, they will have the most valuable collection ever assembled in one place. But if they ever find King Victor Emmanuel's Duesenberg, they will have the crème de la crème, the most treasured classic car in the world!"

"Do you know where the car is?" I asked bluntly.

Maxwell laughed. "I've heard of it," he said, hesitantly. "Duesenberg collectors say it's been destroyed, supposedly cut up after the war. The new Auburn Cord Duesenberg Museum, in Auburn, Indiana, has been acquiring data from all over the world on Duesenbergs. Many collectors I know have been through their archives and found no trace of the car ever being recovered. Those old war cars—most of them have been beat up pretty badly and cost a small fortune to restore."

"Tough to justify a restoration, isn't it?" I asked.

"It is from a dollars and cents standpoint. That's where the emotions come into play. If my clients fall in love with a car, money is no object. Like a beautiful woman, there isn't anything you wouldn't do for her."

When I looked over at Ada, I couldn't tell what was going through her mind. At that point in the conversation, I was ready to leave, but we were only halfway through our dinner.

"Do you have a family?" I asked

"My eldest boy, Timothy, was killed in Vietnam during the Tet Offensive in 1968. My wife blamed me, saying I should have stopped him from enlisting. Her grief was so overwhelming; she became a chronic alcoholic. Later she developed Crohn's disease, among other things." A veil of sadness fell over his face. "I was devastated for a long time," he admitted.

I wasn't sure how much more I should probe. We only met this man a few hours ago. I was surprised by his candor. Ada looked forlorn, as if somehow his melancholy deeply affected her. Neither one of us asked any more personal questions, even though I had many more.

"The exhilaration I get from car auctions is like a drug," he said. "I don't know how I would have dealt with everything had it not been for these auctions."

While Maxwell seemed sincere, something indefinable bothered me about him. Actually, I didn't trust my judgment about these things. How could I ever second-guess a person who experienced such a tragic loss?

We all took a deep breath and exhaled as our discussion reverted back to the subject of classic cars. After dessert, we stood up.

I extended my hand. "Thank you for the wonderful evening, Maxwell," I said.

"It was entirely my pleasure," he said.

A few days later, when we arrived back in Fairchester, I tried to learn more about Maxwell Riter. After calling several of my car collector friends, without success, I asked a close friend of my father's, who was a senior executive at a financial services firm. He sent me a *Forbes Magazine* article. Riter was on the *Forbes* list as one of the world's 500 wealthiest people. The article indicated that a few years earlier he had divested his interest in a few Las Vegas casinos and currently managed his own Real Estate Investment Trust or REIT, as investors refer to them. Some people call them real estate mutual funds. Apparently, it wasn't anything he wanted to mention during our dinner. At the time, I could understand that, but his mysterious demeanor still puzzled me.

FOUR

The 1933 Alfa Romeo 8C 2300 Monza

The following year, in 1976 after the close of school, we boarded a plane back to Italy. We enjoyed Rome, Milan, Florence, and Venice, but we spent most of our time in Sicily visiting and researching the castles, including some of the ones my father lived in when he was stationed in Sicily during WW II. Each castle had an exciting, if not ignominious, past. Many great civilizations of the world occupied Sicily over the centuries. Ada loved all the cultural events and local festivals too, especially the Taormina Film Festival where she met Francis Ford Coppola, who was there to receive awards for *The Godfather* and *The Godfather Part II*.

As we explored the area around Taormina, we discovered Castelmola Castle atop Mount Tauro. Castelmola is a small village high up on a hill above Taormina. The village was built like a fortress to protect inhabitants against aggressors from the sea. By car, the ride is about two miles, or it's about one hour on foot. The village consists of many narrow lanes with small cafes and restaurants welded together on either side.

On our way to Mount Tauro, about fifty feet off the road, we came upon a 1947 International Harvester KB-5 box truck that had been converted into a retail food service vehicle. It had a split windshield on the bright red cab, a long pointed hood, like a pelican's beak, glossy green, twenty-inch wheels with lug nuts the size of tennis balls, and an eighteen-foot long enclosed rectangular white box. Five rows of red and green horizontal stripes were painted on the sides.

"Tell me something." Ada said. "Doesn't that truck look cheesy to you?"

"Cheesy? Where did you dig up that word?"

"Seeing a vintage American truck dressed in Italian garb? Yeah—cheesy!" she repeated. "They have a helluva lot of nerve!"

"It does have *some* redeeming attributes, don't you think?"

"Such as?"

"The smell? You want to stop and have lunch?" I suggested.

The large red letters above the open rectangular serving windows said: *Grande Rosso Cucina – Casa Del Famoso Legna Puttanesca.* Below, in smaller letters, for the benefit of the numerous English speaking tourists who come to Taormina, was the translation: *The Big Red Italian Cuisine – Home of the World Famous Wood-Fired Puttanesca Pizza.*

"Let's check it out, Andy. Maybe we can scrounge up a couple of espressos and a few cannoli."

We drove up to a graveled parking area on the left side of the truck. On the veranda were four tables with two chairs each. As we approached the truck, we noticed four bicycles with small wooden platforms in front of their handlebars.

"Look, Andy. They deliver!"

We had no sooner parked our Fiat, when an oxblood red 1933 Alfa Romeo 8C 2300 Monza Spider, one of my all-time favorite roadsters, drove in right next to us. The second thing I noticed was an exquisite woman in the passenger seat. All I could think of was Mary Goodnight in the latest Bond flick, *The Man with the Golden Gun.* She looked like her twin. Her abundant shoulder-length blond hair was complemented by an inviting smile. She was as glamorous as the Monza was exotic. I had to force myself to stop staring; in fact, I almost forgot the car entirely, which was highly unusual for a die-hard automobile aficionado like myself.

"Ada, look, my anniversary present just pulled in. Did you bring your checkbook?"

"Forget it! We can't afford that car," she said.

"Who said anything about the car?" I laughed.

"Oh, really now," she said.

"I can dream, right?" I braced myself.

"Get this straight, Andrew P. Robinson III. I own you! You are my slave!"

"Till my dyin' day!" I said. "You got me for life! Hey, Ada, the old guy behind the wheel—he must be her grandfather. What do you think?"

"No way," Ada said. "She's sleeping with him. I'd say he's maybe seventy, but blondie there—she's on the sunny side of thirty. Those racing goggles make it tough, but I can tell." I smiled, nodded, and gave her a quick thumbs-up gesture.

Then the deep-throated engine on the Monza rumbled to life. As we stared with admiration, the car backed up and sped up the hill toward the castle. The mechanical symphony produced by the spinning gears, supercharger vanes, and whirl of the valve train amplified into the kind of great music that can only come with a race-tuned, twin-cam straight eight. No matter how many times I hear the soundtrack of the Monza, it never fails to impress me.

"Isn't that about the most beautiful thing you've ever seen?"

Ada looked at me with one of her playful frowns. "The car, Sweetheart? It's the car we're discussing, aren't we?" She shook her head.

I decided not to tempt fate. "Let's get some espresso," I said.

A lanky server with long, curly dark brown hair and curious chestnut brown eyes approached us. His innocent schoolboy look made him appear tentative and unsure, like a puppy adjusting to a new home.

"That was Tazio Nucci in the Alfa," he said. "He doesn't like coming in here if other people are around. As soon as he saw you drive up, he decided to split. He'll be back after you leave." He placed napkins and utensils on the table in front of us. "Please be seated," he said.

"He didn't look very frightened," Ada said.

"Believe me. There's nothing 'frightened' about Tazio. He just gets tired of signing autographs. He's a famous race car driver, you know."

"Apparently," Ada said, "he is known more for his macho qualities. He can't be that famous. I've never heard of him." The young server blushed and nodded, somewhat surprised at Ada's bluntness.

"Ada, if you were into racing, you'd know who he is."

"Maybe I'll get to meet him and learn more about him. He's a handsome dude, that's for sure."

"By the way," I said, "What's your name? Where do you live?"

"My name is Sammy. I'm spending the summer in a villa up on the mountain with my mother and grandfather."

"Where did you learn to speak such perfect English?" Ada asked.

"I just graduated from Johns Hopkins University in Baltimore. I'm traveling through Sicily this summer." He shook his head with displeasure. "I have to work *here* when I run out of money."

"That's pretty tough duty," I said. "What's the story on the truck conversion?"

"Most people around here call the truck *Il Grande Rosso* or The Big Red. It's completely self-contained. It has a wood-fired oven, a commercial refrigeration system, espresso machine, sink, hot-water heater, generator, and a retractable awning. Sometimes, when we cater, we can serve as many as fifty people. That's Greg inside the truck. I have four or five friends who help me out. Tazio actually owns the truck and the business. When he's around, he takes it to local car shows and races, especially the big race and vintage car show over near Enna. People from all over the world show up for The Pergusa Lake Historic Car Festival, and Tazio lets me work The Big Red. Right here, we get business from tourists going up to Castelmola. But the locals show up, too. Working here is okay for now, but my first love is traveling."

"Not a bad gig," Ada said. "Nice to see another Yank with the wanderlust!"

"I'm not really a Yank. I just go to school there. I'll probably spend the rest of my life here in Sicily. If I die in Taormina, looking out on Isola Bella, my life will have been complete." His smile was broad and handsome. "Can I take your order?" he asked.

"Two cups of espresso," I said. "Any cannoli?"

"Only mascarpone today."

"I'm not crazy about the cheese," Ada said.

"Can I make a recommendation?" Sammy asked. "Let me bring you a couple slices of the puttanesca pizza. I think you'll like it."

I looked at Ada. "Shall we give it a try?" I asked.

"Can you tell me the ingredients?" Ada was unusually cautious about food.

"Sure," Sammy said. "The recipe I use is the one I learned from Tazio. I use garlic, anchovy fillets, chopped red peppers, tomatoes, and most important, capers from Pantelleria. That's an island about sixty miles south of Sicily. Their capers are the size of green olives—sometimes even bigger!"

"Sounds delightful," Ada said. She looked uneasy. "Have you ever heard of caper spurge poisoning?"

"Yes, when we go to Mt. Etna, Tazio tells me not to pick the capers with the purple flowers. What do you know about caper spurge?"

"Caper spurge is a poisonous plant with buds that are often confused with the good capers. The only reason I know about them is a friend of mine in Newark got deathly sick from them. She thought she had a heart attack and became delirious, then passed out. She was rushed to the hospital. She nearly died."

"Did you know they are the ones with purple flowers?" Sammy asked.

"Yes, they have a milky sap and the plant bears purple flowers. They're easy to mistake for the edible version. You just have to know the difference when you're picking them."

"Well, no one's ever gotten sick here," Sammy said. "We're careful, so I sure hope no one ever does. Tazio and I pick the best olives in Sicily, the Nocellara Etna olives, and we use the best tomatoes, the San Marzano tomatoes. We pick them on the slopes of Mt. Etna. We get smaller capers there, too. The really good ones—they're imported from Pantelleria."

"We can try a few slices," Ada said. "I'm sure everything is okay." Sammy returned right away with our espresso and ten minutes later served two slices of puttanesca pizza.

"Ada, have you ever heard of the pizza cognition theory?" I asked. I didn't have to wait long for an answer.

"That's when you discover pizza," she grinned, as she cut a small piece of the puttanesca pizza. "That theory claims that the first slice of pizza a child sees and tastes becomes, for him, *pizza*. Any other kind of pizza he has in the future is rejected if it isn't exactly the same as his first piece. Do you remember your first piece?"

Ada slowly chewed a small piece of pizza and then said, "My first slice of pizza was at Hungry Howie's. My mother would take us there for dinner after the five o'clock Sunday Mass. They served those foldable thin-crust pies. We'd typically get our favorite: two large pepperonis. I also remember a place in Fairchester called Alfredo's. Both places definitely defined my thin-crust pizza preferences. Thank God, this abomination I'm eating isn't my first piece!"

"What's wrong with it?" I asked.

"I haven't seen you touch yours yet."

I lifted the whole piece toward my mouth. "Oh, wait a minute! I'm not taking *any* chances. Those splurge capers scare me."

"It's not *splurge*, it's *spurge*."

"That's what I said—*splurge*." I grinned at Ada's redress. "*Splurge* or no *splurge*, here goes!" I took a big bite. After I swallowed, I placed my hands around my neck jerking my head back and forth to simulate choking, trying to talk with no words coming out.

Sammy ran towards the table. Ada raised her cup, sipped her espresso, and aside from her lips drawing in the dark liquid, made no expression at all.

"Are you okay?" Sammy asked.

"Yeah, I'm okay. Just having some fun with my wife."

"The Heimlich maneuver really comes in handy," Ada said, still cool and collected. "You can start with his neck, Sammy." He walked back to the counter but kept looking over at me, making sure I didn't have a relapse.

"Are you upset with me?" I asked.

"Well, it wasn't very funny when my friend from Newark nearly died from spurge poisoning, that's all."

"I'm sorry, Sweetheart. That was poor judgment on my part."

We sat there quietly for a few minutes until Sammy returned.

"More espresso?" he asked.

"Sure," I said. "Bring us a couple more slices of the puttan— whatever you call it—pizza, too."

"He's having trouble with words today." Ada laughed. All was forgiven—for now, anyway.

"Great," Sammy said. "It's puttanesca just in case you might want to order it again. Just remember, we have the exclusive on it right here! No place else in the world makes it!"

"Tell us more about Nucci," I said. "Oh, wait. First tell us about the girl." I smiled and looked at Ada for a reaction.

"You are starting to nauseate me." Clearly, my wisecrack quota for the day had been exceeded.

"The girl is Alexandra Abrahamsen," Sammy said with raised eyebrows. "She's about the hottest Swedish model on the planet. She just landed a multi-million dollar contract with Hilda Girl Cosmetics."

Ada looked over at me waiting for another quip.

"Don't look at me," I said. "I'll behave. Continue, Sammy, if you would please."

"Tazio is a European racing champion. He won four Monaco Grand Prix, including several wins in the 1930s in the Sicilian Targa Florio: You know, the open road endurance race held in the mountains around here. It was the Italian Grand Prix victory at Monza that gave the Alfa he's driving its 'Monza' nickname. That's what made him so famous, too."

"How come you know so much about this guy?" I asked.

"He talks a lot. Ever since he was a kid, cars have been his life."

"And women, too?" I asked with a sportive grin.

"Yeah, that's for sure! If it weren't for all the beautiful women he brings into this place, I'd probably quit and spend my time on Fondacco Parrino beach. The scenery is supposed to be really good there, too! The woman he's with now—oh my God! She's gorgeous! I keep telling him—don't let this one get away. So what if there's a forty-year difference in their ages?"

"You said forty years, right?" Ada asked

"Yeah, Tazio—he doesn't care. And, the girls? Like I said, Tazio is famous. One time I brought my girlfriend here. Tazio was putting the moves on *her*! What really made me mad is that she was actually falling for *him*! Tazio's always been a lothario. A parade of the most beautiful women in the world marches between these tables. Last week he was here with Gabriella Rosini."

"The movie actress?" I asked.

"Yeah, the one who won an academy award for . . . "

"*Dalliance*," Ada said. "It's about an English philanderer who falls in love with an Italian model. He falls so hard it destroys him. She was great. I just wish it had a happier ending. I didn't like it when the English guy died."

"Well, she's just about the nicest person who comes in the place. A few weeks ago, she drove here in a 1957 Ferrari Testa Rossa. I could tell Tazio didn't like being a passenger. He was very edgy—like he was annoyed."

"Maybe she wouldn't let him drive," I said.

"Could be," Sammy said. "That never occurred to me."

"You seem to remember them quite well," I said.

Ada laughed and shook her head. "We *have* to meet this guy, Tazio!"

As we rose to leave, Sammy said, "C'mon back around 10:00 a.m. tomorrow. The breakfast crowd disappears by then, and it's too early for lunch. That's when Tazio shows up with his lovelies. I'll introduce you as my two new friends."

"I would enjoy meeting Alexandra, too!" I said.

"Maybe you should come back alone," Ada suggested.

"By the way," Sammy said. "I never got your names."

"My wife, Ada . . . " I said extending my arm in her direction. "I'm Andrew P. Robinson."

"Hmm, Mr. and Mrs. Andrew P. Robinson, huh? It's been a real pleasure talking to you this morning. Hope you come back tomorrow."

We left the The Big Red more intrigued than informed. Tazio's choice of woman was eclectic enough, but driving an Alfa Romeo 8C 2300 Monza, for a car nut like myself, well, it just doesn't get any better than that. Ada demanded to see this guy in action, although I wasn't exactly sure what she meant by that.

To visit Castelmola Castle, we drove up the scenic Via Dietro Cappuccini, wide enough for one small car—a racecar driver's dream—winding through ancient cultivated terraces, ascending between overgrown cacti and rampant wild flowers. Although they rarely needed them, the quilted grassy banks served as a buffer zone for audacious Italian drivers.

After parking the Fiat, we approached a narrow dirt footpath leading to a steep incline, an old mule-path with mossy, weedy, concrete steps. We headed upwards past the pale brick buildings to an abandoned red schoolhouse. The views to the sea were breathtaking, but our eyes focused on Castelmola Castle. We saw the Monza parked in a field in front of the school building near the main road crossover.

"Ada," I said, "We have to get closer to the Alfa."

I removed my camera from its case. We walked swiftly toward the field. In European car circles, they say Porsche is to Volkswagen as Alfa is to Fiat. Yet, this Alfa defied comparison with anything else on four wheels in Europe or America. Finished in flat oxblood red, the Monza displayed the untamed appearance of a pre-war Italian sports racing machine.

"Andrew, you're right. It's an absolute knockout!" Ada said.

"Yes it is," I responded, "It has that indefinable mystique car collectors love. You know, Ada, every time you look at it from a different angle, you see something new and something seductive. Ada, just think . . . here is a car more than thirty-five years old that has the remarkable distinction of racing in three different eras: the early 1930s, post-war sports car races, and modern historic events. It has always been successful and survived through each generation. How many cars can you say that about?"

As we approached the Alfa, its two big "in your face" Bosch headlights caught my attention first. The long streamlined fenders covering the front and rear wheels gave it its pre-war character. I loved the flat fold-down dual windshields. The low-to-the-ground spare tire behind the sloping rear quarter amplified my euphoria. Being alone with Ada and this monument to racing history was exhilarating. I snapped two rolls of Kodachrome quicker than a hyped-up cub reporter from *Auto-Italia.*

After the photo session, we proceeded up the rocky ridge to Castelmola Castle. We stopped and read the manifest. It was a defensive outpost fortified by the Byzantines in 800 AD. It certainly looked much larger from sea level. With the town of Taormina below, it featured a spectacular panoramic view.

After we had walked to the east end of the castle, I peered downward. I could not believe what I saw next. Parked near the old red schoolhouse, right next to the Monza, was the 1957 Ferrari Testa Rossa Sammy mentioned. Here were two of the most desirable, most expensive cars in the world, worth millions, sitting unattended next to each other in an open field, as if they were a couple of discarded old rust buckets no one wanted.

"Ada, do you see that Ferrari?" I asked passionately.

"Sure. I see Gabriella, too," she said. "Look on the other side of the schoolhouse. She's talking to Tazio and that old man with a cane and a weird-looking hat. I wonder what happened to Alexandra? You know what, Andy? I sure hope you have some of Tazio's wallop when you get to be his age!"

"Yeah, me too!" I said, like a hopeful teen.

Ada ignored me. "We have to find out what's going on here."

"No, we don't." I said. "It's none of our business."

"Let's drive back to the café. Maybe they'll show up."

"No, Ada. Let's go back to our room, sip some Asti, and take a nice long *siesta*. That's what you're supposed to do in Italy, you know—take *siestas*."

"No naps today, Andy. Sorry. Let's drive over and park near the cars. We can walk into the schoolhouse, pretending we are looking for someone."

We reached our Fiat after locating the pedestrian footpath, but by the time we got to the schoolhouse, the Alfa and Ferrari were gone. Ada walked up to one of the windows and peered inside.

"It's a classroom with a screen, overhead projector, and podium." She shielded her eyes from the bright sunlight. "Ten rows of folding chairs are inside."

Ada pointed to a thirty-foot oval area behind the schoolhouse. The landscape was perfectly manicured around the perimeter of the oval. The center had a fifteen-foot circular stone fire pit with dying embers on the surface.

"They must have bonfires or big cookouts back here," she said. "That reminds me, I'm famished; let's stop at The Big Red for a quick snack."

"All right. All right!" I said.

After experiencing a close-up of the Monza, getting behind the wheel of the Fiat 500 was like driving a Hunt's tomato can. We cut through the narrow meandering one-lane road and then, without warning, we were on a collision course with two red cars speeding toward us, kicking up ten-foot high rooster tails.

Ada shouted, "They're not slowing down!" Get the hell off of the road!"

"Where the hell do you expect me to go?" I yelled. Taking evasive action, I turned the steering wheel hard to the right. As the two tires on the left side of the Fiat lifted off the ground, the car hit the dirt mound on the side of the road, became airborne, and plunged nose first into a drainage ditch. I was so incensed by the sound of the Monza and Ferrari speeding by us, I shouted obscenities at the drivers. After we reassured each other we were unharmed, Ada decided that now would be a good time to give me a hard time.

"Ada, are you okay?" I asked.

"Yeah, I guess so," she said. "What about you?"

"I think I sprained my wrist."

"Oh dear, we need to get you to emergency," she said.

"It's just my wrist, Ada."

"The hell with your wrist. I'm talking about your injured pride. You must feel terribly humiliated." Although she never cracked a smile, the devious playfulness in her eyes was omnipresent.

"Is this what they call gallows humor?" I asked. "Okay, Ada, do you want to stay here and smell the 'lilacs' or figure out what to do next?"

Suddenly, we burst out laughing until our eyes teared up. The two of us stuck in a smelly ditch in a tiny Fiat on the Sicilian countryside—we were blissfully entertained by our implausible predicament.

"Let's get the hell out of here before someone sees us," I said. "They might think were doing something we shouldn't be doing."

"In a Fiat?" she asked. "Are you crazy?"

"I'm quite the acrobat when put to the test."

"Oh, really?"

"You'd be surprised. Cramped spaces are my specialty."

"We can call Hertz from The Big Red," she said. "Look. The swirl of dust is still visible, but the two cars are long gone."

That evening Hertz delivered the special Rent-a-Racer Mustang GT 350 I ordered. Black with gold stripes with a four-speed manual transmission, these cars were dispersed sparingly throughout the world. I couldn't have been more excited until I realized, with my sprained wrist, I wouldn't be able to drive it.

"You're benched, Mr. Robinson," Ada said, with the compassion of a cold stone. "Anyway, it's about time someone educated you on the fine art of performance driving. Screwin' up in a Fiat is pretty weak! At least now we'll be on equal turf with the Castelmola boys."

"Except for the driver," I said teasingly. Being doused with a half a bottle of Asti isn't the worst way to end the day. Earlier that evening, we had consumed the other half.

I had trouble sleeping that night. Gazing over at Ada, even as she slept, I understood someday these trips to Sicily would end. We would settle down, have a family, and grow old together. For now, carpe diem ruled, and that was just fine with me.

FIVE

The 1966 Hertz Mustang GT350H Rent-A-Racer

We left the hotel around 9:30 a.m. so we could arrive at The Big Red by 10:00 a.m. We were hoping to run into Tazio and one of his sexy lady-friends. First, Ada had to try out the curves on the Via Dietro Cappuccini, if for no other reason than to prove that her on-the-road dexterity was far superior to mine.

"This thing's a drag racer, not a Grand Prix car," I hollered, as Ada double clutched around a hairpin turn. "You do realize we're going to end up in the ditch smellin' yesterday's gardenias—again!"

"Got to follow the apex," she yelled. "Hold on to your ass!"

"Where the hell did you learn to drive like this?"

"You should know that Newark ain't no Dansforth. While you were growing up in the lap of luxury, I had a part-time job working on go-karts at my uncle's shop. I was the test driver, too."

"Thought you worked at Master Kiyoshi's Gym?"

"I worked at *several* places, Andy. I got so good test driving karts, I raced in the Newark Invitational."

"How did you do?" I asked.

"I won the Miss Congeniality Award!"

"Newark judges," I said, "they can be easily bribed, huh?"

"Yeah, sometimes even with money."

"Watch out!" I yelled. "A small bus just pulled out ahead."

"Oh? I didn't see it."

"How could you not see it? It's a bus!" Placing both hands on the dashboard, I braced myself as she made a magnificent U-turn, sliding the back wheels around in a complete circle. Amid the dust and debris, an important decision was made. It provided immeasurable relief for me.

"Okay, now let's go have our espresso!"

"Fantastic idea," I said. A cold shower and a couple doses of Valium were what I really needed.

When we arrived, the Monza was parked at The Big Red. Sammy was inside the truck behind the counter. Two elderly men, engaged in an animated Italian discussion, with more hand gestures than spoken words, sat at a table in the far corner. We sat in the opposite corner so we could speak with Sammy freely.

"That's Tazio with Alonzo," Sammy said, speaking under his breath.

"What happened to Alexandra and Gabriella?" I asked. "Alonzo seems interesting, but he does absolutely nothing for me."

"Me neither," Ada said. "But Tazio—oh, he's an Adonis!"

Tazio's distinguished good looks were impressive for a man of seventy. Except for minor receding, he had a full head of white hair. It was combed straight back and accentuated with a neatly trimmed beard and heavy moustache of the same color. A tall, thin man, he had thick but not bushy eyebrows, dark but not black eyes. His white shirt, rolled-up sleeves, white trousers, and white canvas beach shoes, made him appear more like a CEO who happened to be on vacation in Sicily.

"Alonzo lives in the village up on the hill near the red schoolhouse," Sammy noted. "I think he's lived there for a hundred years.

He comes here a few times a week, very early in the morning. For the most part, he keeps very much to himself."

The contrast between the two men was striking: one in white; the other in black; Alonzo was obese; Tazio thin and trim, like a thirty-year-old swimming champion. Alonzo's face showed age, with drooping eyelids, sagging cheeks, and wrinkled neck. He didn't smile much. When he did, I noticed a large, conspicuous gold tooth protruding from his upper jaw that he didn't try to conceal. His tight black tweed jacket looked like it required a matching pair of trousers. Instead, he wore brown khakis with rolled-up cuffs. He carried a walnut walking cane, and under his heavy black tweed cap, his pure white hair grew out like a clump of wild dandelions.

"It's eighty degrees out. Why a heavy black hat?" I asked.

"It's a coppola hat," Sammy replied. "I've never seen him without it. In *Sicilia*, it's a sign of obedience. Someone wearing one is considered *una buona coppola*, or a loyal soldier. The *Mafiosi* uses the phrase when referring to citizens unlikely to interfere in any of their criminal activities."

"Alonzo's part of the mob?" I asked.

"Shh. You don't ask *that* question in Sicilia," Sammy replied quietly, placing his index finger on his lips. He looked around to see if anyone was within earshot. "People around here get killed for asking stuff like that."

Alonzo sat with his arms folded high above his waist. The quiet one, the one who listened intently, he nodded often while Tazio maintained a steady stream of lively discourse. As he spoke, he kept looking over at Ada.

"It's true what they say about Italian men, isn't it?" she asked.

"C'mon. They're no different from any other man." I was clearly on the defensive, but knew deep down she had good reason to be concerned.

Ada smiled at me. "Of course they're not," she said, leaving me to wonder why she even broached the subject.

When the two men rose to leave, Alonzo passed our table, nodded cordially, and tipped his coppola hat. When he dropped his cane, it seemed intentional. I caught a glimpse of the holstered *Tanfoglio pistola* strapped to his shin as he bent down to retrieve it. I was staring at him, and he stared back with a still expression until I put my head down. Then he walked away, leaning hard on his cane. He looked back at me when he reached the parking area like he was taking one last mental snapshot for future reference. He still wasn't smiling.

Ada walked over to Tazio and started scolding him in fluent Italian about his driving etiquette, yet I knew it was just an excuse to engage him. He smiled politely, nodded, said something apologetic, took out a pencil, and wrote something on a napkin. Ada pointed to me and blushed a little, her light complexion turning reddish. For whatever reason, the tide had turned.

"*Vediamo Stasera,*" she said, and then walked away.

"Ada, what was *that* all about? It was like you've known the guy forever."

"Because of my artful maneuvering, he invited us to a cocktail party tonight at a place called Villa Christina. We meet here at 5:00 p.m. He said dress comfortably."

"Scantily or comfortably?" I cracked.

"How *you* dress—that's up to you. How I dress—that's my business."

"Oh, you are two lucky people," Sammy said.

"Why us?" I asked.

"I'm irresistible." Ada laughed and shrugged her shoulders.

"C'mon, really. Why us?"

"You'll see," Sammy said, as he smiled. "You'll see. Only very special people ever get invited to Villa Christina!"

SIX

The Villa Christina Classic Car Collection

Our invitation to the Villa Christina cocktail party presented a challenge for us. Ada and I differed on what dressing "comfortably" actually meant. She wore a paisley patterned light blue and pink knee-length sundress. I wore a light blue open-collared dress shirt, dark blue sport coat, and gray bell-bottom trousers. I tucked a blue and green plaid polyester tie in my coat pocket—just in case.

Heading northeast on the Corso Umberto, with Ada's heavy foot, we made the nine-minute drive from Taormina to the base of Mount Tauro in five minutes. Driving his Monza, Tazio arrived at The Big Red exactly at 5:00 p.m. and insisted Ada ride with him. Fortunately, she sympathized with me—my bad wrist, hurt pride, and all—so we followed him up the mountain in the Mustang.

Ada had no problem keeping up with the Monza despite the razor-sharp turns and high speeds attained by Tazio. At one point, I was so transfixed by the sight and sounds of the Monza, I thought we were going around in endless circles, with every bend and turn looking like the last one.

I did see the Church of San Giorgio fly by as if it were re-entering the atmosphere, although we were traveling too fast to notice all the ancient apartment buildings and small shops. Speeding down the Via Della Rabbia to the other side of the mountain, we found ourselves among a large cluster of mature maples, white oaks, and evergreens. We turned onto a narrow dirt road, and after a mile or so, came to a daunting eighteen-foot-high wrought iron, picketed gate guarded by two armed *carabinieri*, members of the Italian national police force. The gate was connected to a red brick wall stretching as far, in either direction, as the eye could see.

As we approached the gate, Tazio signaled, and like Ali Baba saying "open sesame," the gates spread with instant obedience. We continued to move slowly up a steep hill until we could see an elegant two-story salmon pink villa with tan window frames and dark red shutters. We followed the Monza, escorted by white peacocks and peahens, to the right side of the villa, and parked under a cluster of small maples. Ada was immediately captivated by the magnificent gardens at the front of the villa, impeccably groomed and manicured. The azaleas, camellias, magnolias, and rhododendrons were in bloom, making the gardens a kaleidoscope of bright, beautiful colors.

When we exited our cars, my risk aversion tendencies came to bear. "Ada?" I queried. "Are you sure you don't want to get the hell out of here before we make fools of ourselves? I hope you realize we're way out of our element."

"Speak for yourself. I'm stickin' around."

She walked up to Tazio, and clutching his arm above his elbow, she said, "By the way, this is my husband, Andrew P. Robinson III."

"The . . . third?" Tazio asked. He seemed troubled, then quickly recovered. "It is my gracious pleasure, sir. Please, you call me *Tazio*." Only a slight accent was discernable. Most people, I'm sure, would call it charming. I was just glad Ada wouldn't need to be his interpreter.

After retrieving my flirtatious wife, placing my arm around her shoulder, I whispered in her ear. "Stop that stuff."

"What stuff?" she asked.

"Don't flirt with that guy. He's Italian. Remember? He'll think you're serious."

"Hey, maybe I am!"

"Okay, okay. You win, all right? I'll fly straight. No more gawking at Italian women. No more wisecracks."

Ada giggled. She moved closer, reaching for my hand, as we walked toward the front entrance. We lost our balance and almost fell into the azaleas when she placed her arm around my waist and squeezed. Regaining our balance, we prepared for our grand entrance.

A rather diminutive woman stood near the doorway. Despite attempting to look officious and poised, she was overpowered by the grand entranceway, not to mention the palatial villa towering above her. She had a quiet dignity about her. However, at the moment, her mind seemed abuzz with thoughts completely unrelated to us. I wondered what they were.

"Thomasina Nucci, I would like you to meet my new best friends, Mr. and Mrs. Robinson," Tazio said, with the formality of an Italian nobleman.

"Mrs. Nucci?" Ada asked with a puzzled look.

"I'm Tazio's daughter," she said with a tactful smile. "I took my name back after the divorce. Everyone calls me Tommie." Her welcoming response drew my attention to her warm sapphire eyes.

"It's a pleasure to meet you," I said. "Thank you for your kind invitation."

"Welcome to Villa Christina," she said proudly. At age fifty or so, she had light brown shoulder-length hair that was highlighted with streaks of blond. "This place was named after a Sicilian saint, Christina of Bolsena."

"A Sicilian saint? That sounds unlikely," Ada said.

"Christina of Bolsena?" Tommie asked.

"No," Ada answered. "A Sicilian saint. I think they call it an oxymoron."

Drawn in by Ada's humor, Tommie laughed discreetly. "Actually, we have several Sicilian saints. Christina was the most beautiful and had so many suitors that her father placed her in a convent, where she spent her entire life in prayer and service to the elderly."

"That must have been difficult for a beautiful young woman," Ada lamented.

Looking at Ada, Tazio gently flicked his chin with the back of his four fingers, allowing them to linger in the air for a few seconds. With a wide congenial smile, he said, "That's right. It's so sad—all the broken hearts . . . what are you going to do? Some women—they do strange things. What a waste."

"Papa!" Tommie reprimanded. Tazio winked at Ada. "Some women, as you put it, think of things other than men!"

"*Lui e un diavolo!*" Ada laughed.

"Exactly! But this *devil* needs to cool his jets!"

"Mrs. Robinson," Tazio said, "finds it quite objectionable to be forced off of the Via Dietro Cappuccini."

"Well, Mrs. Robinson," Tommie laughed, "maybe you should get some track experience during your stay in Sicily."

Ada nodded and quickly retorted, "Maybe your father needs lessons in driving manners. In America, we shoot road hogs."

Tommie laughed, this time loudly. Thankfully, she was amused.

"Oh, by the way, I'm Ada. This is my husband, Andrew P. Robinson III. He likes to be called 'Andy'.

"The third?" Tommie repeated, as she furled her brow.

"Yeah, like *numero tre*. There's very little originality in his family."

"My high school buddies called me 'Punt.'"

"Hmm," Tommie glanced at Tazio. "Like the kick?"

Ada answered before I could get out the first word. "An unfortunate remnant of his skills at football," she acknowledged. "He actually kicked some ass on the field, though." I jabbed Ada with my elbow and wondered if she was intentionally trying to offend these people. I hoped, by now, she'd soften a little.

"Then I should call you 'Mr. Punt' to show respect!" Tazio asserted.

" 'Mr. Punt' is more than acceptable!" I laughed.

"Tell me." Tazio queried. "Do you know what the most popular sport in Sicily is?"

"Sure," I answered. "Soccer or *futball,* as you call it."

"*Negativo!*" The most popular sport in Sicily is . . . *women!*"

"Just . . . *women?* That's it? Not chasing women?" I asked.

"Oh, Mr. Punt. Sicilians—they never *have* to chase women." Tazio was dead serious, as if he was quoting from some official rulebook on the sexual behaviors of Sicilian men.

Ada could hardly control herself and began to laugh loudly. "That's like saying bears don't poop in woods," she said, nearly choking on her own hysterics. Despite the awkward nature of the situation, I must admit; I nearly lost it too, as I shook my head in total disbelief.

"You think it's funny?" Tazio said. He wasn't finished. "*Women* is the most dangerous sport in Sicily too! You think American football is dangerous? In Sicily, women are more dangerous than the *lupara* (shotgun)!"

"Hmm, where have I heard that before?" Ada asked.

"Don't ask," I said.

Tommie grimaced. "Papa, you've said enough! Our guests don't need to hear about your tainted views on the morality of Sicilian men." Tommie bowed her head appearing to be embarrassed, although I detected signs of amusement on her face. "Please join me in the Great Room," she said. We proceeded through the entrance hall to a spacious living room with vaulted ceilings, a marble fireplace, and Expressionist paintings. The earth tones and yellow highlights of the dining room floor tiles were stunning. It teemed with affluence but was still inviting, comfortable, and cozy.

"I had the villa restored and tried to integrate the décor, fixtures, and fittings with the antique furniture and artwork, but I've been struggling with the rest of the villa."

After we had ascended two floors in an elevator, we came into the area in need of renovation.

"I want to convert this floor to guest rooms," Tommie said. "I am much too busy, though."

She led us to a half oval balcony. We were instantly enthralled by the view of Mount Etna to the west and Taormina to the east. I swear, looking out at the Ionian seascape, we could almost make out the Athenian Acropolis on the other side.

"I understand Mt. Etna erupts almost continuously," I said. "Aren't you concerned that someday it might destroy everything around here?"

"Fear is a very unproductive emotion," Tommie said.

"It's like living in California near the San Andreas fault," Ada said. "The entire California coast is in denial. That would be the last place I'd want to live."

"Maybe so," Tommie said. "People get used to living here. They rarely consider the consequences of an eruption. Just look at the view."

We peered out at Etna, and when our eyes scanned the area, we noticed the plethora of cars parked in an expansive parking lot on the lower right side of the villa.

"Must be a convention nearby, huh?" I said with casual concern.

"They belong to our guests," Tommie said.

"You have *more* guests?" Ada asked.

"They're all in the *cantina* on the lower level. Let's go down and mingle."

The hallway elevator quickly descended three floors. An underground wine cellar the size of a gymnasium appeared before us when the doors opened. About seventy-five people were immersed in cocktail chatter, laughing, drinking, and generally enjoying themselves.

"Please excuse me," Tommie said. "I have a business matter I must take care of." She motioned to Tazio. "Come with me," she said.

They walked to a secluded corner across the room, and engaged in, what appeared to be, a serious conversation. I sensed the conversation was about us.

As we were left to hobnob on our own, I wondered why we were invited to this lavish event. Then I wondered why everyone else was invited. People were dressed in semi-casual attire: men in elegant blazers with silk ascots and open- collar dress shirts, women in stylish dresses. Behind the thirty-foot-long mahogany bar, wine racks extended to a white-coffered ceiling. The casual, indirect lighting was enhanced with soft spotlights that illuminated the expensive signed automotive art hanging on the bronze suede walls. Two rolling ladders that made the top shelf brands readily accessible were in constant motion.

So were the svelte, well-groomed bartenders in stylish red tuxedos and black ties. The hyper-extended elbows at the bar discouraged my longing for a drink, until a beautiful cocktail waitress in a lovely, blue evening gown came by with the *aperitivo*: a pleasantly bitter herbal liqueur called *amaro*. She carried a tray of Tuscan mushrooms, Mediterranean bruschetta, and fig salad wrapped in prosciutto. I was impressed by the grandeur of it all.

Soon after the crowd cleared in front of me, I saw them: the monuments of the classic car universe. Resting on bright red carpeting were twenty-six of the most priceless cars in the world, some of which were so uncommon that their value was incalculable. People hovered over them as if they were rare archeological treasures from another era. It was like a gemologist discovering, in one location, the most cherished, coveted, and expensive diamonds in the world.

In the nomenclature of classic car collectors, there are everyday drivers and concours cars. These cars were in a class by themselves, neither for driving nor for showing. They belonged in a museum behind glass, and as astonished as I was to see them all in one location, I was equally surprised to learn that certain private owners had loaned them out. Then again, the place seemed to be adequately secured with armed carabinieri at every corner. Alonzo was seated in a chair, guarding the rear entrance. That was his purpose, I presumed, to be a guard. Now, I understood why the *Tanfoglio pistola* was strapped to his leg.

It all seemed like a logical assumption at the time. At least, I wanted it to seem that way. There was a surreptitious air to everything, but I just wrote off that impression when I gazed at the magnificent treasures sitting on the red carpet.

In the center of the floor perched the Holy Grail: A 1907 Rolls Royce Silver Ghost, the car knowledgeable collectors considered one of the most valuable in the world, glowed brilliantly under the white incandescent lights of the *Murano* crystal chandeliers. Red velvet ropes, shiny brass stanchions, and four armed guards at each corner surrounded the car.

It was called the Silver Ghost to emphasize its ghost-like quietness. Its aluminum paint with silver-plated fittings was impeccable. The open coach automobile had raised black leather pleated seats in front and back. The windshield was folded down, giving it a roadster-like feel. The long sweeping fenders were rounded in the front, and they extended about two feet behind the rear wheels. The car was priceless and beyond exquisite.

"We brought her here from the Rolls Royce Factory Museum in Derby, England," said one of the guards, doubling as spokesperson. "She's the original AX 201, the 40/50-horsepower model. We guard her twenty-four hours a day whether we're on tour or at the factory, and we love every minute of it!"

"I guess it would be a waste of time for me to make an offer," I said tongue in cheek.

"Who knows what she's worth?" he said. "Some say 30 million, others say 100 million. Lloyds underwrites her for 150. All I know is that the factory would never sell for *any* price."

"Thank God," I whispered. "I need the money for this month's rent."

"I understand, old chap. Being poor means we know *exactly* how much things cost. Only the rich can afford to be oblivious, you know."

We both laughed. "Amen!" I echoed.

Behind the Rolls, I spotted a dark blue 1936 Mercedes Benz 540K Special Cabriolet. As I admired her streamlined appearance, her split swept back windshield, and her long front hood with external supercharger exhausts, an elderly man with a strong British accent approached me.

"The Blue Goose," he said, "is a rather inappropriate epithet for something so beautiful, wouldn't you say? I've been her caretaker for many years. Surely, you've heard of this automobile, haven't you?" He looked worried, as if I might say no.

"Yes, of course," I replied. I assumed it was just another former Nazi car.

"That's their family crest on the doors," he said. Then I realized this was the famous Mercedes belonging to Hermann Goering. "After the US Army's Screaming Eagles entered Berchtesgaden in May of 1945," he said, "the car was used as a command vehicle for General Maxwell Taylor. The old boy then yanked Monty's chain pretty good. When the General gave Monty the small Mercedes 280 that had belonged to Himmler, Monty complained so bitterly they ended up giving him Hitler's 770K Grosser Mercedes, you know, that massive six-seat, eight-wheel touring car Hitler used in parades. Monty was too small to drive it himself, so he hired a Russian female chauffeur to drive him around Berlin. She was nearly twice Monty's size.

It was said General Patton was brought to his knees with laughter when he saw Monty in the back seat, barely able to see out the window, and so large a woman in the driver's seat. Good thing. Otherwise, I think Patton would have shot him. They were archrivals, you know. Patton hated the Russians, too."

"Yes, as a matter fact, I did know that," I said. I remembered the story about the Aberdeen Auction—how in 1956, the US Army auctioned this car at the Aberdeen Proving Grounds in Maryland for $2,167. Before that, it was commissioned by the US Treasury and raised millions on a Victory Bond Tour. In collector car circles, the car was a legend, especially since it is now, twenty-four years later worth in the neighborhood of fifteen million dollars. Another rather impressive ROI!

"Where is Hitler's Mercedes now?" I asked. The man frowned a little, as if maybe my presence at this event would indicate I should know the answer to such a question.

"May I ask . . . was that a rhetorical question?" He smiled, and then walked away, shaking his head. While my question was an apparent intrusion, I still wanted to know the answer.

I walked over to Tazio and Ada, who were admiring a 1930 Blower Bentley. "Tazio," I asked, "Do you know the whereabouts of Hitler's 770K Mercedes?"

"*Si.* It's in America—in Las Vegas—the Imperial Palace Collection. It's worth a small fortune now. No one liked Nazi cars after the war. Now they're worth millions. Hitler's big Mercedes? You probably cannot buy it even for twenty million!"

"I'm curious. What's your favorite car, Tazio?" I asked.

He shook his head. "It's not here," he answered.

"Well, what is it?" I persisted.

"Some day, I find Vittorio's car. Some day soon, I hope."

"Who is Vittorio?"

"Vittorio Emanuele III. You know, the king. . . ."

Before I could learn more from Tazio, Ada ran up to me.

"Hey, Punter. Guess what? A woman named Dorothy Page owned and raced this car back in the 30s. Do you know what that ugly silver thing is in front of the radiator? It kind of ruins it for me."

"That's the blower," I answered. "It's also called a supercharger." I read the placard in front of the Bentley aloud: *"W. O. Bentley, as chief engineer of the company he had founded, refused to allow the engine to be modified to incorporate the supercharger. As a result, the supercharger was placed at the end of the crankshaft, in front of the radiator. This gave the Blower Bentley an easily recognizable appearance and also increased the car's under steer due to the additional weight at the front."*

"This Blower Bentley disappeared just before the war in Europe started," Tazio said. "In 1940, I see it in Sicily at the Targa Florio. Mrs. Page—she's afraid to take the car back to England because of German submarines. She decides to hide the car in Sicilia until the war get over. She died in a train wreck in 1943. No one could find the Bentley. For three years, I chase down every clue. Then I find it in a cave under the Castle of Caccamo, near Palermo. I learn about an underground tunnel where the Italian Army keep guns stored during the war. I see the Bentley covered up in the corner. I was, how do you say it—*ectasktic?*"

"You mean *ecstatic*," Ada said. Tazio laughed and nodded. "Yes, *existatic*! Mr. Punt, you should keep this lady around for a while!"

"How long is 'for a while?'" I asked while laughing.

"When you get tired of her, you let me know, okay?"

"You mean when *I* get tired of *him*!" Ada interrupted.

"Tazio, my *bon ami*, tell me about the Alfa Monza you're driving," I said. "I love it!"

Tommie jumped in to answer, as if she didn't trust Tazio with the facts.

"Count Guglielmo Pavoni, the previous owner of the villa, purchased it in 1943. He was a distant cousin to King Victor Emmanuel. You probably remember from your history classes, he and the king fled to Tripoli after a plebiscite was presented to the Italian people. It was close, but they voted to eliminate the monarchy. The Monza remained here all these years, even after the Italian government took over Villa Christina, which is now a retreat for senior government officials, kind of like Camp David is for your president. Some of them drive the Monza just for the fun of it. We keep it, shall I say, in race-ready condition. I think, in America, you would call it a 'perk.'"

My mouth watered. Maybe, if I played my cards right, I just might get the chance to drive it.

"Please tell us why you invited us here," Ada said directly. "We certainly appreciate the invitation, but it seems like the people here are all very wealthy, and we're a little out of place." I cringed. *There goes my chance to drive the Alfa,* I thought.

Tommie paused for a moment. "Mind if I ask you something?" She looked at me with a curious stare and tilted her head, as if she already knew the answer to the question she was about to ask.

"Not at all," I said.

"You're awfully young to be a judge, aren't you?"

"A judge?" It suddenly dawned on me that she thought I was Andrew P. Robinson II, my father. *Was that the reason we were invited to this event?* My first impulse was to perpetuate the error. It felt good to be thought of as rich and powerful, if only for a few minutes.

"This is a fundraiser, right?" Ada asked.

"Yes, we are raising money to purchase more cars," Tommie answered.

Although it was never our intention to deceive, I felt a bit guilty.

"I'm sorry," I said. "I'm just a poor school teacher from upstate New York."

"Andrew P. Robinson—a poor school teacher?" Tazio repeated. "No, I don't think so! You're a big shot in Washington!"

"He's broke," Ada said. "I can vouch for him."

"Sammy checked up on you." Tommie said. "You know—his Johns Hopkins friends—they said you were a wealthy judge from Washington."

"That's my father. We do look alike." I started to laugh to myself and said, "Unfortunately, my father and I were never the grateful recipients of any of my grandfather's fortune; this was all eradicated by the crash of 1929."

Tazio immediately pulled Tommie aside with a shocked look. His hands were flying in the air as if he were paddling through white water rapids. Shaking his head in disbelief, he was struggling to explain his mistake to Tommie, who seemed totally unreceptive. Poor Sammy. I figured he'd receive the brunt of the blame.

She moved to the intercom near the door, speaking on it just for a second. She wasn't smiling. The time had finally arrived for us to be booted out of the place. I was hoping to learn more about the specifics of the funds they were attempting to raise. I was sure we'd be shown the exit door.

"Mr. Robinson, I'm sorry." I felt a hand reach out from behind me and touch my shoulder. *Here it comes,* I thought.

"You met my son, Sammy, at The Big Red, didn't you?" Tommie asked with a delicate voice. Needless to say, I was relieved, but Sammy squirmed like a teen-ager caught stealing hubcaps at Midnight Auto.

"Well," Ada said, "you should receive an academy award for your performance when we were at The Big Red. It was simply magnificent! But why all the smoke and mirrors? I don't understand."

"I apologize," Sammy said. "We attract a lot of wealthy Taormina vacationers over at The Big Red. Tazio and I invite some of them to fundraisers here at the villa—you know, people we think have money. We never mention the cars but love to see their surprised faces when they see them. They ask a million questions. That's when we solicit contributions. For contributing $10,000 or more, they receive a special gold medallion from the Italian Trade Commission. Mom signs it. Once again, I'm sorry. I feel so foolish."

"Are you kidding me?" Ada said. "I just found a new obsession! In the last hour, I've discovered a whole new world! These cars are fascinating beyond belief! This has been the most exciting experience of my life. You don't have to apologize for anything!" I could hear a sigh of relief as Sammy exhaled.

"So, Sammy, are you really a student in the States?" I asked.

"That's right. Have to start my masters program at Johns Hopkins this fall."

"Have to?"

"Yeah. I've got to get away from my grandfather. Tazio thinks my career should be managing The Big Red full-time." He smiled as Tazio put his arms around him.

"My grandson, he's a smart boy! But it cost too much money to make him smart! I tell him, 'stay here,' we make The Big Red a *francheese.*"

"Franchise?"

"*Si—francheese!* We buy many more trucks and put 'em all over Italia!"

"We have to keep an eye on my father," Tommie cautioned. "He lived with mother in Catania until she died last year. Now he lives here in the villa, taking care of it and working on our classic car project. I stay here too when visiting from Rome. I wish he'd spend more time looking for cars and less time on his extracurricular activities," she chuckled. Tazio grinned and rolled his eyes.

"What can I say?" he asked. "I'm just an old Italian *loafer*."

"*Loafer?*" Ada asked.

"He means 'lover,'" Tommie said. "He gets his shoes and his sex drive mixed up. Lothario is a much better description." After that remark, we all had a good laugh, the mood lightened, and we really enjoyed being with the Nucci family.

"My father left us a long time ago," Sammy said. "Tazio has been like a father to me. Mom *really does* run the Italian Trade Commission. She is a very good friend of Aldo Moro, you know— the prime minister."

"After I graduated from Princeton," Tommie elaborated, "I almost stayed in America permanently. I married a foreign services diplomat, but the marriage only lasted a few years. We were both always traveling abroad and never spent time with each other. One day, he just never came home. That's when I came back to Italia and began my career in government. The commission and the classic car project keep me very busy."

"Tell us more about the project," I said. "It sounds very intriguing."

"During World War II about two hundred of the most expensive cars in Italia were hidden in caves and castles all over Sicilia. Their owners were afraid Allied bombers would destroy them. In many cases, the cars were thought to have been destroyed but several were not. Many owners were high-ranking German and Fascist officials who fled to other countries as the war was winding down."

"Six months ago," Tazio said, "I find Mussolini's 1935 Alfa Romeo Pescara Spyder near Milan—you know, the one that was a gift to him when he save the Alfa Romeo company from a going broke during the Depression. Some Fascist party official hid it after he purchase it from Mussolini. When the bombing start, the guy run to Argentina like frightened *scoiattolo*."

"Frightened *squirrel*," Sammy said, as he smiled at his grandfather.

"I see. Was it as nice as the Monza?" I asked.

"*Molto elegante!*" Tazio replied. "A street car built for the race track. I drive it in the Mille Miglia Retro. The new owner—he's a good friend of mine."

"Think it can make a thousand miles?" I asked.

"With me drivin'? *Naturalmente!*" Tazio asserted. "Listen, Mr. Punt! More of these Alfas are hidden around Europe. The Alfa plant—it was owned by the Italian government, which was the same thing as being owned by Mussolini himself. It was his own private sports car shopping center. He had other great Alfas, too. I'm gonna find two more up near Messina next month."

"Finding these cars hasn't been as easy at my father implies," Tommie said. "In addition to Italy, I convinced the trade commissions of Germany and England to form an alliance to help locate these cars. Villa Christina has become our base of operation, and we intend to create a museum out of the lower level once we find enough cars. You've heard the term, *la bella figura?*"

"If I remember correctly," Ada said, "it has to do with Italy presenting its best face to the world, even if it isn't really true. It's the *appearance* that counts."

"Like I tell you, Mr. Punt, keep this woman!" Tazio said.

"That's exactly correct, Ada," Tommie said. "Tazio and I convinced them a museum of recovered classic cars from the war years would create *la bella figura* for Italy and would attract tourism and commerce. It would provide favorable publicity all around the world for our country."

"God knows," Ada said, "if there is one thing Italy needs after the war years, it is favorable publicity. They certainly were on the wrong side of history during the war, weren't they?"

"Can't argue that point," Tommie continued. "Many of the cars have grown in value since the war and are now worth over a million dollars. Whoever locates them owns them. They're like sunken treasures on the high seas. All this is costly, though. While the government fronted some of the money, we are sustained primarily by contributions. One of our biggest expenses is maintaining a security force. Some people would love to sabotage our project and confiscate the cars for themselves."

"You mean, like the mob?" Ada asked. The silence was deafening.

"In Sicily," Tommie said, "one should not casually toss around words like 'the mob.' I'm telling you this because I want you to be safe during your stay here."

"Oh, sorry," Ada said. "I remember. Sammy told us the same thing."

Leave it to Ada, I thought. She was not the type to be intimidated, despite the fact that Sicily was the most notorious hotbed of Mafia activity in the world. Before anyone attempted to answer, I intervened.

"How do you manage to keep the place secure? With cars like this around here, I would think it would take a small army."

"Remember Alonzo?" Sammy asked. "He provides the best protection money can buy." He pointed toward the corner of the room near the door to the outside parking lot. Alonzo was stationed on a wooden folding chair, resting both hands on top of his curled cane. He was dressed in the same attire as in the morning. When he noticed we were looking at him, he tipped his coppola hat. He still wasn't smiling.

"Does he work for the Italian Trade Commission?" Ada probed.

"He was referred to us by Francesco Mazza, the *Carabiniere General* in Sicilia. He's very supportive of the Italian Trade Commission, as well as our project. Mazza also provides four carabinieri guards around the clock."

"Fascinating!" Ada couldn't suppress her urge for a new adventure any longer. "We would love to help with the project!"

"Ada," I said, we're leaving in two weeks."

"Tommie, we can't give you any money, but we can give you the next best thing—our time. We can help when we get back to America, too."

"Thomasina!" Tazio urged. "We need the help! I like the travel but *hate* the research and paperwork! These people—they can help us!"

"We already have a team of researchers in Rome and Milan working on all the Italian cars," Tommie said.

"What about the Midnight Ghost?" Sammy asked with raised eyebrows.

"That's right," Tazio said. "Vittorio's Duesenberg! That's a full-time job! One day, someone will find her, and when they do, it will be like discovering the *Titanica!*"

Tommie pondered Tazio's comments. "Can I meet you here tomorrow at 2:00 p.m.?" she asked.

"We'll be here!" Ada said.

★　★　★

While it took five minutes to get to Mount Tauro, Ada made the trip back in fifteen minutes. For a moment, I thought the Mustang would die of gasoline deprivation. She was as expressive and ebullient as I had ever seen her.

"Andy," she said, "we have to get involved in this thing. This is the most exciting adventure we could have together. Can you imagine looking for King Victor Emmanuel's Duesenberg all over Europe?"

"Ada, I don't want to burst your bubble, Sweetheart, but we need to be concerned about a few things. First of all, we both have full-time jobs. Second, where the hell are we going to get the money to trek all over Europe? Third, and most important, I'm getting a little suspicious about the whole deal. Does it really make sense? Aren't you suspicious, too?"

I hated to see Ada's joy dissipate. I loved her serendipity, but above all, I respected her clarity of thought when she came back down to earth.

"I know exactly what you're thinking," she said.

"Alonzo?"

"Yeah, he didn't exactly look like the chief of police, did he? Especially with that *pistola* strapped to his leg."

Then Ada became uncharacteristically quiet, absorbed in her thoughts. As we approached our hotel, she began to fidget in the bucket seat. Once inside, eager to exchange our impressions of the cast of characters, I proceeded to the wine rack to find the last bottle of *Nero d'Avola.*

"Please forgive me," she said. "I'm very tired. It's been quite a day."

"Sure. Let's both turn in. We can talk in the morning."

Ada walked slowly into the bedroom, fell onto the bed, and was asleep in a matter of seconds.

SEVEN

The 1935 Duesenberg SJ Emmanuel

Ada and I went for a walk on the beach the next morning. She seemed unusually pensive and nostalgic. A frosty morning breeze blew across the agitated Ionian Sea. It was chilly, but the occasional warmth of the morning sun felt good. We walked hand-in-hand close to the shore, as if we were daring the rolling surf to soak our bare feet. Ada wore solid green Bermudas with a thin red polyester windbreaker, and I wore my khaki cargo shorts and long-sleeved white shirt.

"Andy?"

"Yes, Ada?"

"There's still hope. Look at that beautiful sunrise." She squeezed my hand tightly.

"Would you like to do this again next summer?" I asked.

"We'll see," she said, with a little enthusiasm. I always hated "We'll see." After walking about a mile, we stopped, dropping our thong sandals on the saffron stone terrace of a small cafe named Limoncello.

"Shall we get some breakfast, she asked?"

We sat on blue hassocks surrounding a white marble table. The beach was close enough that we could hear the rhythmic cresting of the breakers on shore. We were the only patrons, which, in addition to Ada's anxious demeanor, added an air of foreboding to the brisk morning chill.

"Nature's calling," I said. "Be right back." When I returned, Ada was gone. After a scan inside the deli, I assumed she also needed to visit the restroom. Then, I felt her two warm arms wrapping themselves around my shoulders, her soft face gently rubbing against mine.

"Hey, honey. I've been thinking." She hesitated, as if she needed to reconsider her words. "Well . . . I've been . . . "

I reached up to caress her arms, but she pulled back and sat down beside me. Uncertainty was in her eyes. Usually, Ada didn't need much encouragement to say what was on her mind.

"Go ahead, Sweetheart," I said. "I could tell something was bothering you last night. Let's talk about it, okay?"

"I was remembering Newark on the way home. All night, I thought about my father, mother, and sister, and how alone I felt growing up. Sometimes, I really struggle with those thoughts." I'd never seen Ada as wistful. "It was a very depressing time in my life. I never want to feel like that again."

"You never will, Sweetheart. Carpe diem—remember? We have love and adventure in our lives. What more could a young couple want?"

"I know. I know." She hesitated a few seconds. "Promise me, Andy, no matter what happens, you will never leave me."

"Of course, I promise," I said. I would never forget the image of her expressionless face last night. Next time, I would recognize it when I saw it. She tried hard not to involve me in her childhood pain, yet I wanted to be involved—I wanted her to lean on me. "You have to promise me something, too," I said. She nodded slowly. "When you get depressed about anything, we will talk it through right away, okay?"

"That's fair enough. I want you to do the same."

"Yes. I will do the same, Sweetheart."

She picked up her sandals. I ran from the café back to the beach. She followed me into the waves. We fell down in the surf and rolled in the waves until they lifted us from the sandy bottom. We were laughing, and romping with joy, never feeling the edge on the morning breeze. Then we walked back to our table, had breakfast, and then returned to our hotel.

We arrived at Villa Christina a few minutes before 2:00 p.m. and took the liberty of walking to a flagstone patio near a kidney-shaped swimming pool behind the villa. We seated ourselves on wicker chairs around a glass table. A shirtless man in his seventies, looking extremely overweight in his swimwear, sat in a lounge chair on the far side of the pool. A cheap cigar drooped from his lips, like it was just another appendage. The same black tweed coppola hat tilted over his eyes. It seemed our friend Alonzo was everywhere.

Tommie arrived carrying a large briefcase. "I'm sorry if we shocked you last night," she said with genuine sincerity. "I sometimes wonder why I even started this project." Tommie looked a bit overwhelmed "What I thought would be an enjoyable diversion has become a major commitment. Sammy and Tazio—I call Papa by his name, Tazio, most of the time—those two—well they talked me into it. I blame them! Not really. I'm grateful for their help even though their methods are somewhat unorthodox, as you discovered last night."

"Yes, but we were the lucky ones. It was a thrilling experience for us," Ada said. "Can't wait to hear more!" Her face was shining with excitement.

"Of the twenty-six cars in the collection, ten belong to other owners around the world. They were kind enough to allow us to display their cars. It really helps our fundraising efforts. The other sixteen were found by Tazio over the last few years and belong to the Italian Trade Commission. We agreed to ship the owner's cars back to them in August, two months from now. I want to thank you for your kind offer to assist us."

"It would be our privilege to help, believe me!" Ada said.

"Your eagerness motivates me, as reluctant as I am to take on volunteers. I worry about the trust factor, especially since anyone can lay claim to these cars once they're found. Whoever finds them gets to keep them. That's the law. I'm a pretty good judge of people though, even though Sammy and his friends had their generations slightly mixed up."

"Don't give it a second thought," I said. "I consider it a compliment to ride my father's coattails. It's not the first time someone made that mistake and certainly won't be the last."

Opening her briefcase on the round glass table, she extracted a thick manila folder. "Did you know King Victor Emmanuel took delivery of a specially made Duesenberg back in 1939?"

"That was about the time the Duesenberg company went under, wasn't it?" I asked.

"That's right. While digging through the archives at the Italian Information Ministry, I learned he ordered the chassis from the Duesenberg factory in Indianapolis and had it shipped to his friend, Joseph Figoni, the famous coachbuilder in Paris. The king wanted a design similar to the 1931 Duesenberg Model J Figoni Boattail Speedster. He saw the car at the 1932 Cannes Concours d'Elegance where it won the Grand Prix.

The king attempted to acquire that car; however, the owner turned him down. The design left a lasting impression on the king and he wanted Figoni to design another car exactly like it. Great coachbuilders disdain duplication, so the king had the chassis sent to John Gurney Nutting, the English coachbuilder. He was the person who built the body for Malcolm Campbell's 1931 Blue Bird world speed-record car."

"Wasn't his son Donald killed back in 1967 while attempting to break his own water speed record?" I asked. "I think he already had the land speed record."

"That's right. Gurney Nutting's fame rose as Malcolm broke land-speed records in Europe and America. The Maharaja of Indore, a well-known classic car collector, commissioned Gurney Nutting to build a 1935 Duesenberg SJ. The car was supposed to be delivered to India, but after Japan invaded China, there was fear Japan might also invade India. Many wealthy Indians, including the Maharaja, fled their homes. With unrest at home and around the world, the Maharaja lost interest. He engaged Nutting to sell his Duesenberg. When the king traveled to London to see the car, he had to have it. The following week, Nutting arranged to have the car secretly delivered to the king's palace in Rome."

"Why secretly?" Ada asked.

"Italy was in the throes of economic decline. Poverty was rampant. Knowing the king had paid one million dollars for an automobile would have been, to say the least, a blatant insult to the Italian people. Had they discovered the king's self-indulgent acquisition, not only would it undermine his respectability, but it would provide fuel to Mussolini, who would like nothing more than to get rid of the monarchy."

"How can a person own such a beautiful car and never drive it?" I asked.

"It really was beautiful, too," Tommie replied. "Look at these pictures."

"It's magnificent!" Ada exclaimed. We both gazed at the pictures, in awe of the car's flowing lines and striking colors. "Andy, it's breathtaking!"

"The primary color is sunglow orange," Tommie said. The orange color swept boldly from the hood ornament over the hood and the slightly raked windshield. It extended from the fenders to the topsides of the doors all the way to the rear deck. Sunglow also graced the pristine leather interior that looked soft and supple as a glove. "The engine is a work of art."

Tommie handed us a picture of a mammoth green engine with a highly polished supercharger under the open hood. "It had a 420 cubic-inch engine with 320 horsepower. It was absolutely mind-boggling at the time! Oh, I almost forgot. That's the House of Savoy coat of arms on the front license plate. Later, I understand that the House of Savoy coat of arms was added to the lower fender right in front of the driver's door.

"The king ruined the color," Tommie said. "He wanted to make it undetectable at night so he could drive it incognito. He had it painted a rather unattractive dark gray—thus it became known as the Midnight Ghost. Today, it is considered the most valuable Duesenberg ever built. The problem is no one knows where it is."

"How do we know it even exists?" I asked. "Maybe it was scrapped like so many other cars after the war."

"I'll let you be the judge of that after you study the paperwork in my file. I've already made up my mind."

"Imagine finding the last Duesenberg made," Ada said.

"And it belonging to the King of Italy during the war years," I added.

"How great is that!" Ada said. "We have to find it, Andy! Remember your campaign promise?"

"Carpe diem?"

"Exactly! We'd love to help locate the Ghost!" Ada declared with a gush of enthusiasm. She was sitting on the edge of her chair, leaning over the table, totally engrossed in Tommie's story of the lost treasure on wheels.

Tommie folded her hands on the table. "Well, I *could* use the help. Tazio has been passionate about finding the Ghost. He really should concentrate on Alfas, and I have other responsibilities back in Rome. Any time you could spend on the project would be more than appreciated. Of course, I'm well aware that you have teaching obligations and have to get back to America soon."

"Yes, teaching obligations," Ada said. She looked at me suggestively, as if she meant to say something else.

"We have to think this through, Ada. In order to make a firm commitment, we need to understand exactly what's involved. It sounds very exciting, sure, and we both love old cars, however, if we are going to do this thing, we need to have some kind of plan, you know, some blueprint we can follow."

"Once you digest the information inside this folder," Tommie said, "I'm confident you'll be able to come up with a game plan."

"That's certainly the place to start," I said. "Will Tazio be helping us?"

"Tazio has some leads on partially assembled production vehicles that were placed in storage and a few racing and experimental cars that were hidden in the caves north of Milan. The war was a disaster for Italy and for Alfa. Occupying German troops commandeered the factory and used it to manufacture weapons, making it a target for Allied bombers. By the end of the war, the Milan factory was entirely destroyed. We do know that many rare Alfas still exist, and Tazio is determined to find them. That's his specialty. If you would like to help us, you can focus on the American Duesenberg. That project can be all yours! Here, take the folder and study the research we have done so far. Feel free to open any unopened mail in the file. I'm just too busy to work on it."

"We would be honored and thrilled," Ada said.

I started to laugh. "Do you think you could show a little more excitement, Ada?"

"Andy, I know you're excited, too. I just show it a little more."

"I must admit, Ada, your passion for the project turns me on. But you know what worries me?"

"I think so, but tell me."

"Knowing how much we both enjoy classic cars, we could easily become totally immersed in it."

"Is that such a bad thing?"

"Ada, we do have a few obligations back home, don't forget."

"Maybe we should apply for a leave of absence."

"Then what do we do for money?"

"That's what I love about my husband. He's always so damned practical!"

"Well, I'm pretty confidant you two will figure it out." Tommie concluded. "I wish I could provide more details about the Ghost. Perhaps, when you get back to the States, going to the Duesenberg Museum in Auburn, Indiana and speaking with the curator might yield some results. Checking records in the Duesenberg Automotive Heritage archives might also provide some clues. Keep track of what you spend; I'll see to it you get reimbursed. I wish we could pay you, but at least you won't have to spend your own money for travel. Any questions?"

"I guess it's up to us to find the answers, right?" Ada said.

"We'll have to dig," I said, wondering what kind of search strategy we would come up with. Then I said to myself, *what if we actually find this car? It would be the classic car equivalent of locating one of Leonardo da Vinci's lost paintings!* The more I thought about it, the more I realized this was an opportunity of a lifetime—even if we didn't find it.

When Tommie stood up, we knew it was time to leave. "I have to drive up to Palermo and catch a plane back to Rome," she said. "Please keep me apprised of your progress."

Ada drove back to our hotel; actually, she crawled back, too busy expressing her jubilation.

"Can you believe it? We can look for this Duesenberg all over the world and get reimbursed for our expenses!"

"That won't last very long if we don't get results," I said.

"Hey, listen to you! Results? You're worried about results? Who do you think you married? C'mon, get with the program, Punter! Carpe diem!"

EIGHT

The 1956 Jaguar XKSS

The following morning, having reached our rental limit on the Mustang, we returned it to Hertz with glowing reviews. Our funds were running too low for another car rental, so we secured a taxi ride back to the hotel. We spent the entire day in our hotel room, buried in Tommie's Duesenberg file.

Ada exclaimed, "I still can't believe Tommie asked us to locate the most valuable car in the world—a rather significant challenge for a couple of ordinary teachers from the States, wouldn't you say?"

"Yeah, I guess. Maybe we just caught her in a weak moment."

Ada smiled and squeezed my hand.

"Oh, by the way, Tazio called," I said. "He wants to show us his latest acquisition. It's a 1956 Jaguar XKSS, just like the one Steve McQueen raced on Mulholland Drive in the early-morning hours. He said it's painted British racing-green, the same color as McQueen's. I remember reading about that car; McQueen referred to it as the Green Rat."

We propped a couple of pillows against the headboard of the bed and stretched ourselves into comfortable positions. Ada reached for the Duesenberg file on the nightstand and positioned her half-frame

91

reading glasses low on her nose. She was well versed in European history.

"The end of the Italian monarchy was Italy's consequence for entering the war on the wrong side," she noted. "Tazio was right. Many Fascist leaders drove expensive Mercedes, Alfas, and even Jaguars and Rolls Royces. When the Allied bombing started, many cars were transported to Sicily and were hidden in caves and even in some castles. When their Fascist owners fled to Argentina, and other parts of the world, many of the cars were left behind. Several were scrapped after the war. On September 8, 1943, Victor Emmanuel announced an armistice with the Allies."

"That must have annoyed Hitler somewhat, don't you think?"

"Yes. I'm sure it did. It also scared the hell out of King Victor, and he took off to Brindisi in southeastern Italy on the Adriatic coast. From there he could make a quick exit to Albania, or even Greece or Egypt. The Royal Navy had several ships in the Brindisi harbor, and the Castello Grande, where the Royal Family stayed, was fortified better than the Tower of London."

"So, did the Duesenberg go with him? Well, that's the question, right?"

"Listen, Andy. In 1944, the king transferred power to his son, Crown Prince Umberto. However—get this—in May of 1946, he formally abdicated, a month before a plebiscite was conducted. That's when the Italian people voted for a republic instead of a monarchy. The Kingdom of Italy was dead. The king donated his multimillion dollar coin collection to the Italian people; it's in the National Museum in Rome. But where is the Duesenberg? *Why didn't he donate the car, too?*"

"Ada, he wanted to keep the car. I don't blame the guy!"

"In the beginning, maybe, yes. Later, I don't think so. The king and all members of the House of Savoy were told to leave the country and never return. I read that the king was convinced he would be arrested and tried for war crimes, so he left in a hurry, taking refuge in Egypt where he died a year later. Look at this." Ada showed me a picture of the king arriving in Alexandria in his royal yacht. "Don't you think if the Duesenberg was on his yacht, someone would have known about it?"

"Maybe he had it shipped later in a freighter."

"From what I've read, when the king left for Alexandria, it was a well-kept secret. He feared assassination. Self-preservation and the preservation of his family were his primary concerns. I don't think the car was on his mind at all."

"He still had connections," I said.

"Then where is it? No one has ever seen this car. King Victor was unwilling to drive it because most Italian people would have rebelled against this. Many blamed him for the country's poverty. Guess he thought driving a million-dollar Duesenberg down the Via del Corso in Rome might annoy some people."

"You're holding something back, Ada. Where do *you* think it is?"

"I think it's in Brindisi, hidden in a cave under the Castello Grande, where King Victor lived for a year after Hitler chased him out of Rome."

"You think there's a cave under the castle?"

"Well, first of all," she explained, "there are caves under every castle in Sicily, so it's a pretty good bet. Look at this letter I found in a sealed envelope in the file. It has Villa Christina's address on it, referencing 'Duesenberg' in the bottom left. Like Tommie said, she was too busy to open some of her mail." Ada handed the letter and envelope to me

"They're in English. Isn't that a little strange?"

"It is. Look at the postmark."

"Brindisi? The ink is a little smudged."

"Yeah—it is Brindisi." I began to read.

Dear Madam Secretary,

I have been following your project with the Italian Trade Commission with great interest, and I'm inspired to think some of the best classic cars in the world will be on display in the great city of Taormina. I am, however, very disappointed that no one has located the most famous car of all: King Victor Emmanuel's Midnight Ghost.

I am writing to tell you what I know about this priceless car. I have a close relative who claims to have seen the car, but he wants his identity protected in order to avoid notoriety and overtures from classic car collectors all over the world.

You might ask, 'What makes you think the car belonged to King Victor?'

Well, my relative saw the coat of arms for the House of Savoy inscribed on a badge on the lower fender in front of the driver's door. It had a big white cross in the middle of it with blue background. I believe that is the correct coat of arms for the House of Savoy.

Now, I think you will agree that I have valuable information here. Nothing would please my relative more than to see the Midnight Ghost occupy the most prominent position in the new Taormina classic car museum.

I am staying at an upstairs apartment at the Castello Grande. You will never find me there. If you are interested in discussing this further, come to the Ristorante Terrazza Buena Vista in Brindisi and tell the maître d' you are looking for Erskine Mayberry. He'll know what to do.

Sincerely yours,

Erskine Mayberry

"What do you think?" Ada asked.

"Erskine Mayberry?"

"Nice Italian name, huh?"

"You know the obvious question."

"We don't know if it's a hoax or not. I understand that."

"So, what do you think we should do?" I asked.

"Let's go to Brindisi and check it out. Let's go tomorrow. I already looked at a map. It's about three hundred miles from us and should only take about six hours."

"Have you considered our mode of transportation?"

"Tazio's new Jaguar XKSS! Ask him. Maybe he'll let us take his car."

"Maybe *you* should be the one to pop that question," I said.

"No problem," she responded.

Tazio arrived at 5:00 p.m. and came right up to our room. Ada and I sat on stools in front of the small bar in the corner. Tazio played bartender and stood behind it with a large unopened bag of pistachio nuts and a bottle of wine.

"*Buoni signori sera!*" he said graciously. "It's my honor to be with you this lovely evening. Here, Mr. Punt! I hope you like this Dubonnet Rouge wine. It's my favorite, full bodied with a ruby red bouquet! *Magnifico!*" He tore into the bag of pistachios, spreading them on the bar counter, and cracking them open with a pair of bent needle nose pliers. "These nuts come a from the village of Bronte. They grow on the lava rocks of the *muntagna.*"

"You mean Mt. Etna."

"*Si.* Everything good to eat in Sicilia grows near the *muntagna.* Try some!"

"Actually, I'd rather see that new XKSS instead of examining one of your pistachio nuts," I said with a wide grin.

"Of course, Mr. Punt!" Tazio led us to the front terrace where he pointed to the exquisite Jaguar XKSS parked by itself in the far corner of the parking lot. "You like the car?" he asked. "It was the last one made!"

"Of course! It's one of the most desirable Jaguars ever manufactured!" I noted. I could already feel the wind blowing through my new haircut on the way to Brindisi.

"Sei bellissima!" Tazio said as he looked at Ada. I think he said she was beautiful.

"Grazie. I feel pretty good, too," Ada said. "How've you been?"

"Grande! I find the French Woodie last week!"

"Woodie?" Ada covered her mouth and began to laugh quietly.

"A 1924 Hispano Suiza H6C Tulip Wood Torpedo! It's known as the French Woodie. My friend, Andre Dubonnet—he race in the *Targa Florio* in Sicilia in 1924—he's an old man now. He said we could keep it in the museum for a year. Maybe I get him to donate it later."

The mounds of pistachio shells on the counter were beginning to look like the ruins of Stonehenge. Clearly, Tazio was a pistachio-eating machine. I marveled at his dexterity. He could crack each one open with one click of the pliers, discard the shells, and store the nuts in his other hand for future consumption—all in one fluid operation.

"That French Woodie is a great addition!" I said. "That's the family famous for aperitifs and cognacs. You know about them, Ada. We had the Zaza cocktail on our honeymoon. Remember? One drink and you were looped!"

"I make one for you now!" Tazo said. "It's just gin and the *Dubonnet Rouge* wine Andre give me. I bring the lemons with me, too!"

"Oh, by the way, Tazio, when will the museum cars be shipped back to their owners?" Ada asked.

"I speak with the transport company on the Radiophone," Tazio said. "In two weeks."

"How many transports are they bringing?" I asked.

"He tells me six."

"Of the twenty-six cars there, aren't there only ten cars on loan from the owners?" I asked.

"*Si*. He'll already have a big load on."

"Oh," I said. "Must be more collectors around here than I thought."

"Alonzo—he will help us, too."

"Alonzo makes me feel uncomfortable," I said.

"It's a sad story about Alonzo," lamented Tazio, who suddenly became grim. "About twenty years ago, his wife and two daughters were killed in a car accident. He hasn't talked much since. Alonzo works for Salvatore Salone at his house in Enna. He take care of his house and his classic car collection. He prepare the meals and fixes things." Tazio put his head down, hesitated a few seconds, and finally said, "No more of this talk! Time for Zazas!"

Like a seasoned bartender, Tazio prepared three Zaza cocktails with a lemon peel curled around the top of the glass. "Queen Elizabeth—she and *sua madre*—they love the Zazas on the rocks!"

I looked over at Ada and elbowed her when Tazio wasn't looking. "You didn't ask him about taking the Jag yet," I whispered.

"Wait until he has a few more Zazas!"

The next morning we left for Brindisi at 6:00 a.m. It was one of those pristine summer days that made you feel all was well with the world, and you wouldn't trade places with anyone. We had informed Tazio of our return in two days and that we would be delighted to assist with the shipment details of the owners' cars. He was so giddy about taking delivery of the French Woodie, I doubt that any of our words even registered. Oh, yes, The Zazas! They played a role too.

As soon as we reached the highway to Messina, Ada said, "Do you think Tazio will remember what he told us last night?"

"You mean about not wasting our time in Brindisi?"

"Yeah, but by that time in the evening, he was pretty well soused. If you need any help driving this thing, please let me know, okay?"

"The wrist feels pretty good. I'll let you know if I need assistance."

"Sure you will!"

I loved this Jaguar XKSS! The Green Rat, as McQueen called it, had 275 horsepower, a dry-sump 3.4-liter straight-6 engine that would propel it to 60 miles per hour in just 5.2 seconds on the way to its 149-mile-per-hour top speed. It was fast!

"Ada, a fire at Jaguar's Brown's Lane factory in February 1957 destroyed all but twenty-five of these Jags. All the necessary jigs and tooling needed to build them were burned up too, so they never manufactured any more of the XKSS. Tazio says this one is the last one made."

"Well then, Andy. Maybe you *should* let me drive it!"

After an hour or so, we boarded the ferry at the Strait of Messina, opposite Villa San Giovanni on the mainland and into Reggio Calabria. As we drove up the Tyrrhenian coast, the stretch between the Strait of Messina and Tropea was breathtaking.

"I have never seen so many lovely beaches," Ada said softly.

"We'll have to come back here when we have more time."

We arrived at the Ristorante Terrazza Buena Vista in Brindisi at noon and were seated at a table overlooking the waterfront. We decided to order wine, have lunch, and discuss our strategy. When I mentioned the mysterious name to the Maitre d', he looked at me quizzically and said, "I'm sorry. I don't know this Erskine Mayberry."

"Are you sure?" I asked. "Erskine Mayberry? You're sure you haven't heard that name?"

"*Si*. I work a here for fifteen years and never hear that name."
He smiled respectfully before returning to his reservation podium.

Ada and I were disappointed. *Maybe the letter was some kind of prank.* We wondered if coming to Brindisi would turn out to be a waste of our time.

"Well, Andy. Let's go check out the Castello Grande, what do you say?"

"We've got nothing to lose," I said, as I shrugged my shoulders.

☆   ☆   ☆

Despite the aggravation of driving in bumper-to-bumper traffic on a small two-lane road, our enthusiasm was rekindled when we remembered that Erskine Mayberry supposedly had an apartment in the castle.

"This is the wrong time of day to be driving through town!" I griped.

"Everyone's going home for their mid-day siestas; that's what happens in Italy every day between the hours of one and four."

"I've never seen so many Fiats in one place! God, they're ugly! I find it hard to believe that Fiat owns a 50 percent stake in Ferrari."

"Actually, I think they're appealing and quite economical."

"Fiat is the acronym *Fix It Again Tony*!" I laughed.

"Yeah, I know." Ada quipped. "That's completely unfair."

"Anyway, I know the Ferrari racing car has maintained its autonomy."

As we inched forward amid the chaos, we were engulfed in a half-mile of new construction and excavation. Add that to the whimpering horns of the Fiats, and I was about ready to park the Jag and walk to the castle.

"Brindisi is one of the fastest growing urban centers in Italy," Ada said, as she read from her travel guide.

"Thanks for the explanation. It's still annoying," I said.

"Andy, look! I can see King Victor's statue over there in the Piazza Vittorio Emanuele."

"Apparently, he's still the big man on campus."

"Guess I didn't realize he's still revered by the Italian people," Ada said.

"I wonder how many of them actually know about the Duesenberg," I mused.

"Very few, I bet. If they knew how much he paid for it, that statue would tumble before you could say Jack Robinson." She was right.

"Who the hell was Jack Robinson, anyway?" I asked.

"I think he was a British guy who changed his mind a lot!" Ada laughed.

"Not the baseball player?"

"No, not the baseball player. I used to think so, but no."

We slowly passed a street sign that said Viale Regina Margherita.

"Hmm. Regina Margherita? Wasn't she the Queen of Italy—King Victor's mother?"

"Yes, Andy. Very good! I remember now—Queen Margherita of Savoy."

I had one of those self-satisfied smirks on my face.

"Looks like the whole family is *in* pretty good here!" Ada remarked.

When I turned onto Via Thaon di Revel Paolo, traffic was still congested; however, the drive along the water became more interesting the closer we came to the castle. We drove past military buildings and a few residential apartments that had laundry hanging above their small balconies. Children were playing in the street and naval personnel were walking to and from the vessels docked in the harbor. *In 1943, when the Royal Family lived in the castle, it couldn't have been much different*, I thought.

"Ada, I can see the square towers of the castle. The place is massive! I had no idea it was such an imposing structure."

"The travel guide says it's shaped like a trapezoid. *Pavement and grass has replaced the moat that used to surround the castle.*"

Getting closer, my initial impression was that the grayish-tan castle looked more like a prison than a regal domicile for a king.

"Says here the Normans built the place during the medieval period," Ada noted. "They used material from old walls and monument ruins, so one might say the castle was a relic when it was built."

Two of three entrance gates on the southern side were closed due to excavation activity. I parked the Jag in a dust-blown parking lot on the west side, making sure the convertible top was tightly secured and all the doors were locked. We walked through the middle gate and immediately found a uniformed tour guide eagerly waiting for us near the ticket kiosk. After we paid the entrance fee, we hired the guide, a college student from the nearby University of Bari, so we could glean as much basic information about the castle as possible.

"My name is Angela Ferre. Welcome to Castello Grande!"

"Good to meet you, Angela," I said. "We are Mr. and Mrs. Robinson."

She bowed her head politely and began her presentation: "The castle was built in 1227 by Frederick II as a fortified palace for his garrisons in preparation for the Sixth Crusade. It has four high towers at the corners, and it was defended on one side by the sea, and the other three sides by a wide and deep moat. In 1488 the Aragonese built the rampart that surrounds the castle. The new wall, the lower Swabian . . . "

"Excuse me, Angela," Ada interrupted, "I don't mean to be rude. Tell me, does the name Erskine Mayberry ring a bell for you?"

It was a long shot, and I was surprised Ada asked the question so soon. Nevertheless, I could tell by Angela's expression that Ada had struck a chord.

"Mr. and Mrs. Robinson, would you please excuse me? I'll be right back."

"She definitely recognized the name," I said.

"Just hope she comes back."

Within ten minutes, a handsome boy of about ten years old greeted us, impeccably dressed in a gray suit, red tie, and blue felt cappello hat.

"Mr. Robinson? My name is Erskine Mayberry," he said politely. He had dark hair and eyes with an irresistible smile.

"Young man," Ada asked. "Your name is Erskine Mayberry?"

"I hate Erskine. You can call me Kenny. Everyone else does."

"Are your parents here?"

"My parents? They're home in London. I'm staying upstairs with my grandpappy. He takes care of the castle. He doesn't go outside much. He told me to invite you to come up and see him."

Kenny led us through an immense wide-open space; the white marble floor was scuffed with ugly black shoe streaks, the gray concrete pillars climbed thirty feet to a light and dark brown arched ceiling, typical of the Norman architecture of the day. Other than a few exhibits, the absence of anything historically significant was surprising. Kenny led us through a long, dark, and narrow hallway, then outside through a dilapidated courtyard in dire need of attention, and then to a door under a protruding arch.

"I have to do this every time I go up or come down," he said, as he inserted a large brass key into an old heavy metal padlock and opened the hasp. "Maybe someday they'll put elevators in this place."

Ada looked over at me and winked. "Smart kid," she said.

"Grandpappy lives in the same apartment where Princess Juliana lived."

Ada bumped me with her elbow. "I wouldn't be surprised if *your* 'grandpappy' lived here, too!" she whispered.

"My ubiquitous grandfather? No way! That's just Robinson family folklore."

After I laughed spontaneously, I began to speculate. I wonder if old "One Stick" ever did see the Princess Juliana's apartment. Knowing him, the question was not if but how many times.

Kenny unlocked another door, and we slowly entered a large, palatial room that was obviously someone's residence.

"You can sit down here on the sofa," Kenny said. "I'll get my grandpappy."

The room, while gloomy, was impeccably neat and ornate. Expensive furnishings harmoniously positioned around the room created a natural symmetry. No space was overlooked. A ceiling fan quietly whirled above us. Closed tan window blinds with two-inch slats made the room dark and unwelcoming. I could almost hear Bing Crosby singing *Don't Fence Me In* on the 1940's style RCA Victrola radio-phonograph across from the sofa.

Several minutes elapsed as we wondered why it was taking so long for Kenny to retrieve his grandpappy. Kenny came out and sat next to us on the sofa.

"My grandpappy, he sleeps a lot during the day," he said.

A tall, well-built elderly man, maybe seventy years old, with long bushy gray hair, walked into the room. He cinched the belt on his light blue terry-cloth robe and limped over to one of the dark brown leather club chairs across from us.

"Bad back. Occupational hazard," he said.

He had a slight English accent and appeared inconvenienced, like an aristocrat forced to deal with a couple of peasants. Ada and I stood up and I extended my hand. He slumped into the chair, completely ignoring my friendly gesture.

"I was expecting someone else," he said tersely.

"Yes sir, I know," I said. "You were expecting Thomasina Nucci of the Italian Trade Commission. I'm Andrew Robinson. This is my wife, Ada."

"I know who you are; don't worry about that. You wouldn't be here if I didn't know who you were."

He had trouble making eye contact with us, staring aimlessly above our heads, awaiting more information.

"Secretary Nucci placed us in charge of the Duesenberg Midnight Ghost project. She has been very busy in Rome and delegated the project to us a few weeks ago. We were given the privilege of opening her mail and that's when we saw your letter."

"You mean my grandson's letter. I don't waste my time writing letters."

"C'mon, Grandpappy, you helped with that letter, remember?"

"All right, so I helped a little," he said. "Go outside and play with your friends, Kenny. I want to speak with Mr. and Mrs. Robinson privately."

"Aw, can I stay? I like them."

"No!"

Kenny shook our hands and left in a huff.

"He's a handsome young man," Ada noted.

"And very polite, too," I added.

"Okay, let's get down to business."

"Excuse me," Ada said. "What is your name?"

"Just call me . . . Tom for now. If there are no more questions, I'll tell you my story. Back in 1949. . . . "

"I'm sorry," Ada interrupted. "Could I have some tea?"

"We both would like some, thanks," I said.

Five minutes later he returned with our tea, not at all happy with the inconvenience.

"Okay, now, back in 1949 I raced the Ferrari 166 S in the 24 Hours of Le Mans race with a man named Luigi Chinetti. That was the first Ferrari ever to win that race." When he said "Luigi Chinetti," I immediately recognized the name.

"Luigi Chinetti! My grandfather introduced me to him in Greenwich, Connecticut. He told me Chinetti was the most famous Ferrari racecar driver of all time. He had the first Ferrari dealership in America, didn't he?"

"Yes, that's right, Mr. Robinson. He had very close ties with Enzo Ferrari. I invested quite a sum of money to help him with his Ferrari inventory." Tom stood up, limped over to the window, and opened the blinds.

"Now we can shine some light on the subject," he said, looking over at Ada and smiling as he eased back into his chair.

"Oh, that's much better," she said. "Thank you."

"Tom," I said. "You have our undivided attention. Tell us more . . . please."

"When I was a captain in the Eighth Army under General Montgomery, he assigned me to a British commando training unit. 'Go learn how to kill Nazis,' he said. I was flown up to Braemar, a village in Aberdeenshire, Scotland for five weeks of grueling combat training. It continued by day and night with river crossings, mountain climbing, weapons training, map reading, and small boat operations. Conditions were primitive. We lived in canvas tents and Nissen huts. The final exercise was a simulated night beach landing using live ammunition. The most comprehensive training was unarmed combat."

He paused for a few seconds. "I was supposed to be sent back to Patton's Seventh Army in Sicily to train a select group of soldiers in the First Battalion, but time ran out. Instead, I was transferred to the Red Commando Unit in General Montgomery's Eighth Army. They were preparing to invade the southwestern shore of Sicily. I went on raids, very dangerous raids. I had to do things—gruesome things.

On July 8, 1943, my commando unit with about twenty soldiers, went in ahead of the invasion force. With high explosives, we destroyed coastal artillery batteries at Cape Murro di Cassibile. Most of the fighting was hand-to-hand combat. We killed over two hundred German and Italian soldiers. Those we didn't kill fled northwest to the caves of Pantalica. Two days later, a full-scale invasion force met with minimum resistance.

While the rest of the Eighth Army proceeded north, I was given orders to destroy arms and munitions stored in the caves around Pantalica. Monty feared the Germans would mount an offensive on his rear flank, and he would be sandwiched between Messina and Taormina. Fleeing Italian soldiers, many who did not have the stomach to fight Americans, were assigned to guard these caves by German soldiers. The problem we faced was that Pantalica was an immense burial ground. Thousands of people were entombed in the caves, not only from the war but also throughout history."

"Like a cemetery?" Ada asked.

"Not at all like a cemetery. It was a convenient dumping ground for bodies going back to the Legions of the Roman Empire, then the Crusades. Victims of Mafia vendettas are the most recent occupants. We had many obstacles. It's a mountainous area. There were no roads. Our maps didn't identify caves. With two Jeeps, each with a .50 caliber Browning machine gun, five armored half-tracks, and an assault team of just twenty men, we proceeded to the town of Sortino, northwest of Syracusa.

When we rolled into Sortino, we stopped at Chiesa Madre di San Giovanni Evangelista, a Catholic Church on the Piazza Matrice.

We were looking for a priest who might be able to help us. After we had walked through the front doors of the church, we were astonished to see about fifty Italian soldiers kneeling in prayer. An older priest pleaded with us not to harm them. That's when I met Major Salvatore Salone."

"Salone?" I asked.

"His family owns the granite quarry in Ragusa between two deep valleys, Cava San Leonardo and Cava Santa Domenica. Allow me to finish. . . ."

"Please do," I said. We were completely absorbed in his story.

"Major Salone approached us with his hands in the air. He said the soldiers in the church were from the local area and were hiding. The Germans forced them to fight, threatening to kill their families if they didn't. After we had explained our objective, they volunteered to become part of our assault team. With Salone leading the way, we searched the caves in Pantalica, killing Germans and recovering ammo.

Now that you have the backstory, on to my main point: We found many expensive American and European cars hidden in the caves. Most were owned by Fascist leaders who fled from Italy after Mussolini was killed."

"You should have confiscated them," I said, rushing to judgment.

"I suppose so. They were too new to be the million-dollar collectible treasures you see at the auctions today. We weren't equipped to handle them, so to show our appreciation for their assistance; we gave them to the Italian soldiers. Salone took the most beautiful one, even though it was a bland gray color. I remember the long flowing lines. It was unlike any car I had ever seen. It said 'Duesenberg' on a small plate on the radiator, but it looked far too streamlined to match any of my recollections of a Duesenberg."

"Oh my God!" exclaimed Ada. "That's it!"

"It's too much of a coincidence," I said suspiciously.

"Coincidence?" he said. "What coincidence? You have to remember—we didn't think anything of it back then. To us, it was just another hunk of metal that would otherwise be destroyed at the end of the war. No one cared enough to figure out who actually owned the car. While the car was unique in its day, we had other challenges to deal with—much more important than researching a car."

"How sure are you that it was the Midnight Ghost? On the king's car," I said, "the coat of arms for the House of Savoy was inscribed on a badge placed on the lower fender in front of the driver's door. It had a big white cross in the middle of it with a blue background."

Tom leaned back against the wall, looked up toward the ceiling, then closed his eyes and slowly nodded.

"Mr. Robinson," he said, "I'm sure of it—I remember the big white cross."

"All right, Tom," Ada said, "time's up! What's your real name?"

Tom made eye contact and for the first time smiled at us. I could see by his expression he felt more at ease than when we first walked in.

"Forgive my rudeness earlier," he said. "I'm a bear when I wake up in the middle of the afternoon." He grinned at me and shrugged his shoulders. "You know the saying, 'when in Rome'? You interrupted my daily *siesta!*"

"So sorry," I said. At least I now knew why the castle was in such disrepair.

"My name is Harland Mayberry. You can call me Harley."

"Now it's all coming back to me. Lord Harland Mayberry and Luigi Chinetti—you made history together!"

"That was a long time ago," he said, sadly. I didn't want to ask why a member of the British House of Lords and the most famous

British racecar driver in the world was a caretaker of some broken-down castle in Italy.

"I'm Lord of the Manor here, so to speak."

"I'd be proud to live here," Ada said, ever the conciliator.

"Thank you."

"Have you shared the Midnight Ghost story with anyone else?" I asked.

"Only our mutual friend, Tazio."

"How do you know Tazio?" I asked.

"We raced together back in the day . . ."

"Why hasn't he pursued the Salone lead?" Ada asked.

"You'll have to ask him that question," he said with obvious misgiving.

"So, tell me, Harley, where do you think the Duesenberg is right now? It's obviously not in a cave underneath the castle is it?"

"I wish that were true. If it were, I'd recover it myself."

"I figured as much," I said. "So where is it?"

"When King Victor agreed to the Armistice of Cassibile on September 3, 1943, Hitler tried to arrest him for treason, forcing the royal family to flee from Rome to this castle. The family lived right here in this apartment for one year. Brindisi was the headquarters for the Italian Navy and, as you can see by the fortifications around the narrow channel from the Adriatic, this place is nearly impenetrable."

"Harley, do you think he brought the car with him from Rome?" Ada asked.

"Rome was heavily bombed in May of 1943. My guess is that the king had the Ghost shipped to Pantalica even before Italy joined the Axis powers."

"Okay, that's important information, but the real question is what Salone did with the car. Did he keep it? Sell it? Give it back to the king? That's where we need to focus our energies when we return to Taormina," I said.

"I agree. We'll have to pay Mr. Salone a visit when we get back," Ada said.

"Oh, one more thing. Our unit was assigned to Brindisi for Operation Slapstick, and also to protect the Royal Family against German retribution. At a reception for King Victor in the downstairs ballroom, I met your grandfather."

"What?"

"And, by the way, your grandfather was smitten by Princess Juliana."

"You've got to be kidding! So much for family folklore," I laughed.

"Listen. On your way back to Taormina, stop at Savoca. It's a commune about nineteen miles southwest of Messina. Few people realize this, but that is the town where Francis Ford Coppola shot many of the *Godfather* scenes. The movie was supposed to be filmed in Corleone, but Salvatore Salone, the boss of the Corleonesi mob rejected the project. When he realized how successful the film might become, he tried to negotiate a large percentage of the film's proceeds for himself. The producers had already moved the set to Savoca. Coppola told him to 'go to hell.' Those were his exact words."

"Is that why you want us to stop there?" Ada asked.

"Not exactly. Coppola is quite the car enthusiast himself and owns a 1948 Tucker, which he drove around the *Godfather* set while filming in Savoca. I heard that Salone was so incensed over Savoca being selected instead of Corleone that he brought the Midnight Ghost to Savoca just to spite Coppola. They used to spend a lot of time in Bar Vitelli. Maybe the owner, Signora Angelina, can tell you something. She was there when *Godfather I* and *II* were made.

While you are there, try their famous *granita di limone*. They have a special machine from the 1930s that makes it."

We spent that evening with Harley and Kenny dining at a small restaurant within walking distance of the castle. While Ada and I were somewhat curious about why such a famous member of the House of Lords seemed so disheveled, all I really wanted was more information about the Midnight Ghost. I was also very intrigued about my grandfather and Princess Juliana. But that could wait.

NINE

The 1948 Tucker Torpedo

During breakfast the following morning, we agreed that our visit with Harley had proved very productive. We now had a path forward, wherever that might lead, and we were anxious to find out where. We agreed on our priorities: We would stop in Savoca and speak with Signora Angelina, and then we'd learn what Tazio could tell us about Salvatore Salone. Next, we would speak with Mr. Salone himself about the Midnight Ghost.

After breakfast, we headed southwest on the Corso Roma to Villa San Giovanni, crossing the Strait of Messina on the ferry again. As soon as we approached Savoca, we could see Sicily's most significant landmark.

"*Mount Etna dominates the island of Sicily,*" Ada read from her travel guide. "*Rising 11,000 feet, you can see it from just about every part of the island.*"

"Hey, Andy, do you know where the name Etna came from?"

"An insurance company?" I quipped.

"It says here, it came from the Phoenician word meaning 'furnace.' Sicilians call Etna *a muntagna,*" she said, "which means simply 'the mountain.' *This mountain has been erupting for a half-million years.*"

"And I thought I had a problem with *my* temper."

"Me, too," she said, smiling.

Following our map, we turned left on Via Pineta and began driving up a narrow one-lane incline with more curves than the Monte Carlo Grand Prix. The Jag felt like a roller-coaster car soaring straight up to the sky and, thankfully, we didn't have to descend on the other side. We were so high; we were looking down on thinly veiled white clouds slightly covering the deep blueness of the Ionian Sea. To our left, the ever-present Etna ascended even higher than we were. I enjoyed the panorama, despite the danger of the rocky canyon below.

The bar Harley mentioned was suddenly in my line of sight. I slammed on the brakes. After jerking forward, Ada fell back in her seat.

"What on Earth are you doing!" she scolded.

On top of its twelve-foot arched doorway, was the sign: *Bar Vitelli*. The piazza in front of the door had a table with three empty chairs.

"Ada," I said, "this is the place Harley was talking about!"

"I can recall nearly every scene in that movie," Ada said. "Michael's wedding reception was right here on the piazza of Bar Vitelli. The table in front of the building is where Michael, Fabrizio, and Carlo sat when Michael asked the *padrone* for permission to marry his beautiful daughter, Apollonia. Remember Michael's famous words when he revealed his identity? 'My name is Michael Corleone. There are people who'd pay a lot of money for that information.'"

I finished the quote: " 'Then your daughter would lose a father instead of gaining a husband.' I hated it when Apollonia was killed by a car bomb. Somehow, I knew Fabrizio couldn't be trusted."

"Hey, let's park the Jag here. I'm anxious to speak with the owner."

As we walked in the front door, we were taken by the amount of memorabilia crammed inside. We passed a couple of fake double-barreled shotguns and pictures of Francis Ford Coppola playing cards with Al Pacino. We were surprised that we were the only people in the place other than a short, elderly woman with snow-white hair who was mopping the floor behind the bar.

"*Mi scusi*," Ada said. "Could we please order two *granita di limone?*"

She flashed a broad smile. "Two?" she asked.

"*Si. Due*," Ada answered.

"You can speak the English here, my dear."

She smiled sweetly and turned on the *granita di limone* machine. It made a high pitch rumble as it devoured five fat lemons with several chunks of ice. She heated water and sugar in a saucepan until the sugar was completed dissolved. Then she poured the mixture into the machine. Soon the machine filled our glasses with a slushy granular liquid. It was a little too puckery for me.

"Could I have a little more sugar please?" I asked.

"Too much sugar—no good!" she responded. I was stuck with what I had.

"This is very refreshing," Ada said. "Thank you for making it for us!"

"Glad you like it, my dear. My name is Signora Angelina."

"This is my husband, Andrew. My name is Ada. What a nice little museum you have here."

"*Si*." Angelina bent down and was out of sight for several seconds. She rose with a three-inch-thick picture album that was held together with black shoelaces. "This is my *collezione*," she said.

Some of the old black and white photos had turned a brownish gray color. The corners had dog-ears and some had been removed from their locations and were floating loosely between the pages of the album. Her favorites were in color and in the front of the album.

"Here is Francesco and me." Francis Ford Coppola was standing behind the bar, holding a wooden pasta spoon straight up in the air with a red, green, and white apron wrapped around him. "They eat here every night. Francesco and me—we do all the cooking." Angelina smiled proudly.

As she spoke, Ada and I slowly paged through the album, trying hard not to ignore her comments. By the time we reached the last page, we had seen several hundred pictures of the people involved in the filming of *The Godfather*. The only automobile pictures were of Coppola's Tucker and the Alfa Romeo that Fabrizio blew up with Apollonia inside of it.

"I have pictures from the war, too." She disappeared again.

When she reappeared, she had another album worn even more than the first. There were several 8 × 10 black and white prints. At first, we were just being polite by looking at them.

"Look! Where was this picture taken?" Ada asked.

"My son, Sergio—he take the picture—in Sortino. He take it right after Italia—she give up."

"Why was he in Sortino?" Ada asked.

"He was a *soldato* in the Italia army! He help the Americani shoot the Germans."

"Sortino! It's right near Pantalica," I said.

"The picture is a little out of focus," Ada noted. "Looks like American and Italian soldiers are taking a break, leaning against a few military vehicles parked at the side of the road. I wonder if one of those cars on the flatbeds is the Midnight Ghost?"

"Where is Sergio now?"

"He take a siesta. We say *breve pisolino*. It means a short a nap!" Angelina laughed.

"Of course. It's that time of day," I said looking at my watch.

"You come back later. Sergio will be here. You go visit the church up on the hill. Michael—he get a married there. Then you come a back!"

We finished our *granita di limone* and began to walk in the direction of the church. We walked uphill with concrete one-story houses on our right side. Each had a single door in the same location. Some houses were yellow and red; most were gray. Few people were on the narrow brick pavement, mostly residents watering plants or simply lounging on their balconies.

Suddenly Ada exclaimed, "Do you see the light colored space next to the door?"

"About the size of a mailbox?"

"Yes. That's where the residents posted their vendettas."

"You mean they actually wrote them out for everyone to see?"

"Vendettas were a serious family matter here. If a family member had a vendetta, it was the family's responsibility to take care of it. They were actually passed down from one generation to the next."

"What do you mean 'take care of it.'?"

"Even the score," she said.

"Revenge?"

"They never called it that, but yes, revenge. Like Harley was saying, most Mafia vendettas ended in one of the five thousand tombs in Pantalica. If they wanted to teach people a lesson, they would create a spectacle using the Sicilian Bull. Have you heard about the "Sicilian Bull," Andy?"

"You mean like the Spanish Bulls that run in Pamplona?"

"Not at all. The Sicilian Bull doesn't run. Most people around here are petrified at the mere mention of the term. It refers to one or even two people being placed in a ten-foot-high brass object in the shape of a bull, and then they are roasted until nothing was left except their bones. A small twelve-inch door behind the bull's ear is opened so the smoke can escape, and their relatives hear their screams. It is the epitome of a horrifying act of intimidation around here."

"Then their bones are traditionally taken to a cave in Pantalica?"

"That's right. Especially in the past, if someone didn't pay for Mafia protection, all they had to do was mention the Sicilian Bull. It was a powerful bill collection technique."

"I cannot believe something *that* outrageous still goes on today. How do you know all about this?"

"I'm Italian. Remember? Actually my uncle's family is from Sicily and he explained a lot of this to me as I grew up. The bull and the bones are used mainly to gain compliance. The Mafia always makes sure there are enough witnesses around to tell the story."

We reached a four-foot red brick wall with unusual rock formations behind it. Stand-alone chunks of limestone were transformed into houses on the adjacent hill. The larger cliffs on the other side had several big rocks dappled with holes, reminding me of a huge beehive. Right before us was a sign that read *Chiesa S. Nicolo,* the Church of St. Nicolo. It was perched high on a cliff overlooking the Ionian Sea. To my untrained eye, it looked like a small Anglo-Saxon castle with square shapes, stone towers, and only two small spires.

"Let's go inside and say a prayer," Ada suggested.

Once inside the church, I was surprised by its modest size. It was quite ordinary, with typical semi-circular arches built into a high cathedral ceiling. Four white concrete pillars surrounded ten rows of pews. Everything was white with peach-colored trim. We kneeled at the altar and looked up at a framed picture of Our Lady centered among the bright rays of sunshine. Ada folded her hands, placed her head down, and prayed. We were the only people in the church.

"I used to go to a small church in our neighborhood in Newark and kneel at the altar—sometimes for an hour. I would ask God to please tell me why. I knew God must have had a reason for taking my father. Then I would move into a pew and continue to pray. Once I fell asleep, waking up hours later, shivering in the cold, unheated church."

After a few minutes, Ada rose to her feet. The light from the stained-glass windows shone on her soft face. She looked pure, clean, almost angelic. The empathy I felt for her was deep and immediate. I gently embraced her and felt a new softness and vulnerability. Her slender body was trembling and she responded by drawing me closer to her. We stood there, neither one of us moving, as if we had become two more statues on the altar. When we separated, I took her hand and led her to a wooden pew. We were quiet for a while, savoring the closeness we had just experienced. Then, sitting next to one another, we began to converse quietly.

"Does it end? Do we ever get over our grief?" she asked.

"I don't know."

"Sometimes I feel corrupt and depraved," she whispered. "My feelings are in direct conflict with my religious values. I've tried hard to be devout and follow the teachings of Jesus. He taught us never to return the evil deed of another, but instead to seek the power of God. *'Do not repay anyone evil for evil.'* This is what I've been taught and always believed."

"Religious values can be put to the test," I said, "especially when a person is dealt the tragic loss of someone he or she loves deeply. When other people cause the loss, vengeance is a natural reaction. Ada, I know the pain is overwhelming and interferes with what my father calls the rational process of thought. I remember the Babylonian code from history class: *If a man destroys the eye of another man, he shall destroy his eye. If a man breaks another man's bone, he shall break his bone.* My father calls it 'a Roland for an Oliver.' He said that code was the most effective crime deterrent in history. Maybe we should rewrite our Constitution."

"Very interesting, Andy. Tell me, what *is* the difference between *revenge* and *justice?*"

"I used to think about this when my father became a mob target in America. *Revenge* is done to satisfy the person who suffered the wrongdoing, while *justice* is done to create fairness for society. Justice is what *should be done,* while revenge is what *you think should be done.*"

"Are they ever one and the same?"

"My father would argue yes, as long as society is the beneficiary, and fairness applies to all. He would say justice is *selfless,* yet revenge is *selfish.* When he taught constitutional law at Harvard, he would tell me justice is all about the government implementing laws to ensure its people are treated with fairness."

"So what if government is unable or unwilling to enforce those laws?" Ada asked. "Can an individual act as a 'government' for the common good, to ensure society is treated with fairness?"

"You mean vigilante justice, like the American frontier back in the 1800s? I suppose getting rid of murderers who are destroying the society around them has more to do with justice and less to do with revenge."

Ada stood up and walked to the aisle.

"I see it differently. Maybe it has something to do with both. My basic desire would be to see the people who killed my father dead! I don't care whether it's called revenge or justice. We'd better head back, Andy." Ada marched toward the front doorway at a rapid pace; I could barely keep up with her.

At first, neither one of us spoke as we started down the hill to Bar Vitelli. Just before we reached it, I said, "Your pain over your father's death and your hatred for his killers is a very private passion, isn't it?"

"I've never let anyone know except you."

"Have you ever tried to get help?"

"I don't want it to go away."

Her answer bothered me. Not only because of the pain it caused her but also because of the range of emotions in which she indulged. I became very concerned. I didn't want Ada to be pain. Somehow, I had to help her.

Sergio was waiting for us in Bar Vitelli when we returned. He was a short paunchy man with considerable nervous energy. He had an Einstein-like appearance, a thick moustache, and was predominantly bald with a ring of gray hair falling over his ears that looked like it hadn't been combed or cut since puberty. Within the first few minutes of our arrival, he had wiped down the bar at least four times.

"That counter must be squeaky clean," I said, attempting to initiate conversation. "There's probably nothing else to do here except wipe down the bar." Sergio stopped wiping, looked at me, and then left the room.

"Now you did it," Ada whispered. "You pissed him off."

"Before we can talk to anyone in this place, they go through some kind of disappearing act." I said. "Let's go. We can meet Tazio for dinner."

As we rose to leave, Sergio returned with a picture. "You ask about the cars?" He held up the picture and pointed to the cars on the flatbeds. "The first car, she belong to the Americana, Capitano Maxwell Riter. The second car, she belong a to that sonama bitch, Maggiore Salone! Salvatore Salone!"

Ada and I looked at each with complete astonishment. "You said Maxwell Riter?" I asked.

"*Si*. When Italia—she surrender, we were ordered to fight the Germs with the Americani. Capitano Riter—he was a the command officer."

Ada and I looked at each other with shock. *Was it a coincidence we met him at the Noble-Dean California auction?*

"It had to be a coincidence," Ada said. "What else could it be?"

"Why did you call Mr. Salone a son of a bitch?" I asked.

"He bring a the car back here when Francesco had his Tucker here to film *The Godfather.* He drive it around here like he was a King Vittorio! Francesco ask him nice to leave, but he refusa."

"What happened?" I asked.

"When they all done a shoot, both cars go home."

"Where do you think home is?" Ada asked.

"Francesco go back to New York. He need to finish *The Godfather.* Salone—he live in Enna. I think the car is there. I don't know—I never see the car again!"

"One more question, do you think Salone is part of the Sicilian Mafia?" I gently elbowed Ada. I was surprised she would ask a stranger that question.

"Shh!" Sergio looked around the room. "You never ask a that question in Sicilia!"

☆   ☆   ☆

We sat quietly in the Jag before we headed back down the hill, still trying to make sense out of what Sergio told us. "I don't know, Andy. There's a side of me that feels like we are being set up. You know what I mean?"

"Set up for what?"

"I don't know. Maybe everything is happening a little too fast."

"Ada, we're supposed to be looking for a famous car. This stuff about the Mafia has nothing to do with us."

We headed slowly away from Savoca. I kept the Jag in second gear until the engine speed increased, then shifted into third.

"Tazio's probably sipping Zazas back at the villa," Ada said.

I increased the speed and shifted into fourth gear.

"It feels like we could drive right over the clouds. This must be what God sees when He looks down from heaven. When I was a young girl, I could draw clear mental pictures of what heaven looks like. Now, I'm wondering what hell looks like." Ada sat back in her seat, clinging to the passenger-side door, bracing herself for our downward spiral. "I know, Andy, I need to get over it."

As we approached the first sharp turn, I applied the brakes. The pedal went straight to the floor without resistance.

"Damn it! No brakes!" I hollered. I swiftly downshifted into third, and then into second. I yanked the emergency brake lever upward. Again, there was no resistance. Our speed increased. The engine revved loudly. When I let up on the clutch, the Jag skidded toward the embankment.

"Stay away from the canyon side!" Ada screeched.

"Grab the dash bar with both hands," I shouted.

Once I recovered from the skid, the Jag gained more downhill momentum. We had to be going at least 60 in a 15-mile-per-hour speed zone, but I was too busy steering to look at the kilometers on the speedometer, much less translate them to miles per hour. If we came to the next curve at this rate of speed, we would surely flip over, and that meant possibly falling off the steep cliff looming on our left side. If we jumped, we would be seriously injured, maybe crippled for life. But jumping was our only chance.

"Ada, get ready! We have to jump before we get to the next turn." I couldn't see her face, but I am sure she was terrified. The next turn was coming up rapidly and only fifty yards away.

"We can do this!" Ada shouted. "It's our only chance. Use the bushes!"

"Get ready! We'll jump together!" I cried out.

A thick cluster of blackberry bushes lined the right side of the road. They were ten feet tall and very dense. Ada had her right hand on the door lever as I drove toward the bushes. I skimmed the Jag along the rough terrain at the side of the road and grazed the thick patches for a few hundred feet. When the Jag slowed to about 30 miles per hour, I steered it directly into the bushes. I leaped to the passenger side and placed my arms tightly around Ada's upper body.

"Ada, open the door now!"

We closed our eyes and launched ourselves out of the Jag. We landed into the heap of bushes, their tangled, twisted branches providing a spring-like cushion for our fall. When I opened my eyes, I could barely see daylight. A complex web of barbed blackberry branches surrounded us. Ada was a few feet away with her back to me.

"Ada! Ada! Are you okay?" She didn't answer. I crawled over to her. "Ada!"

I thought she was unconscious. I gently turned her toward me and felt her whole body trembling. Her breathing was heavy. I was immediately concerned about internal injuries and shock. I didn't notice any serious head injuries, but she had several bruises on her face, legs, and arms.

"Inhale, Sweetheart. Keep inhaling."

"Are we still alive?" she asked faintly.

"I think so," I said. "Those brambles did a number on your legs. They scratched us both up badly. Are you in any pain?"

"No. How about you? Anything broken?"

"Only my perfect driving record is all."

We rose to our feet. After we both calmed down, Ada said, "That was quite a driving achievement. I take back everything I've ever said about your horrible driving. I'd hate to think what would have happened had you been unable to slow down. Thank the Lord for these bushes!"

We walked to a clearing and checked our scrapes to make sure neither one of us had suffered a serious injury.

"We need to get you to the hospital and have you checked."

"Aside from the bruises, I'm okay, Andy. Really, I am."

"Where is the Jag? I don't see it in the bushes."

"It must have spun back on the pavement." When we glanced over the precipice on the other side of the road, we could see the mangled wreck of a formerly pristine Jaguar XKSS crumpled between the sharp rocks about eighty feet below. The first thing on my mind was *Tazio.*

"He's going to kill me," I said. "One of the best cars in the collection destroyed!"

"I just hope he has insurance," Ada said.

"Yeah, even so, they don't make these cars anymore. This was the last one, remember?"

We began walking down the hill. When we reached the curve I was so afraid to confront, we noticed a gravel runaway ramp over to the right.

"Now they tell us!" I said.

"We just need to thank God we weren't killed. Thank you too, Andy, for saving my life!" she said, as we held each other tightly. "Why do you think the brakes failed?"

"We have to recover the wreckage. I'd like to *know* what happened to the brake lines. The older drum brakes in back aren't as reliable as the newer disk brakes in front, but to have them all fail at the same time is almost impossible. Ada, I'm sure of it! Someone out there doesn't want us to find the Midnight Ghost!"

We arrived back at our hotel at 10:00 p.m., deeply shaken over our ordeal in Savoca. We now both understood that if someone was trying to kill us, he or she would try again. We sat on the sofa, pondering our next move.

"They want us killed!" Ada said. She left the room and after about ten minutes returned with two glasses of Nerello Mascalese. "We need to settle ourselves down. This is the wine we purchased a few days ago at Demetrio's. Remember? It's Etna's best-known red pinot. Tell me what you think of the fruit flavors." Ada was trying hard to get our minds off of the accident.

"Dry, but it tastes like raspberries," I replied.

"Don't talk about berries. We've had enough of them for one day!"

"That's for sure," I said. "Glad your sense of humor remains intact."

"It isn't really."

Ada placed her head on the armrest of the sofa, stretching her legs out across my lap.

"Bar Vitelli, huh? Why don't they just say Vitelli's Bar? Actually, Andy, I'm very tired right now."

She yawned and closed her eyes. I knew exactly how distraught she was.

"You know, Ada, we have to be especially cautious now. We are going to . . . "

Her heavy breathing interrupted the beginning of my soliloquy.

"Ada?"

She was fast asleep.

TEN

The Steel Jaws
of the Crusher

Ada woke up early. "A good night's sleep does wonders for the soul," she said. "Do you think we were being a little paranoid over what happened yesterday?"

"We'll learn more once the car is recovered," I said knowing full well that something nefarious was at play. "Ada, I have nominated you to explain what happened to Tazio. He likes you much more than he likes me."

"Yeah, I'm sure he will get his *lupara* (shotgun) out and shoot us both!"

After lunch, we flagged down a cab in front of the hotel and arrived at Villa Christina in the early afternoon. We were both on edge, feeling badly about the wrecked XKSS, not to mention that someone was trying to assassinate us.

The front door of the villa was wide open.

"Who the hell is watching over this place?" Ada asked as we walked through the downstairs area.

"Tazio would never leave this place unguarded," I said.

"He's probably tooling around town in his French Woody. Wait a minute, I hear noises," Ada said. "Backyard noises."

We ambled to the back patio and noticed three men in sunglasses finishing lunch. Their empty plates were still in front of them as they drank tall Bloody Marys and smoked cigars. Bottles of vodka, tomato juice, black pepper, and Tabasco sauce were arranged like tin soldiers in the middle of the table. My trepidation was instantaneous: *Who were the two men sitting next to Tazio?*

"Benevenuto!" Tazio said with enthusiasm.

He attempted to be gracious and stood, but he became unsteady and had to plunk himself back down in the chair, a feat accomplished almost entirely by gravity.

"Andrew and Ada Robinson, I want you to meet my two good friends: Sal Salone and Max Riter."

Once more, my heart raced, only this time from bewilderment.

Max removed his sunglasses. His deep tan seemed deeper with them off. He was dressed in stylish jeans and a polo shirt, in contrast to Salone's less formal attire, consisting of a salmon colored t-shirt, sneakers, and a yellow baseball cap.

"Well," Max said, "it is certainly a pleasure to see you two again! When I learned Tommie put you in charge of the Midnight Ghost project, I came here to offer my services."

He reached for my hand and we shook. Ada managed an abbreviated nod.

"You came all the way to Sicily to help us find King Victor's Duesenberg?" I asked, still wondering why Maxwell Riter was at Villa Christina with Tazio and Salone.

"I call it the Midnight Ghost. Sounds more exotic, doesn't it?"

"I think that name diminishes its grandeur," Ada said.

"We've been discussing the plan for the Pergusa Lake Historic Car Festival to be held in August. My friend, Mr. Salone here, is the main sponsor or, I should say, Salone Granito is the main sponsor. Right Sal?"

"Whatever you say, Max." Salone yawned and looked at his watch.

"I'm honored to judge in the concours event," Max added.

"Oh, where is it held?" I asked.

"The Autodromo di Pergusa is the Formula One racetrack that encircles Pergusa Lake," Max explained. "The Pergusa Lake Historic Car Festival is considered the most prestigious car event in all of Italy. It includes a historic Car race, a Concours d'Elegance, and the Noble-Dean Classic Car Auction. People from all over the world attend this event. Anyone who is 'someone' shows up. Mr. Salone participates in all three events each year. He competes in the historic race, shows off his cars at the concours event, and buys and sells at the auction. This year we will be doing a lot of selling. Right, Sal?"

Salone didn't answer, but leaned sideways on his chair, inhaling his *Toscano* cigar and looking thoroughly disgusted.

"Sal? We *will* be selling there, right?"

"Yes. You know we will, Max! You also know the subject makes me furious!" Max receded in his chair like a two-year-old who was just reprimanded.

"How are things in Vegas, Max?" Ada asked.

"Very good, thanks. In fact, I just secured approval for a Classic Automobile Investment Trust. We call it CAIT. This is our advertising slogan: *Now you can become part owner of one hundred fifty of the most spectacular classic cars in the world for a little as $1,000.* How does it sound?"

"Pretty good," I said. I didn't have the foggiest notion of what he was talking about, but owning one hundred fifty classic cars for a grand captured my attention.

"Is that like a mutual fund?" Ada asked.

"Somewhat. It's similar to my Real Estate Investment Trust, the REIT, but funded with classic cars instead of real estate. It offers diversification and professional management, two very advantageous features for investors. Now all we have to do is acquire some great cars!"

"And find investors willing to take the chance?" Ada added.

"We have to shell out a few million first for the cars, and then we'll sell shares of the CAIT to investors. We'll charge a small management and administrative fee. The history and quality of the cars is what will really attract investors. Right now, we're building a large showroom and road track outside Las Vegas where the shareholders can see and drive the cars. My job is to find high-end, investment-grade automobiles. If I may, I would like to work on the Midnight Ghost project with you."

"Well that's very kind of you, Max!" Ada said. "We can use all the help we can get."

I was perplexed. If Salone *was* in possession of the Midnight Ghost, wouldn't Riter know about it? I simply did not trust either one of these guys. This was a big charade for our benefit.

"Max, he is going to help me find cars all over the world!" Tazio noted.

I wondered if Tazio had just made a deal with the devil.

Salone nodded slowly and finally spoke. *"Sei la ragazza più bella che abbia mai visto"* (You're the most beautiful woman I've ever seen)

"Grazie," Ada said with a wide smile. She seemed surprised and grateful for the compliment.

"Posso mostrarvi un buon momento se venite al mio vill stasera," he continued. (I can show you a good time if you come over to my villa tonight) *"Non rimarrete delusi."* (You won't be disappointed)

"No, no, no!" Ada said firmly. *"Lo non sono in vendita!"* (I'm not for sale!)

"Ha sposato a Andrew!" Tazio said. (She's married to Andrew!) *"Meglio di stop!"* (Better stop!) Tazio was seething and all but ready to pounce on Salone.

That exchange was purposely designed to exclude me. Not only did I feel like the odd man out, but I also knew just enough Italian to realize this guy, Salone, was hitting on my wife. I could also tell that Ada and Tazio told him to stop. What nerve—and we just met this jerk!

"Did you find anything in Brindisi?" Salone asked in perfect English. "I was there during the war."

"No," I said. "Nothing worth mentioning."

I was surprised by Salone's appearance. I pictured a much bigger man instead of some short stack with a full complement of greased down jet-black hair. No gray either. I was annoyed by his pomposity. Napoleonic complex, I think they call it. I've seen it before. Some people overcompensate for their short stature by attempting to exert their power. I knew one thing for sure: Salone didn't like us and we didn't like him.

"I heard recently," Salone said, "the Midnight Ghost was destroyed by a hungry impact crusher after the war. Did you ever see a car crushed to death?" No one answered. "It's fascinating. The hard steel jaws of the crusher open to receive the car then close around it." Salone simulated the movement of the crusher with his arms. "Then the crusher cradles the car, rocking it side to side like it's trying to console it before its violent death. As the jaws bring their full force to bear, the car emits a high-pitched scream then—pop! The windshield blows. And—pop! pop!—the headlights explode. In a matter of seconds, the car is less than two feet tall, and the crusher yawns to accept another victim.

But do you know what is truly amazing? After the car is reduced to its basic elements, it's born again! Who knows, the Midnight Ghost might be a Chevy cruising around Massachusetts or even a John Deere tractor plowing a field in upstate New York."

We were transfixed by Salone's morbid description. Total silence enveloped everyone as Salone was overcome by a sadistic laugh.

I didn't know what was so funny, but then I realized he was toying with us. *Okay*, I said to myself, *I can play this game, too.*

"As far as the Midnight Ghost was concerned, it was a wasted trip. Ada and I had fun, though. She treated me to an enchanting harbor cruise, then a very romantic evening at the Borgo Egnazia for an intimate dinner and a moonlight walk. Then we . . . "

"The massage!" Ada chimed in. Her timing was perfect. "Oh, yes. I learned the fine art of sensual avocado massage in a parlor on 18th Avenue in Newark. The warm oils . . . "

"Yup," I added. "And, you would not believe her stroking technique."

"Stop! You kill me!" Tazio cried out.

Salone just sat there with a cavalier look, realizing that our little massage duet was exclusively for his benefit.

"Very good!" he said, as he applauded slowly. "That was well-done! I must admit; it did turn me on. *Lo tengo a mente quando ci vediamo sta sera.*" (I'll keep it in mind when you join me this evening)

"Mai!" (Never!) Ada said. Now she wasn't smiling. She turned to me. "Can we go?"

"Sure."

"Are you sure you can't sit down for a few minutes?" Maxwell asked.

"Perhaps . . . maybe just a few," Ada agreed reluctantly.

"Mr. Salone is one of my best clients," Maxwell said. "He has one of the finest classic car collections in Sicily."

"Have you ever seen the Ghost, Mr. Salone?" I asked pointedly.

"Never!" He responded with lightning quickness—almost too quickly.

I could tell he was provoked. I was tempted to reveal the content of our conversation with Harley and Sergio but had suspicions about Salone, not solely because I had derogatory information about him. It was his body language, his arrogance, his boorish condescension, and my thoughts about his mob involvement.

"Do you think if I had ever seen it, I would tell you about it?"

"Why wouldn't you?" I asked.

"If I had seen it—I would own it, that's why!" he said angrily. His sudden burst of anger stunned everyone. "Now I have a question for you! You don't have anything better to do than to chase down expensive old cars?"

I hesitated with my answer, unsure how to respond. He was clearly enraged and I had no idea why.

"I don't understand your question," I answered.

"I know about you! You and your goddamned crusade! I work hard all my life, fight for my country, and now everything I own—" He stopped abruptly. "All because of you!"

Salone's face was crimson. The blood vessels on his forehead inflated like balloons ready to burst. Sweat beaded on his brow. *What could have possibly triggered his inflamed rhetoric?* He stood up so suddenly, his Bloody Mary spilled on the table and his dinner plate smashed on the floor. His muscles bulged conspicuously through his salmon-colored t-shirt. "I could break you in half right here!" He charged toward me.

"Whoa!" Tazio yelled. He jumped up to stand between us. "No one gonna break no one in half today!" Salone backed off.

Suddenly, Maxwell also became peeved.

"You really *do* have a lot of nerve, Robinson. Schoolteachers don't bid up Duesenbergs to $900,000! Why did you lie to me? You know, the collector car community is based on honor and integrity, and you already have a bad reputation!"

He stood next to Salone, who still had his fists clenched with his eyes focused on me like lasers. Standing next to Tazio, the battle lines were drawn. The entire episode was so draining that I was speechless. Riter and Salone were like a couple of attack dogs and I was the red meat.

I wasn't disappointed when Tazio's luncheon guests angrily departed. The entire incident cemented the emnity between us and further convinced me our near fatal trip down the mountain in Savoca was far from an accident.

We retreated to the living room area. Tazio was embarrassed.

"I'm so sorry," he said. "I just meet that guy, Riter. I don't know why Salone got so upset."

"Don't worry about it, Tazio," Ada said. "It wasn't your fault."

Ada attempted to break the news about our accident to Tazio, very delicately.

"You know," she said, "two of your dearest friends almost succumbed to the forces of evil over there in Savoca yesterday." Ada was somber with a grave look on her face. She was also very convincing.

"Oh, No! Who was *that*?" Tazio responded with dread in his voice. She hesitated just long enough to increase his uneasiness. "Well, who was it? Are you going to tell me or not?" he asked nervously for the second time.

Ada bowed her head solemnly. "Andy and me," she said contritely."

"What? You and Mr. Punt? Tell me. What the hell happen to you?" Tazio's response fell way short of the frenzy Ada was hoping to achieve.

"Yes, we almost bought the farm yesterday, Taz." she said, matter of factly.

"Bought what farm?" he asked. No farms are for sale in Savoca."

"That's American slang for dying. You know . . . *morente*. We came this far from going over an eighty-foot cliff!" Ada placed her hand near Tazio's face with her thumb and index finger about an inch apart. "That's right, this close!" she said again as if he didn't hear her the first time. "We jumped out just in time!"

Tazio turned his head and looked at me. Then he looked at Ada. "*Bastardi*!" he bellowed. My brand new XKSS!"

"Well, you can always replace the car, but you can't replace us, you know," Ada said. It was a futile attempt. Tazio was already in a rage.

"That XKSS! It was the last one made!" Tazio walked over the telephone in the next room. After fifteen minutes, he returned. "Just call my daughter in Rome. She tell me all our cars are insured with Lloyds of London.

The cars on loan from the owners—they have their own insurance. I make another call."

Tazio left the room again. When he returned he said, "My friend in Palermo is shipping me another XKSS. This one is *really* the last one made! I also call my friend, Francesco Mazza, the Carabiniere Generale and invite him to come over for dinner. We should tell him about what happened to you in a Savoca."

"That's a good idea." I said. *How compassionate,* I thought. Once he got himself another XKSS, he finally got around to expressing his concern for us.

"Guess I know where we rank on the food chain," I whispered to Ada.

"Boy, was I naïve," she whispered back. Then we both laughed.

"Tazio, by the way," I asked, "did you tell Salone and Riter anything about us? Who we were? Where we lived or anything else?"

"*Mai!* I would never tell that man nothing! Believe me, please!"

"Of course. We were just wondering how he knew where we were from."

"Riter! How you say—him and Riter—they're *cahoots*."

"You mean cohorts?" I asked.

"Same thing."

"Salone must have me confused with someone else."

"Tuo padre?"

"Well, if that's true, why is he angry and acting like a pompous jerk?"

"Don't ask me! He just don't like you."

"Short man syndrome," Ada observed. "He has to assert himself at our expense. I used to have a boyfriend like that. When he got carried away with his importance, I would unload a bunch of short people one-liners. That really got to him. I told him once, 'There are advantages to being short.' When he said, 'Yeah, tell me one!' I would say, 'you're always the last person to know when it rains! That would always crack him up and bring him down to earth."

"At least he had a sense of humor. I don't think Salone has one," I said.

We shared Harley's story of how he gave Salone the Midnight Ghost. "Do you think Salone still has the car?" Ada asked.

"Harley—he tell me the same story—about Sortino and how he give all those cars to Salone and his men. No one ever saw the car around here. Salone—he take his best cars to the Pergusa Concours d'Elegance each year. I think if he owned the Midnight Ghost, he'd want people to know about it!"

"Yeah, especially with his ego," Ada said.

"I'm not so sure," I said. "Maybe it will end up being the main attraction in the CAIT showroom. It will be interesting to see where Riter gets the caliber of cars he's looking for. They're not exactly that plentiful."

"Andy, when Mazza arrives for dinner, ask him why he thinks Salone and Riter came down so hard on you, okay?"

"Does it really matter, Ada?"

"I'm just completely baffled, that's all. He has to know something."

Later, there was a loud knocking on the front door. Alonzo wiped his hands on his apron and reluctantly left the kitchen to answer it. We heard the sound of metal hinges and light rhythmic thumping on the floor. A well-built man with horn-rimmed glasses walked toward us with the aid of aluminum forearm crutches. He leaned his crutches against the nearest wall and then hobbled back to us.

"After a year, I'm getting pretty good at this," he said. Before he sat down at the table with us, he removed his Burberry trench coat and smart fedora, placing them neatly on the empty chair beside us. Until I noticed his wide bald spot, I couldn't help but think of Bogart in the movie *Casablanca.*

"I'm Francesco Mazza, Carabiniere Generale," he said.

I didn't understand why the man in command of Sicily's carabinieri was not in uniform, but I had other things on my mind. His face had a noticeable frown. He was clearly annoyed, as if he had enough to worry about without having to deal with a couple of troublemakers from America. *Another moody Sicilian to deal with*, I thought. *Where were all the emotionally stable people like me in this country?*

"You know about the Sicilian Mafia Commission." His words were framed as a reminder, not a question. "You know it's the Cosa Nostra here in Sicilia, otherwise known as *la famiglia criminale Salone*. Why did you have to come to Sicilia? Do me a big favor—go home!"

"Salone?"

"Yes," Francesco said. "Salvatore Salone—his family owns the granite quarry in Ragusa. They sell gravestones all over Italia. Really, you should go home, Mr. Robinson. Sicily—it's no place for a famous American judge like you."

"You, too!" I almost fell off of my chair. "What's wrong with you people? My father is the famous American judge, not me. I'm just a simple schoolteacher! He is Andrew P. Robinson II; I am Andrew P. Robinson III. What the hell is going on here, anyway?"

"You're a schoolteacher?"

"So is my wife! I teach high school English. She teaches history."

Francesco planted his elbow on the table. The palm of his hand combed the wide bald spot on his head as if he had hair. Then it was time for dinner.

Alonzo served an antipasto and then the main course of *pasta con le sarde*, pasta and sardines. *Cassata Siciliana*, a delicious sponge cake soaked with liqueur and sweetened ricotta, was our dessert. One thing I knew for sure about Alonzo; he was definitely a great chef.

During dinner, Ada and I re-emphasized that we really were teachers and shared our background information with Francesco. I proudly explained my father's role in the American justice department and how he helped pass RICO. While I hated to admit it, it was clear his successful legislation against the Mafia had something to do with our current predicament.

After dessert, Alonzo passed around Cuban cigars on a cedar tray. Cigars always made me sick, not only smoking them but also smelling them. There was a time when I would have felt pressured to take one too, especially around men like these. But I politely declined.

When dinner was over, we retired to the living room area. Ada and I sat on the chocolate-colored leather sofa in the middle of the room. Tazio and Francesco sat in plush leather-wrapped Queen Ann chairs facing us. They both still had their Cubans, which had grown soggy with all the conversation.

On the far wall hung a vividly colored painting that Ada and I loved. It was Armedio Modigliani's *Large Nude Seated* in an ornate oak frame with a rich golden patina. Tazio's eyes were riveted on certain parts of the female anatomy—until Ada caught him.

"You should be looking at her face," Ada said. "That's where the action is—her face, Tazio! She will always mislead you. Something is going on there. Do you see it?" Tazio pondered Ada's question while staring intently at the face.

"The artist—he make a mistake," Tazio replied. "Her face has too much skin and her cheeks are fat."

"Not really. Her facial beauty is masked because you are too preoccupied with her other attributes."

"Ahh! Her face!" Tazio said, as he shook his head and slapped his thigh. "She's like old racecars! You need to look under the hood to see the real beauty! The body—she's nice—but under the hood is where everything happens!"

Brilliant analogy, I thought. I was beginning to like Tazio Nucci.

Ada looked over at Francesco. "It seems like you are also preoccupied with the wrong thing," she said.

He nodded and exhaled. "Yes, I believe so," he said. He looked straight at me with penetrating eyes. "But I see the face now."

"Good," I said. "Then tell me why they are trying to kill us."

"They want to kill you or your wife. It doesn't matter. If they kill both of you, all the better. They think *you* are your father."

I placed my hands on my thighs and leaned back. "Okay then, what did my father ever do to them? My father's enemies are in America."

"You don't read the papers? It's been on *televisione* for the last two weeks. A new act providing extended penalties for criminal organizations of racketeering just got through the Italian Parliament. We call it ESCO, *Atto di Estorsione e Corruzione*. Your father—he got RICO, the Racketeer Influenced and Corrupt Organizations Act, passed in America and worked with the *Parlamento Italiano* in Italia to get ESCO passed here. This law gives us the power to hold Mafia bosses accountable for crimes they have their henchmen commit. The big thing, though, is we can take their assets if we even think they are guilty."

Suddenly, Francesco became an intense and passionate man. "Finally! Here in Sicilia! Many corrupt officials have been interfering with the successful prosecution of Mafia bosses. In the Arma dei Carabinieri, we don't have nearly enough soldiers, and many of those we have can't be trusted. It's a disgrace—that's what it is—a disgrace!" His words were accentuated by rapid-fire hand gestures.

"But now," he exclaimed, "how do you say it in America—it's a different ball game! We can confiscate land and other assets owned by the Mafia, and I hear the number-one mob boss in Sicily is scared! Finally, he's afraid of me! The first thing I'm going to do is seize all his assets, including that multi-million dollar car collection he has. Then I'm shipping him off to a dungeon at Asinara prison in Sardinia! It will be the happiest day of my life!"

I looked over at Ada. She was frozen in silence. At that moment, it felt like we were both hit in the forehead by a sledgehammer. *"Salone!"* I said in shock.

"He lives in the Province of Enna," Francesco continued. "It's the largest mob fortification in Italy and probably the world. ESCO will wipe him out! Then it will be my pleasure to indict him for murdering my best carabinieri! He's a desperate man right now, and I can't wait to see the little weasel squirm!"

I began thinking of those few occasions when my father attempted to educate me on the Mafia. "My father told me how the Mafia believes in their principles of honor, solidarity, and vengeance," I said. "They know there is no justice unless they *earn it* themselves. Justice to them is their own brand of revenge, and it is the most honored of all their principles."

"That's right," Ada said. "You have to turn it back on them. Never mind arresting them. Those who live by the sword *should* die by it!"

"Then you know, they *will* execute," Francesco said. "When it comes right down to it, killing you two would be a way for Salone to get revenge for what he believes your father did to him—that's what *his* justice is all about."

"So, it doesn't really matter to Salone whether he kills my father or he kills us, does it?"

"I'm telling you that Salone has contracts out on you and your wife! Every hit man in Sicily—and there are thousands of them— have you in their gun sights. I will take you and your wife to the Palermo airport tomorrow."

"If you leave the villa for any reason—even go outside—without the guards, I can't guarantee your safety. They have sharpshooters with high-powered telescopic rifles who don't miss, so stay away from the windows when you are here. I'll take you back to your hotel this evening, pick you up early in the morning, and we'll head straight to the airport."

ELEVEN

The 1930 Blower Bentley

One day we are basking in the sunshine without a worry in the world, and the next day we're targets for assassination! Ada and I didn't need this trauma in our lives. Looking over our shoulders every five minutes, checking the rearview mirror, not trusting a single soul, is an impossible existence. I knew we had to leave Sicily, but then what? My father had a large security detail protecting him. Perhaps he could get us into the witness protection program. What choice did we have?

Francesco picked us up early for the trip to the airport. Against his wishes, we stopped at Villa Christina to obtain some remembrance photos from the collection. That's when an eruption, rivaling anything Mt. Etna could have produced, gave rise to an even greater trauma in our lives.

As we approached the villa, the wrought-iron gates were wide open with no carabinieri in sight. Suddenly, Dorothy Page's dark green 1930 Blower Bentley sped by us like Secretariat charging out of the gate at the Kentucky Derby. The dark blue Alfa sedan with carabinieri markings in hot pursuit didn't have a chance, but its wildly blinking blue strobe lights and annoying siren put up a good front.

"That car was just stolen!" I yelled. We drove to the back of the villa. The garage doors were open.

"Don't go in there!" Francesco warned. "If anyone is there, they're probably armed. Let's wait until my carabinieri come back." I drove to the front of the house.

"Tazio and Alonzo might be inside," Ada said. "We can't wait!" Ada threw open the door and ran toward the villa. I ran after her.

"Ada! Don't go in there alone!" I hollered. I caught up with her near the front door. "Wait here for Francesco!"

Once inside, with the vigilance of a SWAT team, the three of us walked through the villa, looking around every corner, exploring every room, checking behind every piece of furniture. My blood curdled when Francesco struggled to remove his Berretta firearm from his hidden holster. We rode the elevator to the portico that overlooked Mt. Etna and Taormina. As we peered over the balcony, a fusillade of gunfire came at us from all directions, ripping through the stucco wall with pieces of debris exploding inside the room.

"Get down!" Francesco shouted and shoved Ada and me to the floor and then fell on top of us.

The repeated percussion of 12-gauge shotguns blunted our sense of hearing, and the rapid rat-a-tat-tat of semiautomatic rifles made us wonder how the bullets could possibly miss. When the gunfire ceased, we crawled to the hallway near the elevator and stood up. Francesco leaned against the wall for support, his crutches under his arms, and his right hand holding his Berretta in the air. A ghastly silence enveloped us. We were safe for the moment.

"Anyone hit?" Francesco asked. "Take long deep breaths," he said. "C'mon now, you have to breathe!" I was more interested in comforting Ada than breathing, but she seemed to be all right.

The elevator door opened as if it was tired of waiting for someone to press the button. I placed my handkerchief over my mouth.

I felt like vomiting. I needed water and fresh air. We descended in the elevator to the first floor. Just as the door opened, a man attacked me with a blackjack. Ada dropped him with a perfect kick to the groin, and then somehow intercepted his swinging arm and elbowed him in the face. His blackjack went flying across the floor. The man screeched in pain as he ran out the front door. I was frozen where I stood, staring straight ahead, seeing nothing, feeling nothing, in a mindless stupor.

"Oh my God!" I kept saying. My brain tried to expel what just happened from my consciousness. I lost my capacity to breathe again. Francesco still had his Berretta out and ready to fire.

Ada squeezed the sides of my arms and violently jostled me.

"It's all right! We're okay!" she shouted. "Stay next to me! Let's keep moving!"

"Give me the Beretta," I demanded. Francesco didn't argue. He realized that I might be a better shot, given his incapacity.

While Francesco stood watch on the first floor, I followed closely behind Ada as she combed two floors with scrupulous caution, locking all the doors and windows. Then we descended to the lower level, where the most coveted classic car collection in the world *used* to reside. When the elevator door opened, I will never forget what we saw next. Scattered like fragments from an aerial bombardment was an avalanche of empty wine bottles, broken glass, and pieces of shelving. The expansive red-carpeted floor was a sea of purple wine stains. They were all gone! Millions of dollars worth of the world's most classic automotive treasures—gone!

I noticed blood on Ada's blouse near her rib cage. "Ada!" I yelled. "You're bleeding! Let me check!"

"Just a scrape when I fell. It's from my arm. Don't worry. I'm okay!"

Below her left elbow was a two-inch gash. There was blood all over her arm. I found a first aid kit in a kitchen cupboard. I washed the blood from her arm and cleaned her wound. Then I applied an antibiotic and a bandage from the first aid kit.

"You need stitches," I said. "It's pretty deep."

"Stitches? Just tighten up the bandage, Andy . . . unless you know how to sew."

"At least the bleeding is less now."

"Good. We're lucky this is the extent of our injuries," Ada said.

The realization that our lives were almost shattered was shocking. Also, I was startled by Ada's martial arts skills to say anything more. While I knew she had studied with Master Kiyoshi, I had never seen her in action.

Fortunately, the telephones operated. Francesco dialed emergency number 113. Ada and I sat on the living room sofa while Francesco maintained his vigilance by sitting near us. I still had his Beretta and was ready to use it. After about thirty minutes, the carabinieri arrived with at least five dark-blue Alfa sedans. Converging on the villa like storm troopers, eight of them entered, guns drawn. Francesco retrieved his Beretta and began shouting orders and meeting with his lieutenants. At least ten people were moving in, out, and about the villa like a swarm of hungry locusts. Officials photographed and sampled everything and then dusted for fingerprints. After an hour, Francesco leaned his crutches against the nearest wall and then hobbled over to us.

"You know, Mrs. Robinson, you probably injured a soldier of the *Commissione*," he said. "*Managgia la miseria! Madonna mia!* The *televisione* . . . the *pressione* . . . the *tensione* . . . why did you have to come to Sicilia?"

TWELVE

The Midnight Ghost

Once all the carabinieri and fingerprint officials left the villa, Francesco lit up a cigar and leaned back in his chair.

"Maybe now you realize how dangerous it is to remain in Sicilia," he said. "Just in case you don't, I want to tell you a story. Two years ago, I could walk like you. I could run. Back in 1934 I played in the FIFA World Cup when Italia beat Czechoslovakia. I could still play *futball* until last year."

Francesco breathed deeply. His cigar dangled from the side of his mouth. He kept trying to relight it, as if he needed something to do with his hands.

"I went after Salone a few years ago. I had twenty carabinieri. We followed him to Pantalica—to the Grotta, the necropolis of Filiporto, the cave where most of his victims ended up. Some of them looked like they were still alive. Hundreds of corpses—many were preserved like mummies. They were all killed by Salone's gang. Their mouths were all open like they were trying to tell their own special story of betrayal. It was the most repugnant thing I had ever seen!"

"The Bones of Pantalica," Ada said. "I've read about them."

"That's right." Francesco nodded slowly. "We had carbide head-lamps, but we could only see the bodies in front of us. The bats kept hitting us in the face. We walked a half-mile into the cave. The carabinieri got scared. Some ran back. Then the *grotta* got very wide, almost as wide as the *Romano palestra*. Next, I heard the gunfire. I was hit." Francesco closed his eyes, gathering the strength to continue.

"Francesco," I asked, "would you like something to drink?"

"A glass of water would be fine."

Ada went to the kitchen. She returned with a tall glass of water and a chilled *limoncello* in a small wine glass with a shard of ice and a sliver of lemon peel.

"Thank you," Francesco said. "I do enjoy limoncello."

"It's okay, take your time, Francesco," I said.

"I'm sorry. This is the most difficult part of the story. I get very upset every time I tell it. I was unconscious for several hours."

He dropped his dead cigar on the floor and guzzled his lemon liqueur as if it were a glass of cold beer.

"Everything was a blur; my head was pounding like a jack hammer. I was sitting on a hard wooden chair with my hands tied behind me. I felt the pain of the sharp barbed wire cutting into my wrists. I was dizzy and nauseated and I smelled vomit all over me. I finally came around. I couldn't see everything, but I knew I was still in the grotta. I remember the polished, granite stone walls and marble floors. I saw a large oak desk with big bookshelves behind it. Right in the middle of the floor was a beautiful car. I thought maybe I was hallucinating."

Francesco leaned back in his chair, folding his arms, looking up at the ceiling, pondering the right words to describe what he had seen.

"The fenders were very long. The convertible top was very low and small. It had whitewall tires, but they were covered by long fender slats in back of the car."

"What color was the car?" I asked.

"It was gray. I remember a big white cross on the bottom of the fender. It reminded me of the crest used by the House of Savoy."

"Was it a blue background?" Ada asked. Francesco nodded slowly.

"Salone walked in front of me. He grabbed my chair and spun it around. *'Vedi cosa hai fatto?'* he asked me. 'See what you did?' I saw my carabinieri—fifteen of them sprawled out on the floor—dead and injured. Salone took his *lupara*, and he pumped shots into my injured carabinieri, killing them dead. Then he reloaded and walked over to me and said, *'Lo insegno a voi una lezione non si scorda mai.'* That means 'I'll teach you a lesson you'll never forget.'"

Francesco slumped forward, covering his face with both hands. "Have you ever heard of 'kneecapping?'" Francesco looked down at his knees and began rubbing them. "That's Salone's specialty. At close range, Salone shot me in both knees, paralyzing me for the rest of my life. He didn't want me dead. Salone went to the trouble of transporting me back to Catania to the Vittorio Emanuele Hospital. By the time I received medical attention, an infection had set in and they almost had to amputate both legs. I was there for several months. You can see how I struggle. Not only have I lost the use of both legs but also I have lost all feeling in them."

Francesco turned toward Ada. Tears rolled down her white cheeks. "We are so sorry for your pain Francesco," she said. At the same time I could see fire in her eyes.

With a burst of rage, he forced himself to stand, reached for his crutches, and threw them violently against the wall, and then collapsed helplessly back into his chair. Covering his eyes, he sobbed quietly. Ada tried to console him, kneeling on the floor beside him and placing her arms around his shoulders. She exuded warmth and caring, which eventually brought Francesco enough solace to repeat his familiar refrain, "Go home! Please! I'll take you to the Palermo airport now!"

"C'mon, Ada. He's right. Let's get out of here."

"No, wait!" Ada said. "We need to at least talk to Tommie before we leave. She said she'd be here by noon. We owe her an explanation for everything that has happened. Then we can go."

Just before noon, Francesco reluctantly departed. "Just so you know, I want you both on the five o'clock flight out of Palermo to Rome!" he said adamantly. "This time it's for sure!"

☆   ☆   ☆

We were alone inside the villa. Francesco assigned two of his men to guard the outside, ensuring that no one came through the gate. Ada poured us soft drinks as we sat in the living room area.

"Where did you learn how to fight like that?" I asked her. "I know you trained in taekwondo, but I never realized just how strong you were."

"He blinked!" she said with all seriousness. "Strength is irrelevant."

"But Ada . . . how did you . . ."

Andy, you have to remember, I was the oldest. I had to learn how to protect my family. I had to learn how to survive in what many people called the most dangerous city in the country. It is also the car theft capital of the world. After my mother's car was stolen, and she was beaten when she tried to retrieve it, I committed to the Black Belt program with Master Kiyoshi. I achieved 6th dan and became an instructor. Once the word got out on 18th Avenue, no one ever bothered us again."

"I don't know much about Taekwondo, but 6th dan sounds pretty distinctive."

"I'm a master instructor. If I was going to protect my family, I had to be good at it. I took the oath: "I shall be a champion of freedom and justice and I shall build a more peaceful world." I also participated in seminars on the Principles of War by Sun Tzu and even studied Carl von Clausewitz. For me, Andy, it was purely a defensive strategy. Taekwondo was something I had to learn in order to survive. Oh, and another thing I learned. You don't run away from trouble. You overcome it. You stay and fight!"

☆   ☆   ☆

At noon, amid the reporters, camera crews, and additional *poliziotti*, Tommie, Tazio, and Sammy arrived in a limousine at the front gate. Her initial reaction focused on our well-being. Then she became furious.

"Why did this horrible thing have to happen? Our cars! What are we going to do? The owners! They'll crucify me when they find out! We must get them back!"

"Tazio said they are insured with Lloyds of London," Ada noted attempting to assuage Tommie's wrath. It had little effect.

Tommie shrugged her shoulders and shook her head in fierce denial.

"The owners don't care about cash! Their cars are sentimental treasures, like members of their families. No amount of cash could ever replace them!"

"The goddam carabinieri—they're the ones!" Tazio snarled. "The *bustarella!* Someone got to them! *La burocrazia Italiana è fatta di ladri e bustarelle!*"

"What does that mean?" I asked."

Ada interpreted. "He said, 'the Italian bureaucracy is made up of thieves and people who will bribe anyone to get their way.'"

"What about Mazza?" I asked. "Can you trust him?"

Tazio looked over at Tommie. *"Hanno tutti burattini della Mafia. Si deve sapere che."* (They are all puppets of the Mafia. You should know that)

Their frequent bursts of Italian were beginning to aggravate me. "If you want to exclude us from the conversation, just say so," I said. "Otherwise, will you please speak English?"

"Scusa," Tazio scoffed. "I speak the Italiano when I get pissed off! I said, 'they're all *pupazos* of the Mafia.' My daughter—she should know that!"

"No! Mazza is an honest man," Tommie said. "He's surrounded with a few men he *can* trust. There are many who are deceitful and on the mob payroll. It's hard for him to tell the difference."

"I am sure the people who stole the cars have unfinished business here," Ada said. "We should focus on a defensive strategy."

I looked over at Ada. She was becoming a full-fledged combat soldier. I couldn't believe it!

"What do you suggest?" Tommie asked.

"Can you trust *anyone* around here?" Ada asked.

"Negazione!" Tazio said firmly. "Riter and Salone—I think they steal the cars!"

"Riter and Salone?" Although I was suspicious of Salone, I never factored Riter into the equation.

"Si! They both want a the cars for different reasons."

Sammy was attempting to break into the conversation. "What do you think, Sammy?" I asked.

"Trust is a rare commodity in Sicilia," he replied. "I learned that when I began helping my grandfather at The Big Red."

"The Italian Trade Commission sponsors the classic car project," I said. "What about them?" Sammy hesitated, not expecting the question.

"Sorry, Sammy. I didn't mean to impugn your Mom's integrity."
He looked at Tommie.

"I'd be surprised," Tommie replied, shaking her head. "I know all the senior officials. Of course, in Sicilia, things never are as they seem."

"The government owns the villa?" I asked.

"Yes," Tommie answered. "Strictly for recreational purposes."

"Can we get military protection?"

"Like the carabinieri?" Tazio asked sarcastically.

"Francesco said he replaced the four carabinieri guarding the villa with four of his closest and most trusted friends."

Tazio laughed. "Trusted friends? In Sicilia?"

"Even though we always had the villa guarded, I'd be surprised to learn the Mafia is interested in the cars," Tommie said. "I would think they'd be difficult to convert to cash. I guess we should have tried harder to conceal the fact that the cars were here."

"That would have been difficult, with all the fund-raising projects you have," Ada said.

"For one thing, they're valuable just because of the year and make," I said. Having attended several classic car auctions, I decided to offer my expertise. "All you have to do is trace their appreciation over the last fifteen or twenty years to know they are valuable. Cars with a significant ownership history, they call it provenance, appreciate more. The Blower Bentley that sped by us—it's worth a million now. Whoever stole the cars will re-paint them, re-stamp the numbers, and re-title them. They'll hide them away for a while, make up some phony story about their history, and the cars will resurface at a prestigious classic car auction. That Bentley could fetch five million in a few years. Not a bad return on investment, huh?"

"They can't be traced?" Tommie asked.

"It is very difficult. If their identification numbers are on a plate, they replace the plate with new numbers. If their numbers are on a frame or engine block, they pound them out with ball-peen hammers or grind them down and re-stamp the numbers. They forge new titles. Now the car is essentially reborn and has a completely new provenance.

When bidders bid, winning often supersedes everything, even the truth. It's not always about money or authenticity."

I could see Ada nodding out of the corner of my eye. "Having been to an auction with my husband, I agree. There may be some other motives, though. We should be aware of what Salone and Riter are trying to accomplish. Salone is trying to convert his assets to cash so he can hide money from the government since now they're hot on his tail with ESCO. Riter is looking for cars to fund his Classic Automobile Investment Trust in Las Vegas, so both of them have fairly obvious motives."

"Why do you think Salone would want to steal the cars if he is trying to shed assets?" Tommie asked. "It doesn't make sensc."

"So he can sell them at the Pergusa Festival and pocket the cash," Ada answered.

"Once he converts everything to cash, he can hide it," I said.

"Of course! That's it exactly!" Tazio said.

"Maxwell Riter made a low-ball offer for the cars belonging to the Trade Commission last year," Tommie said. "It was quickly turned down and I never thought anything of it."

"Things are beginning to add up," Ada confirmed

It was 3:00 p.m. Francesco was scheduled to return to the villa so he could shuttle us to the Palermo airport and get us out of harm's way. Ada wanted to speak with me privately, so we found a corner in the villa where we could talk freely. I felt myself experiencing a shift in my priorities, obsessed with only one thought: keeping Ada safe!

"We have to get out of here!" I said. "We have to leave right away! The hell with the Midnight Ghost!"

"Andrew Robinson, I think your fear is clouding the issues, making it impossible for you to think clearly. I'm scared, too, but we have to assess the situation carefully and completely, and then decide what to do."

"What's there to assess?" I asked. "They're trying to kill us! What exactly do you recommend?"

"Listen to me, she said." This was her typical summons when she thought we were moving in the wrong direction. "What happens when we go home to Fairchester? The Mafia in America would be after us just like the Sicilian Mafia is after us here. We will be running for cover the rest of our lives."

"We can always move or even join the witness protection program."

"Come on, Andy. No way! If these people want us out of the picture, it doesn't matter where we live. Running away won't resolve the problem."

"So we should stay here and get ourselves killed? Is that what you're saying?" After I said that, I realized I was being consumed by the fight-or-flight syndrome, but my level of stress was becoming uncontrollable.

"My God, Andy! I grew up in Newark, remember? These two-bit hoods were a dime a dozen, and I kicked many of their asses all the way down 18th Avenue! I could probably kick that little curmudgeon's ass all over Sicily, too!"

"We're not dealing with a 'two-bit hood,' Ada. Salone *is* the Mafia in Sicily!"

"One leg at a time. That's how he puts on his pants. They're all the same to me. Let's figure out a way, Andy. *I'm not running.* Living in constant fear is no life at all. Let's stand up to the bastard!"

"Stand up? Ada! What the hell does that mean?"

"Let's develop a plan. Let's stay and fight! Right now, I need to get out of here. I'm going shopping."

"Shopping? Are you crazy! That's Alonzo's job, Ada! You're not going out!"

"I'm going shopping!" she said. "If they try anything, I'll drop them on the spot. Look what Tazio gave me. It's a Rhino 6-shot .357 magnum. It fits right in my purse! It could drop Luca Brasi with one shot! All I need to do is point and shoot."

"No, Ada! You are asking for trouble with that thing! Tazio! Damn him!"

"You can come with me or stay here if you want."

"All right! All right! I'm coming. You aren't going out there alone."

"Tazio said I could take the new red Jag XKSS. It was just delivered."

We could hear the front door open. "Here comes Francesco," I said. "Wait until he hears what we've decided."

"Let's go Robinsons—before the traffic congestion." Francesco walked in and stood before us waiting for us to rise and follow him out the door.

"We're staying," Ada said.

"Yeah . . . we *are* staying," I echoed remorsefully.

"What? I thought. . . . " Francesco was so startled that he couldn't find the words to say more.

"We're going back to our hotel this evening. It's safer there," Ada said.

"Listen! There are means of entry all over the hotel. If they come in blasting, you'll never see tomorrow. Let me take you to the airport, now!"

Tazio appeared in the foyer with a sawed-off double-barreled shotgun. "I'll stay with you," he said. "When I have my *lupara*, no one messes with Tazio!"

"Great!" I said. "We'll have a regular Fort Ticonderoga in our hotel room!"

"We have guns just in case," Ada noted. "Hopefully, we won't need them."

Francesco pounded his palm on his forehead and left the villa in a rage.

"He'll get over it," Ada said. "He reminds me of my father. I'm off to the grocery store. You coming, Mr. Robinson? I'm anxious to drive the new XKSS."

"You be careful with a my car!" Tazio shouted. "It's the last a one made!"

THIRTEEN

The Automedica Van

Two of the four carabinieri guarding the villa followed us to the grocery store. They were Francesco's most loyal men. At least, that's what Tazio told us. We headed straight back to our hotel. While eating our cold cuts and Italian bread, the telephone rang.

"The Antinori Sangiovese, that special wine we ordered from Tuscany, arrived at Demetrio's. I'm going to pick it up," Ada said. "You rest for a while, okay?"

"Can't we pick it up tomorrow?" I asked.

"Some guy by the name of Angelo said they're closing tomorrow for a two-week vacation. It has to be picked up now. It's just down the street. I'll be back in ten minutes. No problem, Andy."

"Let me go with you," I said.

"Andy, stay here and rest up. The carabinieri will follow me, don't worry. After all we've been through, we *need* that wine tonight!"

As I slumped down on the chaise longue after she left, a gust of wind blew the sheer white curtains inward toward the bedroom, giving me a panoramic view of the Ionian Sea and the busy highway below. Up on the hill, I could see an eight-ton, sixteen-wheel yellow dump truck loaded with granite barreling down toward the parking lot. Ada slowly approached the intersection on the highway in the

Jag XKSS. I was relieved when I saw the two carabinieri following her in their blue Alfa sedan. Having the right of way, she increased her speed. The truck driver increased his speed and headed right for her, oblivious to the red yield sign staring right at him. Frantically turning the steering wheel sharply to her right, Ada slammed sideways into the curbstone and the XKSS tumbled down a steep embankment. It finally came to rest upside down on the street below.

"My God!" I screamed helplessly. "No! No! God! This can't happen!"

I ran down the stairway to the intersection, out of breath and filled with unbridled panic. The wheels were still spinning on the Jaguar, somehow making me think what just happened wasn't real, and I could turn back time. Ada was lying next to the car on her back. Her breathing was heavy and unstable.

I knelt closely beside her, placing my face next to hers, crying so hard I could neither speak nor breathe. A siren grew louder and louder. I hated all sirens, but I especially hated Italian sirens. Their harsh serenade annoyed me. I wanted Ada to have a real siren, a tried and true American siren—loud, frightening, and foreboding. I prayed hard, begging the Lord to save her.

Then I felt a hand on my shoulder. *"Esce davanti!"* a medic in a green jacket said. I knew that meant *get out of the way.*

"You have to save her!" I demanded, as I grabbed his arm.

Three more medics converged around her. I walked over and leaned on the white and orange Automedica van parked in the middle of the road, staring hypnotically at the blue Star of Life emblem on the hood. It was the closest thing to a crucifix I could find. I continued my prayers.

Two men were standing against the granite truck on the upper corner of the road, wearing dirty white t-shirts and smoking cigarettes. That image has been chiseled into my mind. They seemed more inconvenienced than concerned. A logo with three brown asteroids clumped together, followed by a streak of fire, was on the truck's door. *Salone Granito* in large red letters appeared beneath the asteroids.

A man with the name Dr. Lorenzo written above the pocket on his white jacket walked toward me. I prayed he didn't speak English. I didn't want to understand him. I didn't want to hear how badly she was hurt.

"She's bleeding internally," he said. "We need to bring her to San Vincenzo, the hospital near Villa Sirina. You can ride inside the ambulance beside her."

The annoying siren blared, as we sped toward the hospital. The blue strobe light rotating on the roof hummed intermittently. It started to rain hard. The bumps jolted in an uneven rhythm. Everything seemed chaotic and senseless.

Ada was rushed into surgery. I sat alone in the waiting room on a thinly cushioned chair with chrome armrests so cold and hard they hurt my forearms. It didn't matter. My arms were trembling so much that I couldn't sit for more than five minutes. I paced around the waiting area and then walked outside, circling the hospital a few times unable to stop crying. I kept walking, unaware of where I was headed. Once I realized I was at the far end the parking lot, I panicked and sprinted back to the waiting room, horrified that the surgeons may have been looking for me. The waiting room was empty and minutes turned to hours. The prayers I said and the promises I made to the Lord flowed so spontaneously, I felt like I had a new best friend. I always had trouble praying. Now I couldn't stop.

A doctor finally walked out between a pair of double doors. *It had to be good news*, I thought. He was smiling and walked quickly toward me with a spring in his step.

"Mr. Robinson, sir." He spoke perfect English. "We have no reason to believe your wife won't make a full recovery. She has a head injury. We've stopped the internal bleeding, yet we need to watch her closely to ensure no blood clots develop. She also has two broken ribs and a broken arm. She's badly banged up, but she'll recover from those injuries without a problem. Nevertheless, the trauma was significant. Our biggest concern is her head injury."

"Can I see her?"

"She's heavily sedated. I would rather you went back to your hotel. A good night's sleep is what you need right now. Come back in the morning."

"I can't leave until I see her. I'll sleep in the waiting area."

"If you insist," the doctor said.

The waiting area couch was designed purposely for someone who had no intention of sleeping on it. It was perfect for me. My outstretched legs draped over the chrome armrest; my head was on a pancake pillow supplied by one of the orderlies. Hope replaced my terror—Ada was going to be okay. Then, I thought about those two men in t-shirts near the granite truck. I hated their smug, insensitive appearance. Soon their images faded. All I could see was that bastard, Salone. He had just made it personal.

"Mr. Robinson . . . Mr. Robinson . . . " I felt a hand gently shaking my shoulder.

"Yes. Yes," I said, as I swung my legs to the floor and sat up.

"You can see your wife now."

I ran to her room. Ada was barely conscious. I leaned over her bed, pressing her hand against my lips. The stark pallidness of her face emphasized the seriousness of her injuries. Her eyes opened slowly. She squeezed my hand.

"Don't say anything, Sweetheart," I whispered. She ignored me.

"What happened to me? How'd I end up here? Everything hurts, Andy."

"I just spoke with the doctor. You're going to be all right, Sweetheart.

Get some rest, now. I'll be right here with you. I love you."

Once Tommie learned of Ada's accident, she came to the hospital with Sammy to offer her assistance. For people we didn't know very well, they were exceedingly gracious and accommodating. Even more remarkable was Tommie's invitation for us to stay at Villa Christina during Ada's recovery. With the severity of this attempt on Ada's life, it was universally expected that we would return home when Ada recovered. Tommie, therefore, believed that no further attempts would be made on our lives. Sammy was going back to school, and Tommie needed to return to Rome. Tazio would remain at the villa during Francesco's investigation of the car theft. Because of Ada's head injury, her doctors advised against traveling for several weeks. Her broken arm was in a cast and her injured ribs were very painful.

"I would like to demonstrate my appreciation, Tommie, for your allowing us to stay at Villa Christina. Is there anything specific you would like me to do while there?" I asked.

"You stay there for as long as it takes for Ada to get well," she said. "All I ask is that you assist Tazio and Francesco with the investigation. We must get those cars returned! The Italian newspapers are already accusing me of being connected to the mob. Also, if you could oversee things at the villa, I would appreciate it. My father is a good man, but he's not very good with the details, if you know what I mean."

"Yes, I do," I said with a smile. "Please tell him to call his insurance agent. He'll need to order another Jaguar XKSS. I don't have the heart to tell him."

"Enough! No more!" she said. "Anyway, that was the last one made! He's had it with the Jaguar XKSS's!"

On several occasions over the past few weeks, Ada pressed me to call my father and explain the perilous situations we were experiencing in Sicily. I kept telling her I would call him, but procrastinated. I still find it difficult to explain my hesitation. Had he known our lives were in jeopardy, I am sure he would have been on the next plane to Sicily or demanded that we immediately return to America.

For me, neither option was viable. Ada was right. Running away from the problem wouldn't resolve it, nor would calling on daddy to come to Sicily and fight my battles for me. Maybe I was foolishly trying to prove something to myself. I kept thinking, somehow, if we could untangle ourselves from this mess how proud my father would be when he found out I could actually take care of myself and solve my own problems.

As it turned out, a couple of weeks after the car accident, my father called me. My grandfather, who had been in ill health, had passed away. I felt guilty I didn't visit him more often, although he was something of a vagabond. I remembered stories told by my father about some of my grandfather's escapades during the war. It was rumored in our family that he attempted to elope with King Victor's daughter, Princess Juliana of Savoy. I was never too sure about that rumor, although, when he worked at Eastman Kodak, he sold thousands of Beano hand grenades to the Italian army. It was just prior to Italy and Germany declaring war on the United States.

Later, after Italy's armistice, the family rumor mill had my grandfather in Brindisi living with the Princess when they decided to elope. As the story goes, they stowed away on an Italian freighter to Greece. After the Italian battleship, *Venizia*, intercepted them, the unhappy king is said to have immediately deported him back to America. After all those Beanos detonated prematurely, killing thousands of Italian infantry soldiers, he was lucky he wasn't drawn and quartered by the Royal Guard. I laughed when my father said he was America's first secret weapon of the war. Anyway, it was an entertaining family tale.

My father called again, about a week after the funeral. I was surprised and grateful to learn that my grandfather left me his classic car collection, which consisted of an old Buick, a Packard, two Pierce Arrows, and, of course, the Mercer Raceabout, the car I cherished most in his collection. A broker named Aaron, who was representing a Pierce-Arrow collector wanting to purchase the 1935 Convertible Coupe, kept calling. I hated to part with the car, but the $225,000 offer was impossible to refuse. It removed the financial pressure from our lives. I called Fairchester High School and arranged a year's leave of absence from our teaching positions. We had obstacles to overcome before we returned to our normal lives.

And I never did tell my father about our dire predicament in Sicily.

FOURTEEN

The 1937 Mercedes Silver Arrow

The days passed like the pages of a good mystery novel. Ada became stronger, as evidenced by the return of her quick wit. It was four weeks since the accident, and a couple of times each day we would stroll through the beautiful gardens around the villa, feeding the Peacocks and admiring their exquisite feather trains of blue, gold, and red hues.

"You do realize, don't you, Mr. Robinson, that peahens select their mates according to the length of their train."

"Now that's *useful* information!" I responded. "I understand males live in harems with several female sex slaves."

"Not a bad way to get through the day!" she said.

"Almost like living with you!"

After I got elbowed in the side, I said to myself, *Thank God. Ada is getting better.*

"So what's next on the Robinson agenda?" I asked with a degree of apprehension. Ada always had interesting answers to open-ended questions.

"It's very simple. Either kill or be killed. I don't know any other way to say it to you, Andy. Whatever hatred I had for my father's murderers has been shifted to that vicious animal, Salone! I'm ready to take the bastard down!"

"Ada, I'm worried about you. Your hostility for him seems pathological."

"He tried to kill us both! And, what kind of man deliberately cripples another man for life? Yes, I would say pathological is a good word to describe my intentions. I stayed awake last night, conjuring the most expedient means of exterminating Salone. It has to be something overwhelming and decisive, but also fast. I recalled what I had learned about Clausewitz's Principles of War. It still wasn't fast enough to suit *my* needs."

"Ada! We can't take on the entire Sicilian Mafia!"

"If you want to kill the dragon? Cut off the head!"

"The problem, Ada, is that this dragon has many heads!"

Ada and I came in and sat at the dining table with Tommie and Tazio.

Tommie had decided to remain at the villa until the car collection was recovered. Actually, I think she wanted to avoid the pandemonium she would create by returning to Rome. The stolen cars were front-page news.

"I gave Francesco permission to use the downstairs conference room to formulate his plan of action to recover the cars. He was here early this morning with several carabinieri," Tommie said. "He wants Tazio and me to join them after breakfast."

A few minutes later, a loud *"Buongiorno"* interrupted us. Francesco wasn't at all bashful about barging in. He pointed his finger at Ada.

"The man you beat up? His name is Giovanni Moretti—Salone's brother-in-law and *Caporegime!* After my meeting this morning, I'm taking you both to Catania, the headquarters for the carabinieri here in Sicilia."

"Oh, you'll be real safe there!" Tazio sneered.

"You can stay with me in my apartment until Mrs. Robinson is well enough to fly."

"Thank you, Francesco, but no way!" Ada said. "Actually, we would much rather join your meeting and hear about your plan," Ada said calmly.

Francesco mumbled something in Italian. I could tell it wasn't pleasant.

"Francesco," I asked, "so what is the latest on the stolen car investigation?"

"Salone has them. Exactly where is another question."

"Well, where do you think they are?" I pushed back.

"Buried in an underground cave—somewhere deep in Pantalica."

"Impossible!" Tazio contradicted. "How could he transport all the cars across Sicily to Pantalica without being seen?"

"First of all, they transport the cars at night." Francesco was becoming annoyed with Tazio's impertinence. "Who would say anything? They'd end up in the Sicilian Bull!"

Tazio cringed. "That's right, Mr. Robinson. The big brass bull—it has a door and they put people inside and start a fire underneath it. They do that over at the old schoolhouse so the public can hear the screams of people burning inside. Then they take the bones up to the caves in Pantalica."

"Yes, we heard about that," I said.

"Salone is an absolute tyrant in Sicily," Tommie said. "He instills fear in the law enforcement agencies by his barbaric actions. Everyone who attempts to resist him ends up dead, kidnapped, or maimed for life. Stay away from him! That's the best *plan* when it comes to Salone. When I think about it, he'll probably figure out some way around that new ESCO law, too."

"When do we go downstairs and continue the meeting?" Ada asked. "We would like to see the plan you've developed, Francesco."

"My best officers and I are developing the plan," Francesco said. "This time we are going to get Salone for sure!"

We entered the conference room and sat down in the front row.

"Benvenuti nel nostro seminario di guerra!" Francesco said.

"What did he say, Ada?"

"Welcome to our war seminar."

"This should be interesting," I said.

Francesco prepared four flipcharts attached to tripod easels. The top page of each one was an intricate array of colored diagrams and writing. Given the amount of detail on the charts, it was obvious he had invested a high degree of energy and time into his presentation. At the top of the first chart was the heading: The Battle of Filiporto. Below the heading, he wrote: *Gentlemen, the enemy stands behind his entrenchments, armed to the teeth. We must attack him and win, or else perish. Nobody must think of getting through any other way.*

"Frederick II," Ada said, "The Silesian Wars." Her knowledge of history always served her well.

"Thank you, Mrs. Robinson. Frederick II—he was a smart man!"

Francesco folded over the page on the flipchart and began reviewing strategies and tactics he had written out. I was impressed by the detail. Even though all three charts were written in Italian, when he got to the specific offensive tactics they would employ, his carabinieri started to fidget in their seats and became confused and uncomfortable. They challenged Francesco with questions he couldn't answer, not because they didn't want to participate. They simply did not understand his tactics.

"Frederick II was a tactical genius, but he made one big mistake," Ada noted.

"What mistake?" Francesco asked.

"He violated the last Principle of War and was finally defeated."

"The last principle?" Francesco went to the third chart. "Oh," he said, "You mean *simplicity,* right?"

"Prepare clear, uncomplicated plans. Minimize confusion," Ada said. "Frederick II got too predictable, and then he tried to overcome his predictability with too much detail. Instead of a simple strategy, his battle plans became complex. Complexity is the soldiers' first enemy in battle. When a soldier is confused, he can't win. Another thing: The element of *surprise* is missing. You tried to attack Salone in the Grotto *before*, with horrific consequences. Salone will be on high alert. In all probability, he has *his* soldiers permanently assigned to the Grotto. I admire your efforts, Francesco, but there's far too much bloodshed in your plan."

Francesco eased into a wooden chair beside the flipcharts. He appeared grateful to Ada, but the plan he had spent so much time developing was seriously flawed, and he now realized it.

"*Potete andare*," Francesco shouted.

"He dismissed them," Ada whispered to me.

The carabinieri rose to leave, and unless they understood English, they probably had no idea why they were leaving. Yet, a look of relief crossed their faces. The tragic fate of their colleagues from their last encounter in the Grotto was still fresh in their minds. They were clearly relieved this second attempt was aborted.

Francesco looked up despondently and said, "Okay, Mrs. Robinson. Please tell me what you would do."

Ada nodded politely. "Another Principle of War," she explained "was '*always have the choice between the most audacious and the most careful solution.*' Since you are a staunch military man, you know the word *audacious*." He nodded receptively. "The plan needs to be *audacious with the element of surprise.*"

Francesco moved off of the stool. I watched him struggle on his crutches. With all his suffering, he was still determined to confront and arrest Salone, even if the odds were overwhelmingly against him. I admired him, but I felt his plan was a foolhardy solution; in fact, it was no solution at all.

"Mrs. Robinson," Tazio asked again. "What should we do?"

Without hesitation, Ada answered. "Let's go to a car auction!"

I spun my head around, looking at everyone. They laughed politely.

Ada allowed the laughter to run its course and then asked, "Why not? A car auction has all the components of the Principles of War but with different weapons." This time they laughed because they thought she was right.

"Ada, you're not kidding, are you?" I asked.

The room became silent. Once I spoke up, they realized Ada was dead serious.

"Are you surprised?" she asked. They all smiled, yet they were still perplexed.

"If we design a sound plan, Salone will be surprised, too."

"What's your thinking, Ada?" I asked.

"The Pergusa Lake Historic Car Festival will be held in four weeks. It has three events over a three-day period of time: a historic car race, a Concours d'Elegance, and the Noble-Dean classic car auction. Tazio tells me that Salone participates in all three events each year. He races in the historic race, shows off his cars at the concours event, and buys and sells at the auction."

"Pergusa is just a few miles from Enna, where Salone lives," Tazio added.

"Say what you will about Salone, he's definitely not a fool!" Ada said. "Based on the fear he instills in law enforcement, if he does try to sell the Villa Christina cars at the auction, who's going to do anything about it? He could pocket millions, go back up to his fortress in Enna, and ship the money to a Swiss bank account."

"Or," I said, "hide the money in a CAIT, like the one owned by his good friend, Maxwell Riter.

"That's it, Andy!" Tommie said. "I'd be willing to bet on it!"

"The first part of my plan," Ada said, "is to set a psychological trap for him. We're going to entice him to bring the Midnight Ghost to the concours event. We'll find another world-renowned car and tout its historical significance prior to the event. That way, we can exploit the enemy's weakness. That's another Principle of War."

"What's the enemy's weakness?" Francesco asked.

"A massive ego driven by obsessive greed!" Ada answered before Francesco finished asking the question. "He would never ever allow another car to upstage the Midnight Ghost. We can use all forms of media: newspapers, television, and we can distribute flyers to his doorstep. Imagine, a car like that in his own backyard. He'd never be able to keep the Midnight Ghost under wraps."

"It sounds impossible," Tommie chimed in. "Where are we going to find something to compete with the Midnight Ghost at this late date?"

"That's a very good a question." Tazio flashed a big smile, eager to provide an answer to his daughter's question. "My good friend Dante Castronova is the special honoree this year at the festival. He drove the Silver Arrow in the 1937 Grand Prix at the Autodromo. He won the European Championship in 1939."

"What's a Silver Arrow?" Ada asked.

"Boy, Ada!" I kidded, "You've spent too much time in the history books!"

She smiled and said, "Andy, you're the car expert. What's a Silver Arrow?"

"Only the most famous Grand Prix race car in the world, that's all!" I said. "It's a 1937 Mercedes W 125 and one of the most powerful racecars ever built. It has 600 horsepower!"

Tazio was hanging on my every word. "Can you imagine," he continued, "600 horsepower back then? A 1937 Ford V-8 had 85 horsepower! And that was the most powerful model!"

"A car? We are going to war with a car?" Francesco asked shaking his head. "Now I've heard everything. Mr. and Mrs. Robinson, please go home." We laughed at Francesco's characterization of Ada's plan.

"Yes, you're right," I said. "We are merely using the resources at our disposal. The Silver Arrow was the greatest! It broke all the speed records at 269 miles per hour! Do you believe that? 269 miles per hour! Every wealthy collector in the world would spend millions to own this car!"

"You did say millions, didn't you?" Tommie echoed in disbelief.

"Millions!" Tazio reiterated. "The man who design the Silver Arrow—Rudy Uhlenhaut—he was a genius! Special nickel-chrome tubes gave it the strongest chassis of any racecar. I drove it in the Targa Florio in 1938. It was the best racecar in the world! The absolute best!"

"*Racing News* named the Mercedes W 125 Silver Arrow the most iconic race car of all time," I said. "If we're able to get this car at the festival, the Midnight Ghost *will* materialize. It's guaranteed! Then, we'll steal it!"

"So where, if I may ask, do we get the Silver Arrow?" Ada queried.

"Two of my other friends, old Fritz and Manny Blosman, from Mulhouse, France—do they ever have a great collection! But the Blosman brothers—they are a very private people. Me and Juan Fangio—we were the only racecar drivers invited to a special showing of their cars back in a 1972. Their cars—they were *spettacolare!*"

"I remember reading about the Blosman brothers' collection when it made international headlines," I said. "Workers in their woolen mills went on strike because the brothers were withholding pay and benefits. The newspapers went after the Blosmans, accusing them of being greedy and self-indulgent. Their collection was worth millions. They had over four hundred cars and all were in showroom condition. They had another one hundred fifty stashed away in workshops in their mills. The really big thing about the Blosmans was their collection of more than two hundred Bugattis, including one of the six Bugatti Royales."

Tazio jumped in when I took a second to inhale.

"Yeah! And, one of the stars of Fritz and Manny's collection was an original Mercedes W 125 Silver Arrow! And, by the way, I find a perfect replica of the Silver Arrow on display at the Torrington Park museum in England. The curator, another friend of mine—he told me the owner was ready to sell."

"Even though it's 'copy,' that car must be worth a fortune, too!" I said.

"Okay. Let's assume Salone shows up. He brings the Midnight Ghost. Then what?" Francesco asked. "Should we arrest him, shoot him, take his picture, or what?" He was clearly annoyed.

"Shoot him!" Ada quickly asserted. "Then, we'll load the Midnight Ghost into our trailer and head for Palermo. Tazio can ship the Silver Arrow later."

"She's joking," I said.

"Yeah, I'm joking. Once he and the Ghost are at the show, on neutral turf, we can implement the second part of the plan. Any questions?"

"Yeah, what's the second part to the plan?" Tommie asked. "I hope it has something to do with the recovery of the car collection."

"Part two will be tomorrow. Here's what I'm thinking . . . "

Tommie interrupted. "He'll have his own army around him at the show. We don't want any show participants hurt," she said forcefully. "I'm anxious to hear the second part of the plan, but it can't be violent."

Ada nodded her agreement, but, for some reason, refrained from saying anything more.

"Four weeks. That's how much time we have," Ada said, as her directive side continued to evolve. "There's lots of work to do. Here's everyone's assignment: Tommie, we will need your connections. Contact the event organizers and set up all of us as volunteers. Tazio, you contact the Blosman brothers. Ask if they would be willing to loan us the Silver Arrow. Then contact your friend Dante Castronova. See if he would drive a few victory laps in the Silver Arrow to commemorate his European Championship of 1939. Andy and I can help Tommie with a publicity campaign. Francesco, you won't be going to the festival. You'll spook Salone. I would like to meet here, in this room, after breakfast tomorrow for updates and brainstorming. We don't have a lot of time, so let's get going!"

"*Aspetta!*" (Wait!) Francesco exclaimed, "Now you want to do my job? I have my best carabinieri trying to find the cars. I plan on arresting Salone when I get indictment papers from the *Corte D'Assise!*"

A cynical grin swept across Tazio's face. "That's a big joke—the Corte D'Assise!"

"He's right!" Tommie said. "It's a court composed of two judges and six laypersons. Only serious murder crimes are tried by the Corte d'Assise. You can be sure Salone's people will terrorize the six laypersons and their families. They'll be scared to death and will *never* prosecute him. Believe me, Andy, it has happened several times before. I can only imagine what will happen to all of us after he's released, not to mention all his future victims!"

"What about ESCO?" I asked. "I thought that was supposed to change things?"

"It's a masquerade." Tommie answered. "*La Bella Figura!* It's all about appearances, not substance. That's what's important in southern Italy. Fancy cars, fashion, art, history, fine wines, all the proper nuances Italian society demands."

"I disagree," Francesco asserted. "ESCO is different. We can get him!"

"Do you really think so?" Tommie asked.

"Apparently, Salone thinks so, too. When he was here for lunch, he seemed afraid of it," I said. "If he wasn't, why would he try to kill us?"

"Perhaps it's just another one of his ploys designed to misdirect us," Ada said. "Maybe all he cares about is revenge for Andy's father's interference in Italy's criminal justice system. What do you think, Francesco?"

Complete silence enveloped the room as Francesco prepared his response. For him to agree with Ada would mean everything he was doing to capture and prosecute Salone was a complete waste of time. "You are all wrong!" he admonished. "ESCO will work!"

FIFTEEN

The Sicilian Bull

When my father left the house every day by 5:00 a.m., after working until midnight, my mother would often quote William Shakespeare. She would say to him: *"Fatigue makes cowards of us all."* I think my father was immune to any ill effects of sleep deprivation. I wasn't immune. The more I thought about Ada's catastrophic accident, the more fatigue I felt. I also felt responsible. My family's notoriety had become Ada's problem. I now realized that it would be up to us, that no one else could release us from Salone's death grip. While it's hard for me to explain, once we made the commitment to a definite plan, Ada and I found some relief. In fact, much of our anguish was converted to diligence and perseverance. We met in the lower-level assembly area for our second meeting.

"Good things happened since our last meeting," I said. "We became a team. Tazio connected with Manny Blosman, who was at first reluctant but finally agreed to loan us the original Silver Arrow. Dante Castronova was thrilled to drive victory laps in the Silver Arrow. Tazio also had some other interesting news. He confirmed that one of the two Silver Arrow replicas from Torrington Park was really for sale." I paused for a moment. "Ada, let's cash in our NYS Teacher's Retirement accounts and buy that Silver Arrow replica."

179

"Forget it, Andy! Let's get down to business here!"

"The original Silver Arrow will be the showcase car for all three days of the festival," Tommie said. "The organizers already had a Porsche 911 prototype, winner of the 1973 *Targa Florio*. When I told them we had the Silver Arrow, they were eager to modify their original publicity campaign." Tommie's efficiency was not surprising. After all, she managed one of Italy's largest bureaucracies. "I'm working with the show's organizers to secure television, radio, and print coverage. It will be difficult with such short notice, but having the original Silver Arrow there would draw several thousand more people to the festival, and the organizers know it."

"That's great work, Tommie," I said.

"I'm having a big problem, though," she said. "I'm getting a lot of heat from Rome over the loss of the cars. The commission has placed a moratorium on the purchase of any more cars. The project is all but dead. The owners have met and are considering a class-action lawsuit. The newspapers are calling for my resignation. If we don't find the cars soon, I'll have no choice but to resign. I can't stay back in Rome and go to work each day like nothing has happened. I've forgotten how badly the media could treat a public figure."

Tommie was attempting to do something constructive for Italy's public persona, yet she was becoming *another* tragic victim of Salone's brutal machine.

"Francesco," I asked, "any progress?"

"My investigators have been checking the shops around the Church of San Giorgio in Castelmola. They found two people who remember six silver car trailers traveling down the Via Della Rabbia at very high speeds. The investigators—they kept checking and found out the trucks never reached the Vicolo IV Geosafat."

"So they never left Castelmola?" I asked.

"That's right," Francesco concurred.

Tommie was shaking her head and frowning. "Didn't anyone see the cars being unloaded?" she asked.

"Maybe they *never* unloaded them," Francesco said. "We searched all the large buildings in Castelmola and there was no sign of the cars."

"What about the smaller, less conspicuous areas?" Ada asked.

"I still think there's something suspicious about that old school-house," I said. "When I was there with Ada, I can't put my finger on it, it just seemed very peculiar."

Francesco furled his brow, repositioned himself in his chair, and appeared agitated.

"We use the old schoolhouse for carabinieri training every week." He was starting to fume.

"It's the perfect hiding place!" I said. "Tazio, is there a lower level to the schoolhouse?"

"*Si*. But I'm sure you cannot drive the cars down the stairs!"

"Is it possible there might be another method of entry?" I asked.

"Who knows? There might be caves nearby. All the buildings around there—they're too small a for that many cars."

"Maybe they split them up at night," Tommie said.

"That's what I'd do," Ada said. "While everyone's looking for a larger area, big enough for twenty-six cars, splitting them up in smaller locations makes perfect sense."

Francesco struggled to his feet, secured his crutches on his forearms, and as he angrily walked out of the room, exclaimed, "You have all the answers! You don't need me!" He slammed the door so hard behind him, I could hear the chandelier tingle.

"Francesco doesn't like to be challenged," Tommie said.

I waited for a reaction from Tazio.

"Mr. Robinson, you don't know . . . two of the carabinieri who were in the cave with Francesco were his best friends. They were court-martialed because they run away from Salone's soldiers. If they stayed, they'd be killed like the others. Francesco—he feel responsible."

"There is much pain in his heart," Tommie said. "We have to help him. This thing with Salone, he needs to get a grip or it will destroy him."

I turned toward Ada to see if she displayed any kind of reaction.

"It's very easy to say that," Ada responded. "I understand how he feels. Seeing people you care about murdered in front of you, and enduring such a devastating permanent injury, is not something you *ever* get over."

While Ada was taking a nap, I found a lounge chair and sat looking out at the calm azure seascape. At first, I stared at the horizon, wondering what invisible coastline might be in my line of sight. Then I closed my eyes and just listened to the quiet undulation of tiny breakers foaming on the beach.

In my peaceful state, I was able to assess our activities over the last few days and define the current reality. Everything had simply come down to one alternative: The only way to escape the clutches of Salone was for us to end his reign of terror in Sicily. Did I really have the inner strength to kill him? A negative answer to that question meant we should all fold our tents and go home. But killing Salone was the only way to stop him. I could feel a magnetic pull from Ada. I needed her courage. I hated myself for getting her into this situation. Now it was up to me to rectify it.

Despite the effective teamwork displayed at our meeting, after I thought about it, getting the Midnight Ghost out in the open wasn't going to resolve anything. Furthermore, we had no guarantee

Salone would try to sell the Villa Christina cars at the auction. Of course, placing the proceeds from selling them in a Swiss bank account or hiding them in Riter's CAIT made great sense, especially with ESCO breathing down his neck. We still had much more planning to do.

In the meantime, I decided that the old schoolhouse required a visit, if only to look around, possibly find clues, and see if underground access existed. To that end, I thought perhaps Tazio might like to show off his driving skills.

As soon as I re-entered the villa, Tommie said, "Francesco just rushed out. He was going to the schoolhouse with a group of his men. It appeared to be some kind of emergency. He wants all of us to wait here until he returns."

"Sure, Tommie," I said, as I walked past the table pretending to head upstairs to my bedroom. At the last minute I made a sharp turn to the outside door. On the front lawn, I found Tazio reading the newspaper.

"Tazio! You in the mood for a driving lesson?"

I didn't have to ask a second time. Tazio leaped up like he was sitting on a coiled spring. We departed the villa in his new imperial blue Jaguar XKSS delivered only three days earlier. It almost looked like a Shelby Daytona in sheep's clothing.

"I need to tune this beast up for you, Tazio."

"Sometimes—she stall," he said.

"Typical of Jags when they are new. The idle needs adjustment, plus it's running too rich. You should fine-tune the Weber carbs. See all the black smoke coming from the exhaust?"

"Before the festival you can tune it up. We'll race it there, okay?"

"Did you register?" I asked. I wasn't too keen on racing the XKSS with all the other details I had to worry about.

"We race the first day!"

"Well, that's good. I suppose it would provide a good excuse for us to be there."

"Not you! You just watch!"

"What do you mean 'watch'? If you race, I race!"

"How many cars did you destroy since you been in Sicilia? Let's see . . . the Fiat, and, *mama mia,* my beautiful Green Rat, and—oh, my heart—I have a heart attack because of you—my new red Jaguar! What do you think—Sicilia is your own private demolish a derby?"

I started to laugh at Tazio's unique blend of English and Italian. "Now listen, Tazio," I said. "You just received your third Jag XKSS since I've been here. The blue is striking! That leaves the Fiat, and who the hell cares about that thing!"

"Yeah, but the new blue one—she was a the last one made!"

"Yeah, sure it was! Just like the last one and the last one before that!" I loved this give and take with Tazio. "You probably have the surviving 16 locked up in a barn someplace!"

"Aye, Mr. Punt. You give me such a hard time. I still think you need a driving lesson!"

Tazio put the new XKSS through its paces. The double overhead cam XJ 6 engine wound up to 4000 revolutions per minute. Tazio shifted the 4-speed manual transmission deftly, like the seasoned racecar driver he was. The tachometer was large enough for both of us to see, an essential feature for road rallies and general racing.

"Where we headed?" Tazio yelled. The wind noise at 90 miles per hour made it difficult to hear.

"The old schoolhouse," I shouted back.

Tazio placed his hands in the nine and three o'clock positions on the steering wheel, with his palms cupping the outer wheel. His thumbs were wrapped around the ring and resting on top of the cross brace. This man was ready for action! That was fine with me.

Tazio began his driving lesson by explaining one of the critical keys to maximizing speed through corners. "Steady car control," he said. "It comes from my expert steering. If the car travel a smooth, consistent arc, then the steering must be smooth and consistent."

I had learned about steady car control from my racing instructor at Watkins Glen. To help me understand this concept, my instructor took a sheet of paper, put it on a table, and placed a book on the paper. He pulled the paper slowly across the table, gradually increasing the speed. The book stayed on the paper. Then he started to drag the paper again but suddenly jerked it. The book lost traction and slid across the paper.

"The motion of dragging the paper is like your steering input," he would say. "Sudden jerks in the steering wheel would be like sudden jerks on the paper, and the tires will slide. I experienced this sensation during the times I rented an early Porsche 911 at the Glen. The rear end engine bias made it even more challenging around the turns. After I lost control and slid into the open field a few times, I decided to stick with front engine cars.

Tazio was well schooled in this basic concept. It reinforced Sammy's stories about his many European racing conquests.

Suddenly, we were on a road reminiscent of a Grand Prix racecourse.

"Now Mr. Punt," he said, "every time your hand leave the steering wheel, you give up a half of the 'road talk.'"

I knew what he was saying. My instructor called it feedback.

"Both hands on the wheel—always! Never place your hand on the shifter until you are ready to shift. Never grab the shifter too tight! All shifting you do is with your hand open and cupped over the top of the knob, not wrapped around it like a control stick on a fighter plane. You Americani—you do too much drag racing!

Be gentle! Shifting is like making love to a beautiful woman. Never squeeze her too tight! She won't respond right."

I laughed. It was evident my friend Tazio had a multitude of proficiencies, some of which were related to driving.

Tazio increased his speed. We both checked our seatbelts. The wide two-lane highway became a narrow one-lane speedway. As Tazio shifted, the many elevation changes and tight corners made me yearn to be in the driver's seat. Then I observed his true racing acumen as he drifted through a downhill hairpin turn at 80 miles per hour.

"Braking!" he shouted. "That's another thing you Americani need to learn. Braking!"

Tazio was referring more to drifting than braking. That takes *real* skill. Knowing how to drift through a compressive turn, and coming out of it without losing speed, is a thing of beauty. On the next straightaway, Tazio hit speeds in excess of 130. I was impressed with his driving skill but also the performance of the Jag XKSS. It was a true racecar.

"Not bad for the last one made, huh, Mr. Punt?"

"It still needs a tune-up," I said.

"Yeah, yeah, but I do pretty good anyway, huh?"

"Not bad for an Italiano!"

He snickered and shook his head in mock disgust. "All the great Grand Prix and Formula One drivers—they Italiani! The Americani? They drive a go-karts!"

"What about Indianapolis?" I asked

"Ah!" He waved the back of his hand in a dismissive gesture. "*Bambini piccoli*! They go around a big circle. Big deal!"

"Well all I can say, Tazio, is that this is one great car!"

"What's the matter with you? It's the *magish*, not the *wand*!"

"Now I would never argue that point. Certainly not with a racing champion like yourself," I said with a slight chuckle. "I'm looking forward to race day. Then I'll show you what an Americano driver can really do!"

"*Madonna Mia*!" His hand bounced off his forehead in exasperation. After a make-believe scowl, he laughed hard. We both enjoyed each other's banter.

We made a fast move to the corner onto Via Dietro Cappuccini, arriving at the schoolhouse and an all-too-familiar scene. The four white and orange *Automedica* vans parked in the middle of the road put my heart in my stomach. When I saw the blue Star of Life emblem on their hoods, it once again reminded me of a crucifix and my obsessive prayers when Ada was injured. Seven Alfas with their blue and white strobes flashed obtrusively near the back of the schoolhouse. A one-inch-wide yellow barrier tape stretched across a wide area, and uniformed law enforcement people were everywhere. Tazio parked a few hundred feet away, on the other side of street.

"I'm-a getting very sick," Tazio said.

As soon as we began walking to the schoolhouse, an awful, acrid odor nearly asphyxiated us. So repugnant was the coppery, metallic aroma, Tazio began to gag as if a big ball of cotton was trapped in his throat. His eyes swelled with tears.

"I'm going to vomit," he said, then bolted to the side of the road and heaved.

The top of a brass-colored object became visible above the crowd. The odorous assault suddenly changed to the smell of fatty pork burning on a charcoal grill.

"The Sicilian Bull!" Tazio hollered.

We ran to the car, like we were trying to escape from a beast, and turned the heater fan up to its maximum position. Since we were in a convertible, it was to no avail. An unmistakable figure approached the car with a wet handkerchief over his face.

"Now, tell me, what are you two doing here?" A distraught Francesco was trembling on his crutches, too preoccupied with what transpired to be angry with us. "Go back to the villa," he said quietly. "Too much confusion is here. When I return, I will explain everything. *Please* go back to the villa now." He didn't have to ask a third time.

Neither one of us spoke on the way back to the villa. We tried to regain some degree of composure after witnessing such a hide-ous scene. I noticed Tazio's hands were in the nine and six o'clock positions, and he was slumped over the steering wheel like a rag doll. Grandpa and grandma on their way to the corner grocery store replaced the race-happy duo of thirty minutes ago.

We were waiting in the dining area of Villa Christina when Francesco arrived. His face looked broken—like a china doll whose face was just hit by a hammer.

"Francesco, here, sit down," I pleaded, pulling a chair out from the table.

In a rage, he threw his crutches against the wall and collapsed helplessly into the chair. His eyes cast a frozen stare to the floor, as his hands rose slowly to his face. Covering his eyes, he sobbed qui-etly. His forsaken look spelled surrender. I felt a deep sympathy for him. I also felt like a criminal for challenging him earlier. Ada moved next to Francesco to console him. Kneeling on the floor, placing her arms around his shoulders, she exuded warmth, which made it easier for him to describe what happened.

"They were cooked," Francesco stammered, nearly too choked-up to continue. "They were burnt to death. They burned for hours before they died."

He started to sob again. Francesco tipped his head backward and closed his eyes, and then immediately snapped his head forward. His body slouched and twisted in the chair; his eyes were red with misery.

"Their bones! It was the only thing left."

SIXTEEN

The Replica

I'm sure Francesco was a jovial man before all the tragic events encumbered his life. While he didn't know the last two victims of the Sicilian Bull, it still rocked him badly. The paralysis inflicted upon him at the hands of Salone made me wonder how he could go on—or at least how he could continue in his capacity as Caribiniere Generale, much less feel a sense of satisfaction once in a while. And now, a new frailty and fatigue consumed Francesco. His rage expended, all vestiges of aggression against the monster, Salone, had dissipated.

I wasn't surprised when, a few days later, Francesco resigned his position as Carabiniere Generale. It was a significant loss for the law enforcement community, but his paralysis had now infiltrated his mind. The force of the opposition cruelly overwhelmed him. Tommie insisted Francesco stay at the villa so she could watch over him. Despite that, most of the time Francesco sat by the ocean alone. He maintained a hospitable presence at dinners, a deed we all deeply appreciated.

We received bad news about the Silver Arrow. Fritz and Manny Blosman had been issued warrants for their arrest on charges of embezzlement, and the French government seized their car collection. Their woolen mills were in receivership, and they fled to Switzerland to avoid prosecution. Obtaining the original Mercedes W 125 Silver Arrow was now a pipedream. With the festival only ten days away, we were desperate. Tazio tracked down the owner of the replica at Torrington Park museum in England, a Canadian man named Aston Matthews. I felt his asking price of $50,000 was too high for a replica. When he learned I owned the 1910 Type-35R Mercer Raceabout Speedster, formerly owned by Washington Roebling, he became intransigent.

"You must be pretty rich, eh? Can I steal the Mercer?" he asked.

Not only did his solicitation sound arrogant, his rudeness decreased my interest in his Silver Arrow.

"It's not for sale!" I declared. It was a knee-jerk reaction instead of a well-considered business-like response. While I never intended to sell the flagship of my grandfather's classic car fleet, I responded too harshly.

"Fine then, let's trade," he said. "The Mercer for the Silver Arrow."

"You mean a trade plus cash, don't you?"

"No, I'll only do an *even* trade. Do you realize what I have here?" He began to extol the virtues of his Silver Arrow ad nauseam. I hated it when sellers had a blind piety toward their cars, especially when it was completely unrealistic.

"You have a copy," I scoffed. "The Mercer is worth twice the money of your copy." I kept using the word "copy" to diminish its value and enhance my bargaining position. It didn't work. He hung up.

In negotiating with Matthews, I forgot the basic rules: Never diminish the value of someone else's badge of honor. Every car has a unique story, and the seller must be given the opportunity to tell the story. The whole idea of owning a classic car was about exclusivity and prestige. I ignored both in my negotiations with Matthews. Furthermore, I forgot that exclusivity doesn't follow any standard rules about value. Maybe owning this car had nothing to do with its value, only whether or not I *really wanted* it.

I called him back. "Please," I said. "I apologize. Can we start over?"

"That depends," he said.

"I understand you had the original Silver Arrow in your possession when you built the replica. Your car must be perfect."

"It is," he said. "My father helped me build it, and we raced in over twenty historic events. After he died, I just lost interest. We had well over $65,000 invested in the car."

"I'll have the $50,000 wired to you this afternoon if you can arrange shipping to Taormina, Sicily. It's absolutely imperative I receive the car by the end of the week. Do we have a deal?"

"We have a deal!" he said.

Funds remaining from my sale of the Pierce Arrow were dwindling, but it was essential for us to own the Silver Arrow, replica or not. Aside from the Mercer Raceabout, the cars remaining in my collection weren't worth very much. Fortunately, a favorable uptick in the classic car market had received significant publicity: The Kruse Auction Company, from Auburn, Indiana, sold a classic car for a documented $1,000,000—a 1934 Duesenberg Model SJ La Grande Long Wheelbase Dual-Cowl Phaeton. The Duesenberg was sold to Tom Monaghan, founder of Domino's Pizza and owner of the Detroit Tigers. Maxwell Riter brokered the deal for Monaghan and no doubt cleared a cool $100,000 for his efforts.

☆   ☆   ☆

A few days before the festival, while Ada and I were relaxing in our room, she shared a few of her new concerns.

"You know, Andy, after thinking through our options, I'm uncomfortable putting the Silver Arrow on the racetrack. Castronova is an old man. If he has an accident, our entire plan will blow up. It's not too late to modify things."

"He has extensive race experience," I said. "What are you concerned about?"

"He hasn't raced in years. Now he's driving a 600-horsepower racing machine! Do you really think he can handle that much horsepower?"

"I'm sure he can. Salone will salivate when he sees a Silver Arrow on the track. Ada, I think we need to take that risk. Don't you?

"This could backfire Andy. You *do* realize that don't you? They could throw us in a cold jail cell on the island of Sardinia, throw away the keys, and we would vanish from the face of the earth. In Italy, fraud will get us a minimum of 20 years."

"Is that the reason why you want to pull the Silver Arrow?"

"I understand we need the bait, Ada replied. "But . . . "

"Tazio tells me Salone stands up on the auction block with a big fat unlit cigar and buys anything that looks good to him. He actually scares other bidders away. God, how I hate that guy!"

"I just hope the Silver Arrow will look that good to him," Ada said.

"I just spoke with the shipper," I said. "It will be here early in the morning. Ada, will you make sure the guards are aware of its arrival?"

"Sure. Another question for you, Andy . . . do you think Castronova will be able to tell the difference?"

"I guess that will be the acid test. I'm sure he realizes the car was restored, so it can't possibly look like it did when he drove it thirty-five years ago."

"If he finds out, Andy, he'll probably blow the whistle on us."

"I know. Did Tommie get all the stuff for The Big Red?"

"Yeah. She purchased all the food and drinks to serve from The Big Red. We'll be serving a variety of pizzas, along with hotdogs, hamburgers, and salads. By the way, Sammy hired a few of his friends from the University of Catania to serve the crowd."

"They'll be delivering on the bicycles, right?"

"Yes."

"Can we can trust them?" I asked.

"Remember what Hemingway said? *The best way to find out if you can trust someone is to trust someone.*"

"You know how I always hated that quote, Ada! Remember how Voltaire put it? *God protect me from friends, I can take care of my own enemies.*"

"Oh, I don't know if we can trust anybody around here, Andy. Just trying to sort things out is all."

Tommie knocked on the door and walked in.

"Like they say in Vegas," she said. "I had to call in a few chips." She handed us two black wallets. "Here are our new IDs and passports. The three of us are now officially members of the Cruise family: Eben, Mary Ann, and Debbie Cruise. I made one for Sammy, too."

"Perfect!" I said. "But, why 'Cruise?'"

"It was more convincing than 'flow,'" she replied with a grin.

"Ebb and flow?"

Ada laughed. "That was a familiar saying from the old sailing ship days, when tides were used to establish departure times. It means if you have something important to do, don't procrastinate, because neither *tide* nor *time* will wait for you."

"It means we're dedicated to the cause, right, Ada?"

"We're dedicated to the cause, for sure!"

"What about disguises, Tommie?" I asked. "Salone knows what we look like."

"I'll work on that," Tommie said.

☆　☆　☆

Tommie delivered my written description of the real Silver Arrow to the Noble-Dean auction registration desk a few days prior to the festival. I outlined the car's impressive race history, using the actual description taken from the Mercedes Benz company archives.

My Silver Arrow replica arrived as planned in the early hours of the morning. A team of several guards with high-powered rifles stood near the forty-foot trailer with no markings on it. Two men in spotless white uniforms and white gloves untied the nylon wheel tie-downs and uncovered the soft cloth wraps that protected the Silver Arrow. Tazio, Ada, and I watched as the car was gently removed from the trailer and eased down the ramps, allowing gravity to do most of the work. We then pushed the Silver Arrow into the garage. The carabinieri guards would stay with the car until we departed for the festival.

People from all over the world would attend the Pergusa Lake Historic Car Festival—the most prestigious car event in all of Italy. The Silver Arrow was a spectacular car. The world's racing and collector car community would never expect one to appear for sale, much less to be raced in a historic car event. I shuddered when I thought of the consequences if someone found out my Silver Arrow was a replica. We had to make our plan work or Ada was right: It would be a long time before we would see the light of day.

SEVENTEEN

The Pergusa Festival

Francesco was in a wheelchair when he arrived for our Friday morning briefing, the day the festival would begin. I almost didn't recognize him. He looked like a helpless marionette, his legs twisted sideways, his shoulders slumped forward, his arms falling over the side of the wheelchair. He was emaciated. I said to myself, *here is a broken man, broken by a cruel, sadistic person who deserves to die.* Over the next few days, Ada and I would do anything in our power to even the score.

Tommie summarized our assignments for all three days. She asked Tazio to review the details for day one, the Historic Car Races.

"Castronova will be on the racetrack, ready to go," he said. "He'll be wearing the same race suit he wore in 1937, the last a time he race on the *Autodromo*. No helmet for him! He wants everyone to know who he is!" We all laughed.

"You racecar guys—you're so predictable!" Ada said.

"Is he going to race or just drive a couple victory laps?" I asked, recollecting Ada's concerns about the preservation of the Silver Arrow.

Tazio paced the floor, slowly rubbing his chin with his index finger and thumb. "Hmm," he pondered, "what do you think—you can ask a champion race-car driver to go out on a race track not race? *Impossibile!*"

"My Silver Arrow?" I exclaimed with alarm.

"Well, that's the one he come here to drive."

"That's just great!" I groaned. "What if he desroys it?"

"You should talk—after you wreck my three cars! Like you say: you just buy another one! What's the big deal?" Tazio laughed.

"That's not the answer I want to hear, Tazio. We are planning everything around Salone bidding on and buying the Silver Arrow at the auction. If Castronova totals the damn thing up, we're out of business."

"Nah, you worry too much, Mr. Punt! He's a champion!"

"That was a thousand years ago!" I noted.

"No, only forty years. That's all."

"So, how old is he?" I asked.

"I'd say about seventy-five."

"How old are you?" I snapped with contempt.

"I just turn a fifty before you and you wife show up in Sicilia."

"Fifty? Who do you think you're kidding? The last time you were 'fifty,' Garibaldi was wearing diapers!" I shook my head in frustration at Tazio's complete nonchalance. "Okay, Tazio, then why don't you let him drive your new blue Jaguar XKSS?"

"No way. He's too old!" Tazio burst out laughing. "That's *my* car. No one drives it! That includes *you*, Mr. Punt!"

I sat back in my chair, folded my arms, and exhaled in disgust. "Tazio, if anything happens to that Silver Arrow . . . "

"Relax, Mr. Punt! Have you no respect for your elders? *Stavamo correndo quando si erano ancora allattati al seno!*

"Ada. What the hell did he say?"

"He said we were racing when you were still being breast fed."

"That's exactly what concerns me," I said with a sardonic smile.

"Okay. Okay. That's enough zingers from you two for awhile!" Ada was laughing, however, she had no intention of defending my position. "Let's move on. We have a lot to discuss and not much time. How far is the track from here?"

"The Autodromo is about forty-five miles," Tommie replied. "It will take about an hour for us to get there."

"Ride with me," Tazio suggested, as he flashed one of his naughty smiles at Ada. "I make it in half an hour!"

"I'll ride with my husband. We have some last-minute items to discuss."

"Sammy drove The Big Red over last night," I said. "He parked it between the track and the auction tent. It will be right in the middle of the concours field."

"That's a perfect location," Tommie agreed.

"I have the Silver Arrow loaded in my enclosed trailer," Tazio noted.

"We'll haul it to the track this morning and bring it home each evening so it will be safe," Ada said, reassuringly.

"That's if anything is left to bring home," I said. Tazio winked at me.

"We have four carabinieri," Tazio continued. "As a personal favor to Francesco, they have agreed to serve as our escorts."

"Thank you, Francesco," I said.

"It wasn't my idea!" he scowled.

"I hope they'll be armed escorts," I said.

"Mr. Punt, you worry too much! They are four of the best men in the corps." I looked over at Francesco as he struggled to give us a thumbs-up sign and cursory nod.

"Francesco," I said, "you stay here at the villa—out of sight—for your own protection. If Salone sees you with us at the festival, he'll get suspicious."

"The main thing today," Ada pointed out, "is that people get used to seeing The Big Red and the Silver Arrow. Andy, when Castronova does his victory laps, you'll be telling the story of the Silver Arrow over the public address system."

"I wonder if Salone will bring out the Midnight Ghost today?" I mused.

"Don't be too surprised if he has armed guards surrounding the car every second," Tommie said.

"And, Tazio," I said, "make sure to park the Silver Arrow right next to the Midnight Ghost, assuming it shows up! We want Salone to see, feel, and drool all over it!"

★ ★ ★

Tazio, in one of his weaker moments, gave me permission to drive his new blue Jaguar XKSS to the festival. With Ada in the passenger seat, we both sat upright, staring at the road ahead, our minds and emotions fixated on the enormous risk we were about to take. Tazio and Tommie followed us in Tazio's Ford F150, which was hauling the trailer containing the Silver Arrow.

"I'm worried, Andy."

"I am too, Ada. If we . . . "

"I'm worried you might lose your temper."

Ada read me well. Knowing Salone attempted to kill the person I loved most in the world could easily trigger a temper tantrum from me. A calm, cool, collected approach with him would take some discipline.

"Everyone is defenseless against Salone and is getting crushed, while he flagrantly goes on his merry way. I don't feel the overwhelming force of the Principles of War has been implemented by anyone except him!"

"Force doesn't always have to be violent," Ada said. "Simplicity and composure need to be part of the strategy. Not to get too academic on you, but I had this history instructor in college, who had a way of reminding me of this concept. When he taught *The Prince*, by Machiavelli, he read this quote every day. I memorized it: *The lion cannot protect itself from traps, and the fox cannot defend himself from wolves. One must therefore be a fox to recognize the traps, and a lion to frighten wolves.*"

EIGHTEEN

The Prevost Outlaw

The Pergusa Lake Historic Car Festival, held at the Autodromo di Pergusa racetrack, officially opened on Friday, August 3rd, with the Historic Car Races. Saturday would feature the Concours d'Elegance, and Sunday would conclude with the Noble-Dean Classic Car Auction. Volunteers supervised and worked all three events. They included area car hobbyists, retired men and women, nearby college students, and our own contingent of Tommie, Tazio, Sammy, Ada, and me.

The organizers attempted to balance the needs of the events with the interests of the volunteers. Tommie was successful in persuading them to agree with our first choices. At the historic race, our group would serve as flag men and work as pit crewmembers, changing tires, refueling, and assisting mechanics making adjustments to the cars. For the Concours d'Elegance, Tazio would park and position the cars on the field. He would also have a hand in staging the cars before and after the auction. Some of Sammy's friends would be pedal pushers. They would assist by driving the cars up on the auction block. In situations where a car didn't operate, they would be bumper pushers.

The net proceeds from the event would be contributed to the Hospice Comunita di Catania, the hospice in Catania that cares for hundreds of terminally ill children and adults. In past years, between admission and registration fees, memorabilia sales, and a share of the auction profits, the Hospice would be fully funded for the next year.

At the festival, Ada and I wore mirrored aviator sunglasses and nondescript red baseball caps. I added a phony black pencil mustache. They weren't dramatic disguises, but they were adequate, we hoped. We followed directions to the registration tent to sign the paperwork and receive our green volunteer t-shirts and festival brochures, along with our assigned activities for the three-day event. We were told to drive the XKSS to the grandstand and follow the signs to the paddock, where racecars would be prepared for the track. After half an hour in bumper-to-bumper traffic on the narrow, abrasive dirt road, we drove through the gate, past a grandstand large enough to hold four thousand people. The total number of people at the festival would exceed one hundred thousand. The PA system in the grandstand would reach all of them, no matter where they were on the grounds.

On the right side of the grandstand, several colored race status flags blew in the wind. Drivers received signal instructions from flag-men stationed at various areas around the track. When we reached our racing garage that was labeled Box 15, five other volunteers, friends of Sammy's, were waiting for us. They would change tires, refuel, and clean windshields. The track supplied one mechanic for every three cars, which was adequate, given the fact that pit time wasn't as critical for a historic race as it was for a Formula One contest. Tazio had unloaded the Silver Arrow and was right next-door in Box 14.

"We're ready to go!" he exclaimed. The vintage race would run from 11:00 a.m. to 4:00 p.m. Awards would be distributed at 4:30 p.m. "I already reserve my place on the podium!" I loved Tazio's optimism, if not his steadfastness.

"He's been asked to drive the pace car, too. The victory laps in the Silver Arrow come next. That means—you and me—we can drive the XKSS and the Arrow!"

"Really? Great news!" I replied. "Just keep an eye on old man Castronova!"

The paddock covered about five acres and was already abuzz with race-day excitement. Pit crews, mechanics, and drivers, all huddled in their boxes, were preparing the cars. Vintage Porsches, Ferraris, Alphas, Jaguars, Mercedes, MGs, and Triumphs were among the most common cars. Many cars were daily drivers. Some, known as "trailer queens," were rarely driven. Service vehicles, tow trucks, and *Automedica* vans were becoming acquainted with the track by following the pace car, a Ferrari 312T Formula One racer, driven around the track by Dante Castronova. It was the car that won the 1975 F1 World Championship and was driven by Niki Lauda. He was supposed to drive the pace car here today, but a few days ago, Lauda had a terrifying accident at the Nürburgring track in Germany and had been seriously injured.

The Pergusa track is 3.076 miles long and is considered one of the fastest tracks in Sicily. Sixteen tight corners and three chicanes make the difference on time around the ring. Chicanes are sharp curves located at the end of long straights. I remembered the chicane at Watkins Glen where many drivers wiped out trying to overtake other cars.

The racetrack serves as the boundary for Pergusa Lake. From the right and left sides of the track, drivers have beautiful views. The banks of the lake are laden with thick sunflower and purple snapdragon beds; other parts have light tan beaches. The southeast side has a large cluster of pine and maple trees. The northeast side has an incredible view of Mt. Etna. In the summer of each year, the water in the lake undergoes a remarkable reddening phenomenon due to red sulfur in the water. Some say the late afternoon sunset reflecting off the red lake combined with a spectacular view of Mt. Etna is the most picturesque panorama in all of Sicily.

I noticed numerous birds landing on the track. "I don't like seeing all these birds on the track. They pose a threat to the drivers," I complained to a flagman.

Ada, who was sitting on a stack of tires, got up and peered out at the lake. She looked at me and nodded her head in agreement.

"They can inflict a lot of damage," she said.

The flagman responded. "The lake has become a refuge for thousands of migratory birds. We've had no problems yet, but it's an accident waiting to happen. Environmentalists blocked every attempt made by race officials to remove the birds. Maybe, when a driver gets killed, they'll do something."

"Are you paying attention, Tazio?" I asked.

"Forghetta-about-it! I drive a hundred times on this track. Listen, do me a big favor; drive my pick-up and trailer to the parking lot on the other side of the registration area. Maybe that will calm a you down for a while."

Good, I said to myself. That will give me a chance to look around. The Big Red should be open for business. The auction pavilion should have cars already staged, too.

"Be back in an hour. C'mon, Ada, let's take a ride and check things out."

"*Favoloso*!" Tazio said, gratefully. "The cars—they be ready when you come back. Don't get lost."

Sammy had The Big Red almost set up for business.

"We have enough food and supplies for all three days," Tommie said. "We have the ingredients for five types of pizzas, including our special recipe for puttanesca."

Ada helped Tommie organize the supplies on the shelves. A couple of Sammy's friends mounted two of the bikes and attached small pizza placards on the handlebars.

"Meet Burt and Greg," Sammy said. "They're two good friends who are exchange students from America. They volunteered to help us with deliveries."

"Where are you from in America?" I asked.

"I'm from Boston," Burt answered. "Greg, here—he's from Buffalo."

"We won't hold that against him, now will we?"

"Hey!" Greg objected. "Last year, O.J. had 1800 yards and 23 touchdowns!"

"Yeah sure, and the Bills missed the playoffs again," I said.

"Don't count them out in '76!" Greg asserted.

"Next year. It's always about next year with the Bills. I see they picked up big Ben Williams in the draft. Maybe you're right about next year, but I doubt it. Anyway, Burt and Greg, thanks for volunteering. Tell me, do people here eat pizza this early in the morning?"

"We have an egg, sausage, and cheese breakfast pizza. Here, try out a piece, Mr. Robinson." Sammy placed a small piece on a paper plate and handed it to me. The cheese was still simmering.

"Looks delicious," I said. The heat from the bottom of the plate made me juggle it until I could rest it on one of six tables in front of the counter. "We're going to sell a ton of these!"

"Okay Ada," Tommie said. "Thanks for the help. I think we're organized."

Burt and Greg rode off toward the racetrack. "Go get those orders!" I shouted, as they sped by me.

"More of my friends are over at the registration area making placards," Sammy said.

"Make sure they make enough for the puttanesca pizza!" Ada laughed.

"With extra capers, right?" I added.

"Yes, indeed. We know the drill!" Sammy responded.

★   ★   ★

Driving around the festival grounds, I almost forgot our dangerous mission.

"Ada, maybe someday we can do this again—without all the tension."

"We will; don't worry. You look worn out."

"Feeling a bit weary is all." I stretched my arms and rotated my head. "I just want to get this whole thing over with and go home." I exhaled, staring straight ahead, nearly oblivious to all the activity around us.

"I understand," she said.

"But we're not giving up, Ada. Not now."

"We've reached the point of no return—in more ways than one."

I stopped the truck in front of the auction pavilion and turned to face her. "I was thinking about our conversation in Venice the night I talked you into marrying me."

"Carpe diem?"

I nodded. "I think we've had enough carpe diem for a while, don't you?"

"Plenty!" she said and began to laugh heartily.

"It wasn't *that* funny!"

"I was just thinking about *Peepee* and our *keese* under the Bridge of Sighs, and it just occurred to me that the Bridge of Sighs is an entrance to a prison!"

"Yes, it is," I said. "And, that's exactly where we're going to end up! In prison! Seriously, I'm glad we're not running away, though."

"Me, too. Anyway, maybe we can get adjoining cells."

"I love you," I said.

"I love you too, Andrew." She moved to my side of the truck, grabbed my arm, and placed it around her shoulder. "We'll get through this. Don't worry."

The auction pavilion was the size of an American football field, with over one hundred fifty auction cars neatly numbered in chronological order. The first two auction cars were already staged on the auction runway. We walked through the aisles, looking for any car that might resemble one of the stolen cars from Villa Christina.

"Salone wouldn't dare to bring the cars out too soon," I said. "He'll wait until the last minute. Bidding on a stolen car is bad news not only for the bidder but also for the auction company. Bidders count on the auction company's due diligence before they accept a car on consignment. I know of several auction houses that were shut down because they attempted to sell stolen vehicles. They didn't even know they were stolen until the bidders complained after the auction was over. Salone will probably have them driven right from the haulers to the auction block."

"Speaking of car haulers, let's drop ours off," Ada said.

We drove the trailer to the other side of the field to a gravel-laden parking lot. Row upon row of car haulers lined both sides. We saw everything from 18-foot flatbed twin-axle open trailers for one car, to fifty-foot tractor-trailers capable of hauling ten cars. Owners wanting the ultimate protection for their classics used closed-carriage trailers. Wealthy collectors owned motor homes and generally attached car trailers behind them. Owners from the mainland used ferries from Rome or Naples to Palermo and then drove to Pergusa.

"Finding a parking spot here is going to be challenging," I said.

We circled the entire area and passed six identical closed-carriage tractor-trailers. A forty-five-foot long Prevost Motor Coach was parked on the grass behind the tractor-trailers. Its polished stainless steel wheels, tinted glass, and immaculate gold, black, and burgundy graphics reeked of opulence. I had seen these motor coaches at classic car auctions in the United States, and only the most affluent collectors owned them. This particular model was called the Prevost Outlaw and sold for nearly two million dollars. It was the epitome of elegance and self-indulgence. Its twenty-foot retractable patio awning stretched over several lounge chairs and a small bar. Five men dressed in summer sportswear were seated at the bar.

"Look, Ada. There's that lousy viper, Salone!" I said. "See him? He's the one with the yellow baseball cap and green t-shirt, with a cigar in his mouth. How I hate that bastard!"

Ada began to squirm in her seat. "Keep driving. Go to the other end. I think I saw some open spots. If not, just park over there on the grass."

I looked at Ada and then looked at the motor coach again. *That's the bastard that tried to kill my wife!* I slammed on the brakes.

"Andy! Forget it! We wait and execute the plan! Come on! Step on the gas! Let's go!" I jammed the shift lever into park. "See. They're looking at us. You're going to ruin everything!" I started to get out of the truck. "Andy!" Her voice was several octaves above normal. "We are not going to accomplish anything by going over there! Stop it now! Do you understand me?" I closed the door and placed my head down on the steering wheel.

"I can't help it. Seeing his arrogance does something to me. Realizing he was the one who tried to kill you, I can only . . ." Sweat beaded on my face. I reached for Ada and embraced her.

"You have good reason to be upset, but let's not mess up the plan!" she said. We have to stand by each other and honor our agreement—no matter how difficult that may be."

"Just stay very close to me the next few days."

"That's one thing you can count on for sure!" I said.

NINETEEN

The 1935 Duesenberg SJ Mormon Meteor

The atmosphere was electric when we returned to the paddock. Racing enthusiasts and journalists flooded the area. The historic races, compared to other racing events, had a more receptive feel. Race fans were allowed to stroll through the paddock to view the cars and mingle with the drivers. Racing legends like Tazio and Dante Castronova were on hand to sign autographs. Fans loved it when these icons of the racetrack drove the cars they had previously raced.

A crowd was swarming around the Silver Arrow. Fans wanting Dante's autograph were persistent. When he drove the Silver Arrow on the track, the grandstand crowd erupted into thunderous applause.

"Ladies and gentleman," bellowed the announcer, "please welcome the 1939 European Grand Prix Champion, Dante Castronova, driving the most famous racecar in the world, the 1937 Mercedes W 125 Silver Arrow."

Again, the crowd cheered as Castronova began his three victory laps. The Silver Arrow's shimmering aluminum finish reflected everything around it. When Castronova accelerated on the straight, the roaring high-pitched whine coming from the supercharger was unmistakable. Race enthusiasts call it a symphony, one that could only be orchestrated by the Mercedes Silver Arrow.

Tazio, a few of Sammy's friends, Ada, and I moved to the pit area where we would service the Silver Arrow and the XKSS during the upcoming race. I learned from Tazio that the original Silver Arrow was painted white. During its first race at Nürburgring, it didn't qualify. Race specs of the day required a maximum weight of 1,653 pounds, excluding tires, fuel, and driver. When the Silver Arrow weighed in at 2.2 pounds over the limit, the pit crew removed the paint and primer, so it would qualify for the race. Ever since then it was silver.

"We used to call it the 'Naked Arrow,'" Tazio laughed.

"Andy! You need to get up to the press box to publicize the Silver Arrow," Ada said. She pulled me aside. "Remember," she said, "make sure you announce that the Silver Arrow will be competing in the concours event and will be for sale at the auction on Sunday."

On my walk up to the press box, the full impact of what we were doing hit me like a bag of rocks. I thought about my father, how hurt and disappointed he would be to learn I was spending the rest of my life in an Italian jail, not to mention the international incident the press would make of it. I stopped, turned around, and walked back down to the pit area.

"Andy! Get up there!" I heard Ada shrill. "What happened?"

I slowly shook my head. "I don't know if I can do this," I sighed.

"Okay! I'll go. You stay here!" Ada was angry. She started up the stairs.

"No!" I shouted. "I'll do it!"

"Well then, get up there! The race is about to start!"

When I entered the narrow press box, the announcer seemed inquisitive. "I'm the owner of the Silver Arrow," I said. He covered the microphone with his hand and asked my name. I was about to lie to one hundred thousand people.

"Ah . . . Eben Cruise," I stammered. I tried to purse my lips and force the sound upward so my voice would have a nasal quality to it, a technique I learned when teaching voice acting in my high school English class. The last thing I wanted was to be recognized by Salone.

"Oh, you must be new to the high-end collector market. Where do you live?"

"I'm from Brooklyn."

He moved his hand away from the microphone, "Ladies and gentlemen; I would like to turn the microphone over to Mr. Eben Cruise, the proud owner of that magnificent Silver Arrow!"

"Good Morning," I said, and then pulled back. Hearing my bogus words reverberate through the throng of seasoned collectors made me even more flustered. "The car you see on the track . . . " I continued to explain its "history" and provided background information on Dante Castronova. I pointed out, "This car will compete in the concours event tomorrow and then will be sold at the Noble-Dean auction on Sunday."

The crowd buzzed, speculating on how many millions the Silver Arrow would bring at Sunday's auction.

"Can you share your reserve?" the announcer asked. That was the one answer a smart auction seller would never reveal. Otherwise, the buy and sell auction dynamics are rendered completely ineffectual.

"Sorry. That would be totally foolish on my part."

The rumbling from the crowd heightened. This time they were most likely wondering, *if it was such a valuable car, why would the seller even bother with a reserve?*

Then I caught a glimpse of one of the stars stolen from the Villa Christina collection. There it was: the oxblood red Alfa Romeo 8C Monza. It was being driven from the paddock to the pit area. Three bloated Bosch headlights immediately caught my attention.

The dual Brookland windshields were folded down and ready for racing. When the silver-gray front wire wheels turned into the pit lane, exposing the massive front drum brakes, I gleaned a better look at the driver. He wore a leather skullcap with racing goggles and a pair of plain white cotton coveralls like the zip-up "siren suit" worn by Winston Churchill during the war. It was standard attire for vintage racecar drivers these days. When the driver parked the Monza and exited the car, he removed his skullcap and goggles. It was Salone! I stopped talking and handed the microphone back to the announcer.

"Thank you, Mr. Cruise," the announcer said, "and good luck at the concours event and the auction! Ladies and gentlemen, we all anticipate the Silver Arrow will fetch an astronomical price at Sunday's auction, well above anything ever paid for a classic car to date!"

I was still focused on Salone, studying the man who had caused so much misery for so many people. He began walking up the stairs toward the press box. I pulled my red hat down to my ears and checked my mirrored sunglasses and pencil mustache to be sure they remained intact. My heart thumped. I needed to control myself. *One must therefore be a fox to recognize the traps, and a lion to frighten wolves.* My mind understood the words, but my emotions were not nearly as compliant. I was afraid everything could crash down on me at the mere sight of this degenerate animal.

"Hello, Mr. Salone," the announcer said, as he covered the mic again.

Salone poked me with his elbow. "You finished with the mic, buddy?" His small size and tight siren suit made him look acrobatic, almost like a gymnast.

"Yes." I stood up, allowing Salone to be seated, and then headed toward the exit. I couldn't get out of there fast enough.

"Wait!" he yelled, pointing his finger at me.

He reached into his upper pocket and pulled out a folded sheet of paper. The dark black frames of his reading glasses made him seem bookish, even scholarly. As I stood behind him, I resisted a powerful urge to strangle him, to clamp a death grip around his neck so tight, he would be asphyxiated right in the press box. He was much smaller than me but had bigger muscles. I didn't care. Fortunately, somehow, I remained in control.

"Ladies and Gentleman, Mr. Salone has an announcement."

Salone removed an unlit cigar from his mouth, placing it on the edge of the counter near the microphone. He flattened the fold on his prepared text.

"Good Morning, everyone. The Alfa Monza you saw me drive on to the track was manufactured in 1933, one of only ten Monzas built. It had numerous wins in both the Mille Miglia and Targa Florio. This car won against the Mercedes Silver Arrow in the 1935 German Grand Prix at Nürburgring. In fact, the losing driver, Tazio Nucci, is on the track and, for some strange reason, is working with the Silver Arrow crew. Fair warning! My car has a top speed of 140 miles per hour. So, just a note to my fellow drivers: Stay the hell out of my way!" The crowd laughed, but Salone gave no indication he was joking. "This car will also be for sale at the auction on Sunday and will be offered at no reserve."

The crowd oohed and aahed loudly. In the last few minutes, they learned two of the most coveted racecars in the world would be sold at the Noble-Dean auction, one with a reserve and one without a reserve, which simply meant the highest bid would take it, no matter how low or high that bid turned out to be.

Salone handed the microphone back to the announcer and looked at me, squinted, and shook his head inquisitively. I'm glad he didn't remove his reading glasses. He might have recognized me.

"I've never seen you at the American shows and auctions. Are you new to this racket?"

"Racket?" I asked.

He picked up his cigar, lit it, and tapped the middle so the ashes could fall on the floor. "Listen, maybe we can help each other drive the price up on our cars and protect each other's investment. Are you corruptible?" He wasn't smiling.

I shrugged my shoulders. Had I said no, the conversation would have been over. I wanted to hear more.

"Listen, this is a big shell game, you know." He snickered with self-righteous arrogance. "It just takes a little cash and you and me—we bid on each other's cars to drive the price up. Then, at the right time, we back out. The auctioneer makes sure we're not the last ones to bid."

"How does he do that?" I asked.

"The chandelier bids."

Even though no chandeliers were in the auction tent, I understood the parlance. Essentially, the auctioneer would pretend he was receiving real bids in order to sustain demand beyond the last bid.

"I'm selling some other cars. You can help me there, too! Oh, by the way, Mr. Cruise, I *have to own* your Silver Arrow! It's an absolute requirement for my collection!"

I almost screamed *bingo!* I'd love to rap him for a cool 20 mil for a replica. The publicity alone would ruin him. Of course, it might not matter much to me. I would be dead!

"Let's see what happens during the auction," he said curtly.

"Gentlemen, please. Can you take it outside? I have a race to announce."

"When we're finished, we'll leave!" Salone's caustic response made the announcer shrink as if a bench vise was squeezing him. "As I was saying," Salone continued, "maybe we can strike up a deal after the auction and avoid the commission."

He waited curiously for my reaction, trying to determine whether I would be of any value to him.

"Sure, Mr. Salone," I agreed.

I don't know why I said "sure." I'd like to think my subconscious mind told me that bidding on each other's cars might present an opportunity I hadn't considered. Actually, in truth, I didn't want to risk it. Yet, I figured, since the auctioneer was probably in his pocket, he could control the bidding on the Silver Arrow as well.

"Call me Sal," he said. "You have any cars in the concours event tomorrow?"

"The Silver Arrow. Maybe a Jag XKSS my friend owns. And, you, Sal?"

Salone laughed. It was a loud, pompous, and imperious laugh that quickly turned into a harsh cigar cough. He removed his glasses and placed a handkerchief over his mouth. His eyes welled up with tears.

"Damn *sigaros*!" he exclaimed, throwing his cigar on the floor. "Just want you to know I win every year." He coughed again. "So maybe you should keep the Silver Arrow in the barn tomorrow. What do you think?"

That was the last straw. Such blatant arrogance!

"I'm going to pulverize your butt! That's what I think!" Suddenly, I was proud of myself and smiled at him. "Really, I said. I don't think you have a snowflake's chance in hell!"

"Or ghost of a chance, maybe? Like in Midnight Ghost?" He smiled suspiciously and lit up another cigar.

"What do you mean?" I asked.

Salone looked at me contentiously, as if he was unaccustomed to being challenged. "You're all right. I like you! I'll be at the west end of the field near the judges' stand when you want to talk."

As I walked down the stairs to the pit area amid a cheering, boisterous crowd, I felt emboldened. While I wasn't ring wise to auction manipulations, I hadn't cowered in the face of his sinister offer. I could actually sell a replica to Sicily's most notorious crime boss and make millions. And the Midnight Ghost? Salone's avarice just might blind him. Now I was getting all psyched up for the main event.

Castronova was driving into our pit area when I returned to the track. Photographers swamped him, as if he had just won the European Grand Prix Championship all over again. Pandemonium had broken out in the stands, as the uproarious crowd cheered wildly.

"Dante," I shouted, "they sure love you!"

"No!" he shouted back, "It's the car!"

The time for the vintage race was drawing near. Cars were lining up three abreast as the track announcer called out their numbers. Race marshals and track technicians had checked the brakes, seat belts, fire extinguishers, tire treads, and overall race worthiness of each car. It was time consuming, but safety was always a priority at these events. Dante Castronova, in the race red Ferrari 312T Formula One racer, moved to the front of the pack. While waiting in the pit lane, Tazio and I donned our fire-retardant Nomex racing suits and fastened our helmet straps. While some drivers preferred to emulate the racing regalia of the '30s, we wanted helmets. Our pit crews were busy finalizing their pre-race checklists for the Silver Arrow and the Jag XKSS.

Salone's revelation through the PA system to a festival crowd of 100,000 people that Tazio lost the 1935 German Grand Prix to the Monza was making him seethe with anger.

"That sonna ma bitch!" he growled, pounding his fist on the rear wall. "That was the *only* race I lost that year!"

Racing legends like Tazio tended to associate their self-esteem with the number of championships they *won,* not *lost.* His ego was clearly bruised.

"Tazio," I said. "It was a cheap shot. Forget it!"

"We'll see what happens on the track," he said in a retaliatory tone.

"Look what Salone is driving!" I said.

"That's a 1935 Duesenberg SJ Mormon Meteor," Tazio noted.

"Why is he racing that instead of the Monza?" Ada asked. "That thing looks like it belongs on a battlefield, not in a vintage car race!"

"The Meteor is unrestored. What a crude-looking car!"

"Yes, Mr. Punt. Just be careful out there. That Meteor is a beast and Salone—he couldn't care less if he wrecks it. Stay out of his way!"

The big pale yellow Duesenberg growled to the starting line. Was it ever ugly! The announcer referred to it as a supercharged speedster, but it didn't look anything like a speedster. It had a bulky appearance, like a boxcar. If the European sports cars were gazelles, the Meteor was a rhinoceros. The Cyclops headlight placed below its waterfall grill only emphasized its unsightliness. The Plymouth-like hubcaps made it appear as if the manufacturer had run out of parts. The long chrome tailpipe on the passenger side and the veiny supercharger bulge on the hood seemed like afterthoughts. The tear-drop designs of fenders, while attractive in their own right, were completely out of place on the bulky body.

Nevertheless, this was the car that set speed records on the Bonneville Salt Flats with an average speed of 153 miles per hour for twenty-four hours. That speed record didn't last very long. Some classic-car advocates, nonetheless, claimed the Mormon Meteor was the most important car America had ever produced. I could never understand why. It certainly wasn't my kind of car.

Tazio and I couldn't resist the temptation to race. With Tazio in his blue XKSS and me in the Silver Arrow, we were positioned on either side of Salone in his Mormon Meteor. The pace lap gave us time to test the steering and get comfortable with the track and the cars. Salone purposely revved the engine, swerving the car from left to right, attempting to intimidate us. White smoke spewed from the louvered engine cover, creating the biting smell of burnt oil. His Duesenberg sounded like a B-17 taxiing down the runway. It looked like one, too.

As I viewed the cars on the track, the standard colors applied: Germany was silver; Italian cars were red; French were blue and, with the exception of Tazio's XKSS, British were green. The sounds of chugging, roaring, and rattling were everywhere. Castronova increased his speed in the Ferrari pace car. Anxious spectators cheered and applauded frenetically. The experience was titillating, as I set my sights on beating the bastard Salone.

Once the race starter waved the green flag in a figure eight motion, we were suddenly immersed in the hissing superchargers and the whip-cracking sounds of backfiring. I wondered which additives caused such a noxious smell from the old motors. Even Tazio's XKSS and my Silver Arrow contributed their share of smoke and noise. As I accelerated to speed, I reviewed in my head the basic historic car-racing rules. *Over-aggressive driving, blocking, or risk taking, which could result in another competitor's car being damaged, will not be tolerated. Any driver going four wheels off, making contact with a barrier or tire wall, or having car-to-car contact in any session is strictly prohibited.*

Actually, the unwritten rule was more generally acknowledged: while it was a competitive event, it was more of a "gentleman's race," where the primary objective was enjoying the thrill of driving a vintage race car, not beating your opponent. *Sure it was,* I said to myself.

After passing the grandstand, we headed through a short straight and then around a sharp corner. I braked hard, followed the apex, and accelerated. As I came out of the turn, I felt the tremendous throttle response of the Silver Arrow, as if I were being launched in a surface-to-air missile. Now I knew why the Silver Arrow was such a legend. *Wait a minute*, I had to tell myself, *this car is a replica, not the genuine article.* It sure didn't feel that way!

We circled the three-mile track four times. The full race was fifty laps. I was in no hurry to prove anything. Too many former champions were in this race for me to be over-confident. I just loved driving my Silver Arrow. In fact, on a few straights, for a few seconds, I felt like I was in a road rally instead of on a racetrack.

On the long straight on the northwest end of the track, Tazio passed me in the Jag XKSS. Even though I was becoming accustomed to the track, I was afraid of the chicane at the end of the straight. I looked in my mirrors for the Meteor and was surprised that it wasn't in my field of vision. At some point in the race, I figured Salone would try to bully me with his Loch Ness monster. Only two cars were ahead of me, Tazio's XKSS and a Bugatti Type 35B driven by Jean-Pierre Fabre, the winner of the Monaco Grand Prix a few years ago. If I could shoot out of the chicane, maybe I could take them on the next corner. Was I dreaming? Andrew P. Robinson III, taking the lead away from two seasoned Grand Prix champions? *Why not?*

Tazio saw me coming and slowed down, allowing me to pass him on the straight. The adrenaline was pumping through my every limb. The wind was pounding against my goggles, and it was all I could do to keep my head forward. I quickly converted the kilometers to 140 miles per hour. As I approached the chicane, I braked hard. Fabre was on my front right-hand side. *Now was the time!* I put the accelerator to the floor. Without warning, a large yellow "bus" sandwiched itself between Fabre's Bugatti and my Silver Arrow. I was immediately tempted to fight back and turn into the car but knew that would be the end of the Silver Arrow. Instead of accelerating out of the turn, I was forced off of the track, plowing into mounds of bald tires and bales of hay. Then I slid sideways across the white turtles spread near every corner to slow down cars that were flying off of the track.

As I was sliding and spinning at more than 100 miles per hour, I braced myself for the inevitable roll. Even though the Silver Arrow had a built-in roll bar, I could still break my neck or be thrown from the car. Thankfully, the turtles slowed me down. Amid the smoke and smell of burnt rubber, I sat motionless in the car. I heard those damn Italian sirens again! I rotated my head waiting for the pain. My shoulders, arms, and legs moved, but I had a stabbing pain in my back, and my knees were pretty banged up. The Silver Arrow was much worse off than me. Not only were the front wheels lying on the ground behind the car but also the grille assembly was hanging off the left side. There I sat, dead in the water, with a shattered car, broken spirit, ruined plans, and maybe, a broken back.

Concours d'Elegance

The vintage race culminated with a victory celebration in front of the grandstand. The good news was that Tazio won by one car length, and Salone and his dinosaur were disqualified. A victory wreath, a garland of white and red carnations, and a bottle of milk were awarded to Tazio. I was glad for him and hoped his esteem would be restored after Salone's cruel remark.

I spent the night in the hospital at Enna with a slightly sprained back and badly bruised knees. My knees hurt more than my back. My pride, however, was shattered. But even that was eased with the prospect of seeing the Midnight Ghost at the auction. Tazio and Ada picked me up at 7:00 a.m. He delivered more bad news.

"Guess Salone scored another punch, didn't he?" I carped.

"I won the race, but Salone—he come out on top! We're finished," Tazio conceded. "The Silver Arrow—she won't be competing in no Concours d'Elegance anytime soon!"

"The auction is out of the question, too! Damn!" I moaned.

"C'mon, you two! I'm not ready to throw in the towel just yet!" Concession wasn't part of Ada's DNA. "Where is the car?" she asked.

"She's locked up in the trailer behind us."

"Then let's get it fixed!" Ada exclaimed. "What's so hard about that?"

"What the hell good will it do?" Tazio asked. "The concours is today!"

Ada leaned forward. "Forget the concours!" she shrieked. "The auction is our focus! Let's get the front wheels put back on. The grille assembly can be repaired and repainted. You must have some connections around here, don't you, Tazio? For God's sake!"

"It's not that easy. We need parts for a Mercedes Silver Arrow. Where do we get them around here?"

Tazio's excuses were wearing thin with Ada. "Well then, Tazio, determine what parts we need and we'll go from there. We're not performing brain surgery!"

"Listen, the wishbone assemblies—they got mangled," Tazio said. "A good welder—he can a fix or make a new ones. Helical springs and other suspension parts—they're hard to find."

"Tazio," I said, "all that stuff—brake parts, torsion bar springs, hydraulic shock absorbers—should be available at any automotive store. These cars get banged up all the time on the track. As long as we fix what's wrong and get the thing back the way it was, we can enter it in the auction. Anyway, we are selling a replica, remember?"

"Where's the closest race shop?" Ada asked.

"Enna," Tazio replied. "Negozio di Velocità Amedio. Amedio's Speed Shop, the same one Salone uses for his cars."

"Okay," Ada continued. "Drop us off at the festival, pick up a couple of volunteers from the track, and take the Silver Arrow to Amedio's. Tell him we'll pay him three times his hourly rate, but we need the car done by this evening. If you have a problem, *don't* come back to the festival!"

"*Si, signora generale* Robinson!" Tazio's eyes darted nervously side-to-side. *Who was this harsh demanding woman anyway?*

Lucrezia Borgia? "I'll get right on it!" he said. Ada meant business and he knew it.

We arrived at the parking lot for the concours event at 9:00 a.m. The field was filling up fast. Hundreds of cars—all kinds of marques from all eras—were arriving at the main gate. Some were in trailers; others were being driven. Cars had pre-assigned numbers on their windshields, and parking attendants were directing them to their respective class locations. The long line at the entrance gate was frozen in time, just like the classics waiting there.

Ten classic car categories were in the Concours d'Elegance. Each category highlighted the details of the cars and included the historical contributions of each marque. Placards positioned directly in front of each car provided ownership, restoration, and racing information (if appropriate) on each car. Owners, dressed in the regalia of the era their car represented, stood by their cars and answered questions, but most of all, smiled proudly for the cameras. Everyone was taking pictures, but with so many people hovering over the cars, it was impossible to get unobstructed views of the cars

"Ada, let's check out the postwar European sports car category."

I knew her first love was the sport cars of the '50s. We viewed a 1961 Porsche Roadster with an exquisite powder blue exterior and a bright red interior, a British Racing Green 1957 Aston Martin DB 3/4, and an incredible red 1951 Jaguar XK120 with biscuit interior.

"Ada, a person by the name of Max Hoffman imported thousands of these cars to America. In fact, in 1949, he arranged for the first steel-bodied Jaguar XK120 to be delivered to Clark Gable. With all the success of that car, General Motors and Ford were inspired to design their own sport cars of the '50s: the 1953 Corvette and 1955 Thunderbird.

"When we get home, I want you to buy me a brand new Corvette," Ada said.

"Sure. If we ever get home, that's the first thing I'll do! Promise!"

We moved over a few rows to visit the pre-war antiques.

"Andy, what is that?"

"Wow! A 1908 American Underslung Roadster! The placard says: *This car was designed by Fred Tone and Harry Stutz and was America's very first noteworthy sports car. It received its name from its unorthodox chassis layout, having axles above the frame, essentially flipped from the usual design. It caused frequent tire changes, which led to the car's early demise.*

"Look at this brass car!" Ada exclaimed. "A 1906 Pope-Toledo Type XII Roi des Belges 7 Passenger Touring car. It's pure art!" The bright-green paint with a gold pinstripe against the highly polished brass radiator and light was captivating.

Next, we saw a Mercer similar to mine, a 1913 Mercer Model 35 J Raceabout—yellow with black stripes on the fender and a big one-foot-wide brass kerosene light in front of the windshield. How grateful I was that I didn't trade mine for the Silver Arrow replica.

"Look! The Big Red bicycle team is out in full force delivering Sammy's breakfast pizzas." Greg, the young man from Buffalo, was delivering near the parking area. "Hey, Greg," Ada asked. "Do me a favor, if you would please?"

"Sure, Mrs. Robinson."

"See that big parking lot over there?" Ada pointed.

"Yes, I do."

"You will see men sitting under an awning of a Prevost Motor coach at the far end of the parking lot. Bring them a few pieces of puttanesca pizza with extra capers. Don't charge them. Just say it's on the house. I'm sure they will appreciate it and tip you well."

"I can do that for you, Mrs. Robinson. No problem."

"Thanks, Greg. Here's a few American dollars for your trouble."

"Thank you, Mrs. Robinson!"

"Let's hope he likes it," she said.

As we approached The Big Red, Tommie ran up to us. She was ebullient.

"It's here!" she cried out. "It's really here! Find space G21, but oh, forget the numbers. You'll see it right away. Just walk to the judges' tent. It's on a four-foot-high revolving pedestal with brass stanchions surrounding it. Salone's thugs are stationed at each corner, so it's difficult to get up close. I've never seen anything more exquisite! I could sit there for hours and just stare at it!"

"So our plan actually worked!" I lifted Tommie from the ground and twirled her around, and then I hugged Ada tightly.

"We found it!" she said in a loud whisper. "We actually found the Midnight Ghost!"

"I was beginning to worry," I said. "Never underestimate the power someone's ego, especially Salones!"

Between all the twirling and hugging, I was out of breath and sat down on one of the picnic tables in front of The Big Red. The combination of elation and trepidation was becoming a familiar sensation for me.

"Let's go look at it," I said. "Tommie, did you see Salone near the car?"

"No, I didn't," Tommie replied. "I didn't want anyone to read the jubilation on my face. I did meet a distinguished man, someone named Maxwell Riter, at the registration desk. He's one of the judges. I must say, I thought he was George Hamilton."

Ada was pulling my arm in the direction of the Midnight Ghost.

"Let's get over there, come on!"

We power-walked along the perimeter of the lake and eventually joined the mass of people on their way to view the Ghost. When we arrived, the crowd surrounding it was nearly impenetrable and teeming with curiosity, as if it were the leading candidate for eighth wonder of the new world. Ada followed me as I knifed my way through the throng, one body at a time, finally arriving at the front row.

I used to wonder what my reaction would be if I'd ever become lucky enough to see the Midnight Ghost. It reminded me when I was a kid and saw Niagara Falls for the first time, or when Ada and I saw the statue of David in Florence a few years earlier. It seemed incomprehensible that steel, rubber, and leather could be amalgamated into something this ethereal. Gone was its ugly gray paint. Sunglow orange covered the fenders and swept across the top of the car from the hood ornament to the rear bumper.

"Ada, this car does not deserve the trite nickname of Midnight Ghost. It diminishes its grandeur and the last thing it looks like is a ghost!"

"You're so right," she said. "We are now officially renaming it: the 1935 Duesenberg SJ Emmanuel, the car owned by a king!"

"And, with the final glorious touch of the revered Duesenberg marque," I added, "it's a masterpiece of design and engineering."

"Rolling sculpture, Andy. No description can do it justice."

The black platform on which it was resting was rotating slowly in a clockwise direction, allowing the crowd to remain stationary and admire her incredible design from all angles. Shiny brass stanchions held a black velvet rope extending around the platform. In front of the platform, positioned at each corner, four men dressed in black tuxedos and dark sunglasses stood with their arms folded. "Ada, we don't want to mess with these guys. They think they're guarding the Crown Jewels."

"How fantastic this car would look in the Villa Christina collection." Ada observed. "I can see it now—sitting in the middle of the floor, rotating on a platform with hundreds of people around it spellbound by its beauty. They'd come from all over the world to see King Victor's car."

"That's where it belongs, not hidden away in some cave in Sicily, that's for sure. It certainly would restore Tommie's reputation with the car collector community, too."

"At least the world now knows this car actually exists," Ada noted.

Miles Noble, one of the owners of the Noble-Dean Auction Company, was standing beside me.

"You know," he said, "back in the '30s someone wrote, 'The man who *arrived* drove a Duesenberg.' It was a case of the ultimate people owning the ultimate car. This Duesenberg is the ultimate of the ultimate! It's the most stunning automotive design of the 20th century!"

"Do you think it will ever come up for auction?" I inquired.

"To tell you the truth, I'm surprised it's in the show today. No, I don't think it will ever be sold at an auction. See that ornament on the hood? Collectors call it the The Duesenbird because it resembles a bird in flight. Do you know how much we've auctioned the ornaments for?"

"I haven't the faintest. If I had to guess, I'd say around $400 to $500?"

"Try $5,000 to $8,000—not the cheap imitations, but the real ones."

"I thought the real ones were only on cars."

"They were. In America and Europe, some Duesenbergs were scrapped after World War II. That's what most people thought happened to this car. Even I didn't know it still existed until now. You asked if it would ever be auctioned. We are seeing history being

made here today. Once the word gets out that this car has been discovered, I can't imagine what it might be worth. Not only that, it
will raise values of all other Duesenbergs and, in general, the entire
classic car market. As far as classic cars are concerned, this car repre-
sents the discovery of the century!"

"Got to get back to work," he said. He started to work his way
back through the crowd, then turned around and said, "Do you
have anything going through the auction?"

"Yes, the Silver Arrow."

"Oh, *you're* the one with the Silver Arrow. Mr. Salone asked me
what I thought he could buy it for. I told him fifteen, maybe twenty
million. I've been in business for twenty years and still get surprised
with auction prices. Well, good talking with you."

Once again, the magnitude of the crime we were about to commit hit me hard. *Fifteen, maybe twenty million* for a replica? I could
already feel the heat from the Sicilian Bull.

After Mr. Noble had left, I started taking photos. Then I noticed
no one else was, but I didn't think twice about it.

"Stop!" someone yelled. "Can't you read, buddy? The sign says
no pictures! Give me the film—NOW!" One of the guards, a giant
of a man, with hands the size of frying pans, was standing in front of
me. The people around me became silent. Without a word, I opened
the back of the camera and gave him the film. The man quickly
returned to his station.

"Hey, Bubba!" someone in the middle of the crowd shouted,
"if anyone wants to take a picture, you can't stop them!" The man
crumpled my film in his huge hands, as he peered through the crowd
looking for the heckler. Then he moved away to the other side of the
platform and disappeared.

A judges' canopy, maybe fifty feet away, was behind the
Duesenberg's platform. Six judges sat behind two rectangular tables.

Maxwell Riter was seated directly behind the trophies for Best of Class and Best of Show. The man who confiscated my film was having an animated conversation with Salvatore Salone near one of the tables. Salone raised his head and looked toward me.

"What a joke," Ada said.

"You mean the judges?"

"I mean it's rather obvious which is the best car here. It's like a beauty contest. The winners are determined at the cocktail parties."

"Really?" I asked and grinned. "Miss Congeniality, huh?"

Ada speared me in the gut with an elbow. Then we quietly ducked away.

TWENTY-ONE

The 1924 Hispano Suiza H6C Tulip Wood Torpedo

It was late when we dragged ourselves back to the villa. Tazio was sitting alone at the dinning room table, pounding down one Negroni cocktail after another. An open bag of fat pistachios with a mound of hollow half shells littered the otherwise immaculate tabletop. His face was beet red, he couldn't sit up straight, and he slurred his words. We caught him mumbling something indiscernible. *Not one, not two, not three, but four.* He was moving shells, one at a time, to another pile as he counted. He kept doing it—over and over again like he was in some sort of hypnotic state. We pulled out a couple of chairs and sat next to him.

"Tazio, hope you don't break any teeth on those shells." I cautioned.

"Quiet! I need to concentrate! That's four!" he said.

"Four what?" I asked.

"That's one, that's two, that's three, that's four. . . . "

"He's starting to sound like Lawrence Welk," Ada laughed.

"Too many pistachios saturated with Negronis." I quipped.

Tazio tilted his head sideways, giving us an incredulous look. "That is how many beautiful cars you two destroy since you been in Sicilia!"

"Not true," Ada observed. "I only get credit for one of them."

"All this time," I teased, "I didn't think you were old enough to drink."

"I am at least six-a-teen!" he dribbled. "And, I just sip!"

"Sipping is more common than drinking in Sicily," Ada noted.

"Ada! C'mon! Our friend Tazio isn't sipping or drinking—he's guzzling!"

"Mr. Punt, I make you the best Negroni you've ever had!" Tazio garbled.

"I've never had one and don't want to start now. Thanks anyway."

"Tazio," Ada asked, "I hate to change the subject, but do we have a green light on the Silver Arrow? The auction is tomorrow, you know."

"That guy Amedio—he refuse to work on the Arrow. He give me trouble!"

"Oh, no!" I said, quickly deflated by the prospect of failure.

"Hey, wait a minute, Mr. Punt," he mumbled as he teetered precariously on his chair. "Tazio—he never let you down! Bow your heads! We bury the beast today!" He lowered his head piously and closed his eyes.

"Tazio, maybe you should call it a night," Ada advised.

"The Mormon Monster—it was in his shop for repairs, too."

"No way!" I said.

"Amedio—he work for Salone, you know. He had orders to fix it right away."

"Of course," I said. "He wanted it ready for the concours event."

"You mean Salone would allow himself to be embarrassed by entering that contraption in the Concours d'Elegance?" Ada said, astonished.

"It shows his arrogance," I said. "He's immune to embarrassment. So, Tazio, tell us what the hell happened before we all fall asleep."

"Well, me and my two *assistenti*—we throw Amedio in the grease pit and remove the ladder. Then we *cannibale* the Monster. The front parts—they're the same thing. I weld on the wishbones. We take the tires off of the Monster and hide them, just in case Salone get more ideas."

"I'd love to see the Meteor now!" I said, laughing.

"Without wheels, it look like a *scarphacliff*!" Tazio laughed.

"You mean a *sarcophagus*?" Ada asked.

"*Si*! A *sacrapiss*! Smart woman, Mr. Punt. You keep!"

Ada and I broke up. Tazio snickered, totally amused by his feat.

"We deliver the Silver Arrow to Noble-Dean early in the morning. *Salone! Ha! Telling everyone I lose the Grand Prix at Nürburgring!* I teach that sonna ma bitch a lesson he won't forget! He don't wanna mess with *il grande* Tazio!"

"Would I ever love to be around when Salone figures out what happened to his Meteor," I said. "That little runt will have a stroke!"

"I do have sympathy for the mechanic, though," Ada said.

"Salone will think a guy named 'Eben Cruise' had something to do with it," I said. "Let's just hope he doesn't try another stunt before the auction."

Francesco entered the room in his wheelchair. He began to yell.

"You all are going to get yourselves killed! Whatever you are doing, stop!"

"Don't worry, Francesco. No one's getting killed," Ada said.

"You cannot do this thing!" Francesco exclaimed. While his fragile body slumped in the chair, I could see the impassioned anger in his eyes.

"Tell me the plan for tomorrow! Tell me!"

"We are going to do what Sicily's law enforcement community hasn't been able to do for decades." My answer was too spontaneous and inconsiderate. It came across as arrogant. I was sure I had insulted Francesco. "Listen, Francesco, we are just trying to get the cars back. I didn't mean to offend you."

"That's right," Ada added. "We have a plan in place."

"And what if it doesn't work? The lives of everyone here are in danger!"

"We believe it's worth the risk," I said. "We have to try."

"You have no idea who you are dealing with here! Salone is not some hood from America. He's a killing machine that goes into action when anyone, and I mean anyone, gets in his way."

Ada and I looked at each other and said nothing. We understood the futility of a response. We also had a deep compassion for a man who lost everything because of Salone.

"It's late," I said. "We can all discuss this in the morning. Goodnight."

Prior to falling asleep, Ada and I made one last review of our plan.

"You know, Ada, Francesco *was* right about one thing. We are placing other lives in grave danger. I'd be lying if I said that didn't bother me very much."

"Of course. It concerns me very much too, Andy. But I can tell you what motivates me. Just think about how many other lives would be in great danger if we did nothing. Or conversely, how many lives we will save by ensuring Salone's permanent incarceration."

Early in the morning, Ada and I joined Tazio, Tommie, and Sammy for a meeting at the dinning room table. Francesco sat beside us in his wheelchair.

"Good morning," Ada said cheerfully, as if we were having a routine breakfast.

She was wearing black slacks and a lavender summer sweater. She never looked better. After being seated, she smiled at me affectionately with her beautiful hazel eyes.

"Did everyone have breakfast?" Her congeniality helped put everyone else at ease. I knew she was churning inside.

Tommie smiled politely. "We were waiting for you and Andy."

For the first time I noticed a genuine harmony among everyone at the table. We were a team bonded together with a common objective. It felt good. At the moment, the only weak link was Tazio. He suffered from mental gridlock from his merrymaking the night before. Like the stacks of pistachio shells scattered across the table, it seemed like Tazio's brain was also out of order.

"Clean up your mess!" Tommie ordered. "We have important things to discuss this morning."

Tazio didn't respond. He leaned back in his chair, and for a moment I thought he might pass out. Tommie walked around the table with a wastebasket sliding piles of shells into it.

"In case you haven't noticed, my father is still a kid!"

Ada and I started to chuckle. "Yeah, a fifty-year-old kid at that," I said.

"I think he was fifty when I was born," Tommie cracked.

"Now Tommie," Ada said, "you have to admit, after he was able to save the Silver Arrow, your father was entitled to celebrate a little bit last night."

Tommie was amused. "I don't care if he gets drunk; I just hate those messy nut shells all over the villa. I find them in the bathroom, the bedroom between his sheets, and in the closets. I even found a bunch in his underwear!"

"Okay," I said. I waited until I had everyone's attention. "We are about to embark on a dangerous mission. We need to focus." I sensed their concern as well as their quiet confidence.

"We're anxious," Tommie said. "We absolutely have to get these cars back!" Sammy quietly nodded. Tazio started to snore. "Papa! Pay attention! This is the most important project of your life! This is no time for a siesta!"

"*Sì,* I'm sorry." He stretched his arms and rubbed his face. He was ready.

"Oh, by the way, Mrs. Robinson," Sammy said. "My friend Greg told me to tell you—your friends with the Prevost loved the puttanesca pizza."

"I'm glad we could accommodate our old friends." I said.

"Yup. Me, too," Ada added. She looked in my direction and nodded.

When Tazio described his encounter with Amedio, Francesco's eyes bulged.

"When Salone finds out what you've done to his Mormon Meteor, the montagne is going to erupt!" Francesco barked. "You have unleashed his viciousness! I know this man! I know what he will do to you! Don't go to the auction today! I beg you! Stay here!"

A long silence enveloped the room. Then Ada spoke. "Francesco, I hear what you are saying, and Andy and I are well aware of how dangerous a man Salone is. What this sadistic monster has done to you and the crimes he has committed against society are unforgiveable. This man cannot be stopped by ordinary methods."

"There's been enough bloodshed! Francesco asserted. "No more!"

"Most of us will be staying here today," I said.

"Sammy," Ada asked, "are all the extra phone lines installed here and at the auction?"

"I had four installed with unlisted numbers, like you said."

"That's one for each of us—Sammy, Tommie, and me; we're the three anonymous telephone bidders—and one more line to communicate with Andy at the auction. We have twenty-six cars to buy, ten belonging to the owners, and sixteen belonging to the Villa Christina collection. Punt will be bidding in person and he will have access to the bidders' phones. I will coordinate things here at the villa. Tommie has registered us as bidders under fictitious names. Eben Cruise has been listed as a bidder. He is also the consignee and seller of the Silver Arrow."

Francesco struggled to his feet. I could see the exasperation in his eyes.

"Get me my crutches!" he demanded. Ada rose from the table, removed his crutches from a nearby closet, and handed them to him. "I can't listen any longer!"

He jerked the wheelchair against the wall with his elbows, and then moved his crutches in front of him one at a time, trudging laboriously toward the back door. He walked out to the patio, slamming the door behind him. Ada went to the window to check on him.

"He's on a chaise longue staring at the pool," Ada said. She followed him outside, sat down next to him, and began talking.

When Ada returned, she said, "This entire ordeal has been tumultuous for him. He's way beyond bitterness. I'm worried about what he'll do. When we finish with this meeting, let's spend some time with him. I have some ideas."

"Good," I said even though I knew neither one of us would be able to alleviate Francesco's considerable angst.

Tommie shuffled uncomfortably in her chair.

"Okay," she said, "let's get back to business. My father's all signed up to drive the cars on and off the stage."

"Tazio!" I said. He didn't move. "Tazio! Did you hear that?"

"*Si*! You want me to drive the cars off of the stage."

"We want you to drive them *on* and *off* the stage and then park them all together in the same location," Tommie said.

"One thing I can do is drive! Call me the wheel man!" Tazio added.

"Terrific," I said. "Tazio, just remember, after you drive the cars down the auction block, bring them to the west end of the parking lot, on the opposite side of Salone's trucks. We've arranged for five Genaro World Wide Transport trucks to wait there for the cars. The drivers will load the cars and lock them up. After we give the drivers payment receipt vouchers, they will transport the ten owners' cars to the Palermo Ferry Port, a two-hour drive from Pergusa, and then ferry them to the Automobile Terminal at the Port of Naples. They will take the sixteen Villa Christina cars back to the Villa. I'll be in direct communication with the Genaro World Wide Transport dispatcher."

"Francesco, despite his objection to the plan, arranged for a few loyal carabinieri to be stationed at each truck and guard the cars once they're back inside the Villa," Ada noted.

"We were able to get a list of the cars being auctioned today," I said. I passed copies around to everyone. "Tommie and Tazio, please asterisk any cars that were in the collection. I recognized most but don't remember them all."

"Fortunately," Tommie said, "some of the more priceless cars like the Rolls Royce Silver Ghost and Goering's Mercedes went back to their museums before the other cars were stolen. We should have a total of twenty-three cars, not twenty-six."

Tommie put on her reading glasses and scanned the list. Tazio was looking over her shoulder.

"Oh my God!" she exclaimed. "All of the twenty-three are on the list!"

"Well, of course!" Ada said. "Salone is that arrogant. He has no qualms about selling the cars at a public auction. He thinks he's untouchable."

"So did Capone," I said, with a smirk.

"I'm pretty good at assessing classic car values," I said. "I also have the latest Hemmings and a couple of reliable price guides to work with. Let's come up with the presale estimates and jot them down. I know it's just a projection, but it will give us an idea when the bidding *might* stop. Then again, some bidders will become completely obsessed and pay *any* price. I call it 'asset infatuation.' It's like a drug. No matter how hard they try, they simply cannot live without it. They're the ones that worry me. They could bid up our cars so high, we'd be forced to pay way too much for them."

"Yeah, but sooner or later, they'll run out of money, right?" Tommie asked.

"Well, yes. Things usually slow down near the end of the auction. By that time everyone's broke! Most bidders plan in advance. They make their decisions from the cars listed for sale. If any cars are auctioned that are not on an advance list, they probably won't do too well. Bidders don't like surprises, especially when we are talking this kind of money."

"Okay, now let's assign the cars." I continued. "Ada, Tommie, and Sammy, you take five cars each. We don't want one person doing all the bidding. The auction people will get suspicious. I'll take eight and will be sitting near the phones at the auction so I can coach you, if necessary. Ada, you can coordinate things here and then come to the auction and help with the last two cars, the Hispano Suiza and the Silver Arrow. Using an average of eight minutes per car, we can project the approximate timing for each car. I am familiar with this auctioneer and have timed him in the past. Once you have your approximate time frames, spread out your bidding assignments, so you'll have time to help each other, if necessary.

"Remember, Salone has the auctioneer in his pocket. Some of the bidding will be simulated or I should say 'make believe.' That means the bids will be phony. It's called chandelier bidding. Don't bid too early. Wait until the bidding slows, and the car approaches its market value. This should work in our favor as long as someone else doesn't decide to bid the car up beyond its value. Okay, let's prepare."

Over the next hour, we wrote the current value next to every car on the list, calculated an approximate auction time, assigned the bidding responsibility for each car, and then arrived at a total.

"How much?" I asked.

"We have $16 million," Tommie answered. "That doesn't include any surplus from over-anxious bidders."

"Which is impossible to predict," I said. "We might have a few cars come in under market value, too. It's hard to forecast either way. We have a reasonable blueprint to follow. If the unpredictable happens, and it will, I'll make the call. The Silver Arrow is sched-uled to be the last car auctioned. Salone should be flush with cash by then. Once his greed kicks in, who knows how high he'll go? I'll put a $16-million-dollar reserve on it and then drop the reserve when it gets close. That should bring it over the top. Additionally, we will have a buyer's commission, but no seller fees, typical for high-end cars. Whatever we sell the Silver Arrow for will be the net number."

"Wait a minute," Ada cautioned. "That works in our favor with the Silver Arrow, but what kind of premium do we have to pay to purchase Salone's cars?"

"They won't negotiate the buyer's premium. It's 6 percent," Tommie said. "So that's another $960,000," she quickly calculated. "Instead of $16 million, we should be projecting $17 million, right, Andy? Doesn't that sound like an astronomical amount of money to pay for the Silver Arrow? What's the market value?"

"Market values for one-of-a-kind classic cars are nonexistent," I replied. "There's no sales history on which to project a price. The real question is, what's the bidder willing to pay?"

"Then it's a crap shoot!" Tazio chimed in.

"Glad to see your paying attention, Conte Nucci!"

"I pay attention very well, Mr. Punt."

"Listen everybody," I said. "It really all boils down to one thing. I'm counting on Salone's ravenous appetite to own something no one else in the world has: simply the most sought after racecar of all time! I really believe he won't be able to pass it up!" I hesitated a few seconds, tilting my head back.

I said to myself, *if this works, it will be the rip-off of the century!* I was actually getting excited. I looked over at Tommie. She still appeared worried.

"What if he doesn't bid on it or discovers it's a replica?" she asked.

"Then, we'll all be cooked!" I said impatiently.

Sammy and Tommie traded expressionless glances. Overall, I know they were supportive of the strategy and would work hard to achieve our objective. However, that did not allay my concerns. I needed a full boat with everyone going in the same direction.

"We will make it work!" Tommie asserted.

"All my people are on board, Mr. Robinson!" Sammy said.

"Let's go talk to Francesco," Ada said. We have to try and diffuse his anger."

After I affixed my disguise, Tazio and I jumped into the truck with the trailer still attached and left for the auction. When we arrived, we checked with Greg and Burt at The Big Red. They were busy making breakfast pizzas. Two young women were preparing to deliver the pizzas on the bicycles. While I spoke with Greg and Burt, Tazio entertained the young women.

"You guys okay?" I asked.

"Everything is going well," Greg said.

"We're running low on peppers, capers, and anchovies," Greg said. "We mentioned that to Mrs. Robinson last night. She said she would bring a supply over later today."

"She'll be busy most of the day," I said. "I'll be speaking with her later."

"We'll be okay until three or four."

"Great. Thanks for the help, fellas."

"Let's go, Tazerino!" He was so engaged in conversation, I had to repeat myself. "Tazio! We need to make sure the Duesenberg is still here. C'mon!"

"Okay. I am coming, Mr. Punt."

When we reached the Duesenberg platform, I said, "Look, Tazio! Fresh exhaust stains are on the ramp. That means the Duesenberg moved back and forth from its trailer under its own power."

"So, someone must have driven it from the trailer."

"Probably in the middle of the night," I said. My mind began to buzz with possibilities, like stealing it after the auction, or when everyone became distracted when the Silver Arrow came up on the block. The fact that it was drivable would make things much easier.

"I can drive it out of here, Mr. Punt! I can hot-wire it, too! You figure out *when,* and I will drive it to my trailer and load it up!" I loved Tazio's enthusiasm, if not his practicality.

"You think Mr. Salone and his cronies might object to that idea?"

"You have to cut the head off the dragon, Mr. Punt."

"Yeah, I've heard that before. Any good ideas on how, my good friend?"

"I do not know! You are the brains of the outfit; I am just the wheel man!"

"That reminds me, you should get yourself to the drivers' meeting over at the pavilion."

"Okay, Capitano Robinson. I'm outta here!"

The auction was scheduled to begin at 10:00 a.m. This meant it would actually begin around 10:30 a.m. The auction folks liked a full house and usually waited until the stragglers arrived. The first fifteen cars to be auctioned were lined up on the runway. Hundreds of people were inspecting the cars. Some were selecting candidates on which to bid; others were simply admiring their elegance, charm, and historical significance.

Under the auction tent, thirty rows of folding chairs were set up classroom style, enough for about five hundred people. Another few hundred would be standing around the inside perimeter of the tent. One cocktail bar was in the rear; the other was on the front left side next to the stage. Bartenders were preparing to serve wine, beer, and mixed drinks. I sat in a middle row, near the telephones, which were on a table right next to me.

As I perused the auction list, I noticed the 1924 Hispano Suiza H6C Tulip Wood Torpedo, the French Woodie Tazio had located before all the cars were stolen. It looked just like a wooden torpedo. This car, I thought, might pose a problem with our presale estimates. While the Duesenberg became the most expensive car in America, the Hispano Suiza H6C became the most expensive car in Europe. Although Hispano Suiza was a Spanish company, many of its cars were manufactured in Paris. Andre Dubonnet, Tazio's friend and heir to an aperitif and cognac fortune, designed and raced this car in the 1924 Targa Florio.

It had an extraordinary appearance along with great provenance. Similar to the Silver Arrow, it was one of a kind. I had no idea what number it would actually bring. It would be auctioned just before the Silver Arrow and would be the last of the cars from the Villa Christina collection. Even though it was near the end of the auction, as long as it was on the list, bidders could prepare for it.

When Malcolm Carlisle, the auctioneer, appeared on the stage, many collectors went over to shake his hand. Carlisle was famous. It was important for collectors to be on a first name basis with the venerable Carlisle. In reality, the only thing Carlisle cared about was selling cars, and if he had to shake a few hands and slap a few backs in the process, it was all part of the charade. Oh, I almost forgot: his cut from Salone—that mattered, too. As lines formed near the stage to shake Carlisle's hand, I wondered, *perhaps I should say hello.*

"Top of the mornin' everyone! Top of the mornin' indeed!" Carlisle was a man with boundless energy. He was moving across the crowded stage with the self-assurance of someone who had done this a thousand times before. When I reached him, I said, "I'm Eben Cruise. I'll be bidding on quite a few cars today."

"Oh yes, Mr. Cruise! Mr. Salone told me to pay particular attention to you today. He said you were a *player.*"

"What does that mean?" I asked.

Carlisle laughed brazenly, as if to completely nullify my question. Then, like he was gathering votes for a presidential run, he moved sideways to shake the next hand in line.

Walking back to my seat, I was struck by the disingenuous nature of the auction mechanics. Actually, I was in no position to judge. Today, I would be the most reprehensible perpetrator of bidding manipulation in the history of classic car auctions. In fact, today, if our plan worked, I would be responsible for hijacking millions of dollars worth of classic cars. I relished the thought of catching a glimpse of Salone's face when he realized how badly he had been taken.

Putting my head back into the auction list, I memorized all the market values of the cars. Then, I continued to watch the auction participants assemble. The first five rows were VIPs, collectors, or dealers who had purchased five or more cars from Noble-Dean in the past. I noticed four chairs in the front row were separated from the other chairs. One of the individuals seated there was Salone. I'd recognize *his* profile anywhere. He was dressed in a green t-shirt, jeans, and a yellow baseball cap. When he turned his head, his trademark unlit cigar protruded from his mouth like a rusty weathervane. Three people, apparently friends or associates, were with him.

Seeing Salone made me uptight. Controlling my desire to attack him with whatever weapon I could put my hands on was the most difficult task I had for the day. A mad dog was inside me that wanted to tear him limb from limb. I started to perspire and couldn't remain still. I walked to the bar.

"You look rattled. Can I get you something?" the bartender asked.

"Whiskey on the rocks," I answered. "Any kind, it doesn't matter."

Hard liquor was not part of my early-morning diet, but I needed something to settle me down. My eyes remained fixed on the auction stage, watching Carlisle campaign for bids. I recognized some of the people from past auctions, like Peter Shultz and Brad Ward. They had multimillion-dollar collections and, in all probability, would be bidding on the Villa Christina cars, maybe on the Silver Arrow, too. I took a large sip of my drink. Then, someone tapped me on the back. It was Salone.

"Mr. Cruise!" he said. "I wanted you to know they just placed my Alfa Monza on the runway. It's car number five. If you're interested, I'd be happy to answer any of your questions. Fistfuls of people plan to bid on it."

His own fist was clenched. He was stiff and formal and had a nasty glare, like all he had to do was blink, and he could murder me with his eyes.

"Is it still for sale at no reserve?" I asked.

"That's right. How about the Silver Arrow?"

"A car like that? I'm not selling unless I get my price."

"Oh, by the way, Mr. Cruise, you can remove your sunglasses. I don't see any sun inside the tent, do you?"

"I have photophobia. My eyes cannot handle the light."

"Mr. Cruise. Listen, I'm sorry about our accident yesterday. I hope you understand it wasn't intentional. Despite that, you also have to get it through your head the Silver Arrow isn't worth the money any more. I presume you have a low reserve on it. We can work something out right now. Come with me. I'd like to introduce you to my classic car broker. Maybe, one day, you could use his services."

I was nervous. I didn't know how well my disguise would hold up, but I agreed to follow him. We walked through the crowd to the front row.

"Mr. Cruise, this is my friend, Maxwell Riter. He travels all over the world finding classic cars for me. Last year he bought me several cars at the Blackhawk Inn auction on Fisherman's Wharf. Were you at that auction, Mr. Cruise?" Salone stepped back with a taunting grin, like he just dropped a bomb and was waiting for it to explode.

"Mr. Cruise," Maxwell said, "it is indeed a pleasure to make your acquaintance."

"Thank you," I said with a deep voice.

"Honey," he said to the voluptuous woman who was seated near him, "this is Mr. Cruise."

She stood to shake my hand, yet all the while her eyes were locked adoringly on him. That sob story about his son being killed in Viet Nam and his wife being sick . . . now I was sure it was all a big ruse. Traveling to auctions with his girlfriends and buying cars for the mob, that was his game. He was nothing more than Salone's puppet.

"Care to join us?" he gloated.

His insidious tone telegraphed a cold impudence. I had to move away. Up until now, I could harness my temper. In another few seconds, I *would* explode.

"I have to get back to my seat," I said.

"No deal on the Arrow?" Salone asked. "You probably won't get your reserve, you know. A smart man would face up to the situation and get what he could now."

"I'll still take my chances with the bidding," I said.

"Well, good luck, ah . . . Mr. Cruise." Salone said. "I think you're going to need it!"

His nostrils flared like a bull getting ready to attack. I detested his arrogant, venomous look. Then his sardonic laugh resonated throughout the auction tent. He placed the wrinkled unlit cigar back in his mouth and walked away. Four black suits encircled him, glaring suspiciously at anyone who came too close.

"Nice meeting you . . . Mr. Cruise!" Maxwell said. "If you need help bidding, let me know."

"Thanks. I can handle it. Good day, Mr. Riter."

I couldn't have been more naïve! This was all a set-up right from the start!

TWENTY-TWO

The Noble-Dean Auction

I spent the next half hour fuming and then went into the men's room, removed my flimsy disguise, and splashed cold water on my face. That always sharpened my awareness and got my mind back in the game. I combed my hair, adjusted my moustache, and positioned my mirrored sunglasses. *How futile was this disguise!* For a moment, I wanted to toss it in the waste bin. What's the use? Salone and Riter—I was sure they already must know my identity. I returned to my seat to concentrate on the job at hand—with my worthless disguise intact.

The first four cars were auctioned off below market value. They were considered warm-ups and not highly desirable. When the Alfa Monza came on the block with Tazio behind the wheel, the auction tent was full—a good sign for Salone; a bad one for me. According to our plan, my purchase budget was 17 million, and it had to last through twenty-three cars, including the 1924 Hispano Suiza H6C Tulip Wood Torpedo, which was the last car before the Silver Arrow. This car and the 1957 Ferrari Testa Rossa could easily crush our plan.

"Ladies and gentlemen, please welcome the 1933 Alfa Romeo Monza 8c, winner of Le Mans, two Targa Florios, and several Grand

Prix races. Former Grand Prix racing champion, Tazio Nucci, is driving the car that made him famous."

When the crowd applauded, Tazio waved as if he had just received the checkered flag at the Targa Florio. For a brief moment, he was back in the 1930s reveling in his many racing victories. I was glad for him, especially after Salone attempted to diminish his grandeur.

"This car has been restored to perfection and is in race-ready condition," Carlisle said. "Do I hear $10,000,000?" The crowd grew silent. "C'mon, now. Don't be shy." Carlisle's habitual use of the Queen's English added a degree of prestige to the event. "Okay, everyone, I'll come down, just trying to be fair. $5,000,000?"

As Carlisle tossed out the bait and no one snatched it, he was quiet for a few seconds. Experienced bidders knew that when bidding started at a lower price, future bids were always more robust. That was dangerous, too. At no reserve, this Monza had to be purchased for our pre-determined price. Our presale projection was between $800,000 and $1,300,000. My guess was $1,000,000 would take it, but maybe I could get it for less. I had to try.

"Okay, who wants to start out the bidding?" Carlisle suddenly had three rapid-fire bids for $800,000, $850,000, and $900,000. "Now $1,000,000 anyone?" The bidders were quiet again. "Okay, it's $900,000—fair warning! $900,000 going once . . . "

My arm shot straight up. "$925,000," I yelled.

"Thank you, Mr. Cruise, and welcome to the Noble-Dean auction, the largest most successful classic car auction house in the world!" He enunciated every syllable, as if he were teaching a class in phonetics. Carlisle pointed to the back of the tent. "Okay, now we're up to $950,000."

I couldn't determine who was bidding against me.

"Do I hear $1,000,000?"

I signaled to halve the difference, using the basketball time-out sign, and quickly turned my head to catch a glimpse of the bidder behind me.

"Okay, we have a bidder at $975,000. C'mon, now! Ladies and gentlemen, I would like to point out that this car has won all the major European racing events. Only 190 of these Alfas were built during the depression era. These cars were known for their long distance endurance racing ability, and this one is the pick of the litter! Ladies and gentlemen, what are you waiting for?"

While I continued to glance at the back of the room, waiting for a bidder to raise his hand or nod inconspicuously, a bid came in from somewhere else.

"$985,000!" Carlisle shouted.

It had to be the chandelier. Despite my being manipulated, I was still within budget.

"Now, we absolutely and positively must have $1,000,000, ladies and gentlemen!"

The crowd was hushed with anticipation. All eyes were on me. I had to make a decision. I waved my bidder paddle in quick short motions with my wrist.

"Yes! Mr. Cruise!"

The crowd broke out into spontaneous applause. Reaching the million-dollar mark was always a significant milestone at a classic car auction and worthy of recognition. I must admit—bidding with money I didn't have seemed to make the entire process unreal.

Carlisle persisted, "Do I hear $1,100,000?"

He paused, apparently content with my million-dollar bid. Then he looked at Salone.

"Fair warning!"

He paused again. Salone took off his yellow baseball cap.

"Sold! Sold! Sold! $1,000,000 to bidder number 25! Thank you, Mr. Cruise!"

His voice reverberated through the PA system and the speakers shook. The crowd applauded again. Salone and Riter turned to me and gave me thumbs up signs. Salone priced the Monza at one million. Carlisle made sure it didn't sell for one penny less.

At first, I was thrilled. My winning bid for the Monza, although finessed by Salone and Carlisle, was within our presale estimates. For a fleeting moment, I was the proud new owner of one of the monuments of racing history. When I came to my senses, I was anything but proud. Eben Cruise was the lucky man. Regretfully, neither Eben Cruise nor Andrew P. Robinson III had the money to pay for it!

The next car on my list, the 1957 Ferrari Testa Rossa we had seen that long-ago day in front of the schoolhouse, was about an hour away from the bidding block. I had to find Tazio in the auction pavilion and make sure he understood the drill. The sooner the Monza was in a Genaro World Wide Transport trailer, off the festival grounds, away from Salone's people, the happier I'd be. Two guards still loyal to Francesco, were located near the rear doors of each of the Genaro trailers.

Now for the tricky part: all the paperwork! Security required sales vouchers before they would release the cars. Cars had to be paid in full before Noble-Dean would release the sales vouchers. With the proceeds from the sale of the Silver Arrow playing such a critical role in our plan, the paperwork formalities could easily become an obstacle to our success.

Once the Monza was safely tucked away in the trailer, I checked with Greg and Burt at The Big Red.

"We have enough peppers, capers, and anchovies for an hour or so," Greg said. "Mr. Salone ordered four large trays of puttanesca pizzas to be delivered to the auction tent at 5:00 p.m. I just want to make sure we don't run out. He's one guy I don't want to piss off."

"I hear you loud and clear. Thanks for letting me know." *Here I am bidding on million-dollar cars, and I have to worry about peppers, capers, and anchovies? Of course, if our plan succeeds, I will be very glad I worried about peppers, capers, and anchovies.*

When I returned to the auction tent, the Testa Rossa was next up on the block. Five auction volunteers on the telephones accepting bids were seated behind a table across from me. Carlisle would treat them like any other bidder. The volunteers merely had to raise their hands to bid on behalf of the person on the other end of the line. Another table had five telephones available for bidders, mostly dealers, who wanted to stay in touch with their customers. I went to one of the telephones and called Villa Christina. Ada answered.

"We got the Monza for a million," I said.

"Good job," she said. "We have to spread the remaining $16 million over twenty-two cars. Do you think we can do it?"

"Two cars worry me: the Testa Rossa and that Hispano Suiza. Either one can break the bank." I actually thought we had a bank to break.

"Tommie is on the Testa Rossa," she said. "Do you think it has a reserve?"

"I don't know. If there is one, Salone will remove it when the bids get close."

"I don't think he has a reserve on any of the cars," Ada said.

"Why not?"

"Any amount of cash he gets makes him a winner. How much cash did he invest, anyway?"

"Zero, of course!" I replied.

"So, speaking of return on investment, anything he receives is 100 percent profit. Why have a reserve?"

"That makes good sense, Ada. Listen, stay on the line with me. We'll coach Tommie if she gets in trouble."

"Okay."

"Oh, here comes the Testa Rossa. Tazio is behind the wheel again."

"Ladies and gentlemen!" Carlisle bellowed. "Just feast your eyes on this Italian beauty. The most exciting Ferrari ever to come to auction! This car's restoration has won multiple awards. This exact car won the Best of Show Award at the famed Pebble Beach Concours last year. Just looking at this car is a visceral and breathtaking experience! Designed by Scaglietti, it is one of the most successful racecars of all time! Who would like to open the bidding at $15,000,000?"

"Ada, tell Tommie to wait! I'll tell her when."

"She's cool. Don't worry."

"I have $2,000,000! Thank you, Mr. Ward! Is there a bid for $2,500,000?" Several hands went up. Okay, $2,500,000 . . . now $3,000,000 . . . now $3,500,000. Okay, now $4,000,000?"

I couldn't believe how quickly this car blew past our presale estimate of $1,500,000.

"Tell Tommie to get ready!"

"She's ready!"

"Someone here wants the Testa Rossa and wants it badly, but paying more than twice the market value will ruin our plan!"

"We have no choice, Andy. Buy the car!"

"I'm waiting, but I don't have all day now."

Carlisle had stepped away from the podium placing both hands on his hip.

"Okay, it's $4,000,000 now! Thank you, Mr. Shultz!"

"Tell Tommie to bid $4,500,000! Now!" I hoped Shultz's bid was his limit.

"Ladies and gentleman, I have just received a telephone bid for $4,500,000! Is $5,000,000 out there? Okay, we can do that! I have $4,600,000. Thank you again, Mr. Shultz!"

"Shultz is attempting to keep the total price of the car, with the buyer's premium, below $5,000,000. So now I know that's his budget. We might be able to get it for $5,000,000 plus commissions. Tell Tommie—bid $5,000,000 now!"

"Another telephone bid! This time for $5,000,000!"

I heard the tumultuous applause from the audience. Then, an abrupt silence filled the room.

"Are we finished? I could use a bid for $5,500,000."

Carlisle studied the crowd for another bid, and then looked at Salone with a conspicuous stare.

"Fair warning!"

Salone tipped his yellow hat. Carlisle slammed the wooden gavel down hard on the podium.

"Sold! Sold!" he shouted. "Another sale at the fabulous Noble-Dean auction, the largest classic car auction house in the world!"

"I know we had to have the Testa Rossa, but now we're in trouble!" Ada warned. "We've already spent $6,180,000, including the buyer's premium, and we have twenty-one cars to go!"

"Hey, Ada."

"Yes, Andy."

"Eben Cruise is having a ball."

"Yeah?"

"Andrew P. Robinson III? He's scared shitless!"

After loading the Testa Rossa, I returned to my seat and buried myself in the sales projections. Twenty-one cars left with $11 million in the "kitty." That's $524,000 per car. Of course, that was only an average, and what mattered most was the cumulative total. I had no idea what the Hispano Suiza would bring, and I feared our estimate was far too low. I felt like Wild Bill Hickok holding a dead man's hand. *Everything,* and I mean *everything,* depended on Salone purchasing the Silver Arrow. I prayed his bloodthirsty greed would appear at just the right moment.

"Talk to you later, Ada. Something's happening here."

Several auction participants suddenly stood and ran toward the entrance. Salone's four hooligans created a lane near the entrance of the auction tent. The unmistakable deep-throated rumble of a supercharged Lycoming engine sounded like no other car in the world. I stood on my toes and stretched my neck to see above the throng of impassioned collectors gawking over the car. Duesenberg SJ Emmanuel, the king's car, Fred and Augie's final iteration, had just appeared at the entrance. Even at idle, the whine of the super-charged engine defied hyperbole. It was raw power, brute force, and a gentle whisper, all rolled into one exhilarating sound. *Will it be sold?* I wondered. *Impossible! Salone would never sell this car! He just wants to mark his territory, that's all.* Nevertheless, the car Ada and I were going to travel the world to locate was now sitting twenty feet away from me. It was exhilarating!

Carlisle stepped aside. Miles Noble himself came to the podium.

"After thirty years of conducting classic car auctions all over the world, I've been privileged to observe unsurpassed automotive great-ness. I must say King Victor's Duesenberg is beyond great! Collectors have searched tirelessly for this car since the end of World War II. But for the first time ever, courtesy of Mr. Salvatore Salone, it is on display here at the world-famous Noble-Dean Pergusa auction. For enthusiasts, this discovery is the classic car equivalent of locating the Santa Maria! The blue ribbon on the windshield says Best of Show. I submit to you, ladies and gentlemen, that it is the Best in the World! Thank you, Mr. Salone, for displaying your treasured automobile for us!"

Once everyone settled down, the auction resumed. Our team of bidders managed to buy the next twenty cars on the list. Bugattis, Aston Martins, Ferraris, and Jaguars were all now owned by the new world-famous collector, Eben Cruise. I purchased Ada's favorite, the 1930 Blower Bentley, which threatened to obliterate my estimates for $1.8 million. The bottom line? I had three million remaining and still had to purchase the Hispano Suiza Torpedo. I went to the bar for extra courage. I felt another tap on my shoulder. It was Ada.

"Thought you might need some moral support, so I came over a little early. I delivered the peppers, capers, and anchovies over to Greg too."

"That's good. One car is left before the Arrow. That's the Hispano."

"Tommie and Sammy are on their way over."

"Have you heard anything from Francesco?" I asked.

"If the carabinieri do their job, Francesco will be safe," she said.

"I'm still worried about him."

"He'll be fine."

I placed my arm under hers and gently pulled her away from the bar. "Salone is over there seated next to Riter. Do you see them?"

"Yes, I saw them when I came in."

"Are you prepared?"

"Yes, everything is taken care of. Don't worry. Listen Andy, we have about an hour before the Hispano comes up. I'm going back to The Big Red to help out."

"Go ahead. Be back in less than an hour, so I can have your 'moral' support with the Hispano bidding."

"Oh, another thing . . ." She looked at me with a calm reassurance. "I'm very, very proud of you."

"Thank you, Sweetheart. That means a lot right now. Let's just hope we can pull this thing off. Right now, I'd gladly trade in *carpe diem* for a La-Z-Boy and a hot wood fire!"

"Funny," she said with a broad smile, "I would too, Andy, I would too."

I prepared for the Hispano Suiza. After the Hispano, the Silver Arrow, the star of the auction, would be at bat. *How great it would be to recover all the money I spent that I didn't have.* We only had three million left. Our spending spree consumed $14 million!

It suddenly occurred to me, Salone hadn't bid on anything for the entire auction. Of course, one never could tell for sure with all the secret body language going on between him and Carlisle. Apparently, his need to raise cash superseded his need for more cars. Still, I believed the Silver Arrow would be his Armageddon. He had to have it.

Carlisle read from a prepared text: "The 1924 Hispano Suiza H6C Tulip Wood Torpedo, also known as the French Woodie, was commissioned to be built and was raced by Andre Dubonnet. It has a frame of wooden ribs covered with a wooden veneer. Strips of mahogany or 'tulipwood' were fastened to the veneer with thousands of brass rivets. The body was then sealed, sanded, and varnished. The Torpedo tail enclosed a 46-gallon gas tank for long distance racing. Ladies and gentleman . . . now I ask you . . . have you ever in your entire lives seen anything more beautiful?"

Carlisle asked a great question. The car *was* exquisite. It seemed to change colors. From one angle, it had a reddish burgundy look, from another, a blondish appearance. The crowd was mesmerized into a frozen stare, anesthetized by the automotive art they were observing. I knew I was in trouble.

"Do I hear "$10,000,000?" Carlisle was pushing it to the limit.

The French Woodie is still going to blow the lid off, I thought. However, the bidding was somewhat sluggish and stalled at $2,000,000.

"Do I hear $2,500,000?" I placed my hands in the halving position.

"Thank you, Mr. Cruise, for your $2,250,000 bid."

I still had room. Another bid came in immediately after mine.

"$2,500,000!" Carlisle bellowed.

My mind churned like an atomic calculator. He waited for any kind of reaction from the crowd.

"Okay, now, may I have a bid of $2,750,000? Thank you, Mr. Thomas."

"Now, I absolutely must have $3,000,000!" Carlisle waited patiently. "How about $2,830,000? Okay, no takers?" He waited a few seconds. "Well then, $2,750,000 going once . . . "

"$2,830,000," I yelled. I could feel the strain in my vocal cords.

"This one's gonna be a struggle!" Carlisle said. "One last time for $3,000,000?"

Carlisle waited and again looked at Salone. I could see him touch his yellow baseball cap. I had a deal.

"Sold to Mr. Cruise!" Carlisle's wooden gavel came crashing down on the podium.

I did it! I couldn't believe it! But, where was Ada? She left more than an hour ago. . . .

TWENTY-THREE

Overwhelming and Decisive Force

"Ladies and gentlemen! Now, for the most renowned classic race-car known to mankind! Our headliner, the vehicle already immortalized by racing legends all over the world, the original Mercedes Benz Silver Arrow!"

When he said "original," I felt a twinge of anxiety but made sure to project a confident air. Carlisle waited for the audience to quiet down.

"Noble-Dean is honored to offer this incredible vintage racecar at our auction. It is the best of the best, ladies and gentlemen! This is a momentous occasion for all of us at Noble-Dean!

I would like to summarize the description taken from the Mercedes Benz company archives: *The front wheels were steered by double wishbones with helical springs, as in the celebrated 500 K and 540 K production models. The wheels at the rear were mounted on a De-Dion double-jointed drive shaft providing constant camber adjustment, with longitudinal torsion bar springs and hydraulic lever-type shock absorbers. Shear and braking torque was transferred to the chassis by lateral links.*

The first outing of the Silver Arrow was not in Europe, but in the vitally important Gran Premio di Tripoli. Up until 1939, the race was

263

part of Italian leader Mussolini's dream of recreating the glory of the Roman Empire. After it had won its initial race in Tripoli, the Silver Arrow wrote its way into the record books, winning the Grand Prix of Switzerland (Bremgarten), Grand Prix of Monaco, and Grand Prix of Italy (Livorno), with Silver Arrow drivers finishing first, second, third, and fourth in the European title."

Of course, his glowing commentary was actually for the original Silver Arrow and not my copy. I had to keep reminding myself of that fact.

"Ladies and gentlemen, this is the main event, the coup de grace, the fait accompli. . . ."

Or the final deathblow, I thought. I stood up scanning the crowd for Ada. When I didn't see her, I became more nervous.

"Mr. Cruise, shall we start the bidding at $25,000,000?" Carlisle perused the crowd for a bid. I sat back down. "Okay, no takers? Let's try $20,000,000? My friends, no matter where we start the bidding, we all know where we're going to end up, so someone please bid and save us all the trouble! Mr. Ward sir, this car belongs in your collection! Oh, c'mon now, Mr. Ward. Only $3,000,000? Okay, I'll accept it! I have another bid at $3,500,000 from my good friend, Marc, the distinguished gentleman and renowned collector from Charlotte, North Carolina."

Then disaster struck. Salone was leaving! He disappeared behind the red curtain that separated the stage from a lounge area. I started to breathe hard. *Stay focused!* I kept saying to myself. *Stay focused!*

"We have $4,000,000!" Carlisle said. "This might be a good time to plug Mr. Riter's new Classic Car Investment Trust! Now you can become part owner of one hundred fifty of the most spectacular classic cars in the world! See Mr. Riter after the auction if you are interested or better yet, just write him a check!"

What a crock! Now Riter was bidding for Salone to divert attention!

"I have a $5,000,000 bid from Mr. Kelly. C'mon Mr. Riter! It's your call at $6,000,000. What's a million dollars between friends anyway?"

The bidding quickly soared beyond $15,000,000.

"Mr. Riter, do I have your last bid? No hurry. I'm a patient man—it's okay!" I walked near the stage where one of the bidding assistants, or ringleaders, as they are known in auction parlance, could see me. Their job is to find bids in the crowd. I motioned with the cutthroat sign by sliding my flat palm horizontally across my throat. It meant "Drop the reserve now!"

Carlisle read my signal even before the ringleader. "The reserve is off! The reserve is off! The owner just lifted the reserve! The Silver Arrow will sell today! Time to talk turkey everyone! Yes, Mr. Ward, I will gladly accept your $16,000,000."

The bidding continued up to $25,000,000 but then stopped cold. I studied the list and added the numbers. At first, I thought something was wrong. My God! We were up eight million!

Carlisle's eyes moved slowly from left to right like those of a well-trained Labrador retriever marking its prey. His gavel was frozen high in the air.

"Fair warning!" he said.

Again, he waited a few seconds, trying to coax one more bid from a reluctant crowd. Then his gavel plunged to the podium.

"Sold for $25,000,000 to Mr. Maxwell Riter!" Holy shit! I was beyond astonished. After all was said and done, would we really walk away with an eight-million-dollar profit? Was this possible? God! Salone just bought a $50,000 replica for $25,000,000, and he has his good friend Maxwell Riter to thank! That ought to do wonders for that relationship! I was delirious with joy!

Tazio leaped from the car, ran over, and began hugging me like I was one of his Italian "loafers."

"Mr. Punt! You did it!" He hollered, lifting me in the air.

"Tazio, *stai zitto*!" I placed my index finger on my lips. "I'm Eben Cruise, remember?"

"*Si.* Now Eben Cruise owns the most valuable car collection in the world!"

"*Tazio!* Never show your hand," I said quietly. "Or I should say Eben Cruise's hand.

"Mr. Cruise, you are amazing!" he said. "We make Zazas tonight and celebrate!"

"I'll buy the pistachio nuts!" I joked.

"Well, everyone," Carlisle said, "thank you for your participation in another . . . wait a minute! Wait a minute! I was just handed a note. We're not finished yet, ladies and gentlemen! Excuse me while I compose myself! I don't believe what I just read. No, there must be a mistake!"

An auction official motioned to Tazio. I watched in amazement as Tazio got into the driver's seat of the Duesenberg SJ Emmanuel.

"What the hell are you doing?" I asked.

"They just tell me this minute to drive it up."

"It's going through the auction? Can't be! Impossible!"

"Mr. Cruise! Now you have to buy it!"

"Buy it with what? My good looks?" I asked.

"Then you be in big a trouble!" Tazio snickered.

Although Tazio was laughing almost too hard to drive the Emmanuel onto the stage, he finally managed to get the mighty power plant to roar to life. Then he drove very slowly toward the auction stage. Driving the Emmanuel up the ramp was a challenge. The car simply did not want to go there. He finally gunned the engine, lifted the clutch, and the Emmanuel labored, the engine showing signs of being overworked. With the clutch slipping, the pungent smell of burnt rubber permeated the auction complex. Tazio eventually parked it in the middle of the stage; however, a large cloud of black exhaust smoke congested the immediate area. Carlisle placed a handkerchief over his nose and mouth to avoid ingesting the fumes. My guess is that the fumes were from stale gas, a common occurrence when cars are not driven for years at a time. Many participants ducked out, unable to bear the acerbic combination of odors.

Salone emerged from behind the red curtain and whispered something to Carlisle, who was still holding the handkerchief near his mouth.

"Mr. Salone tells me he will contribute the proceeds from the sale of his Duesenberg Emmanuel to Hospice Comunita di Catania. I'm sure they could use it to make their patients comfortable. Thank you, Mr. Salone!"

The crowd applauded wildly. Like one of mankind's illustrious heroes, Salone walked to center stage and bowed several times, then disappeared again behind the red curtain. The whole thing made me sick to my stomach.

It had to be some kind of tax dodge, I surmised. *He must think he needs one to offset his 100 percent profit on the Villa Christina cars. Wait until he discovers how much he lost on the Silver Arrow! The last thing he'll need is a tax deduction!* I smiled. It was a pleasant thought. On the other hand, my cost was $50,000 and Salone purchased it for $25,000,000! *Looks like Eben Cruise is the one who will need the huge tax deduction!* I stopped smiling.

Back to business. I had $8 million remaining. I'd never be able to buy the Emmanuel for anywhere near that number. Nevertheless, there were three new circumstances in my favor: First, people had been leaving; second, the Emmanuel showed signs of sickness going on the stage; and third, it was an unscheduled auction car. I had to try. Just bidding on it would be a memorable experience. Carlisle's long-winded oratory about the virtues of the Emmanuel gave me time to run to the bar and get a full glass of Chivas on the rocks.

I tried to prepare myself for what no car collector in the world had ever experienced. The range of emotions I was feeling was impossible to describe. I told myself, *just make believe it was the Green Latrine, that old '49 Ford I won from a guy named Torpedo Fidanza in a game of 8-Ball.* It didn't work. I was still awed by the overwhelming significance of the moment.

The neon lights cast a warm glow on the Emmanuel's beautiful exterior, making the car look even more streamlined and dynamic than it already was. The remaining crowd was silent, mesmerized by the spectacle unfolding before them. Several potential bidders rushed onto the stage to take a closer look at the car. Salone and Riter reappeared from behind the curtain to a private corner.

There was my bride! Just as we planned it! Ada was disguised as a ravishing golden-haired woman, dressed to the nines with her skirt five inches above her knees and her blouse tied five inches above her waist. As she flirted with them, Salone and his entourage wolfed down several pieces of The Big Red puttanesca pizza she had served on a tray. It was 5:30 p.m., and the most significant car of the century was about to be auctioned, yet my wife was engaged in a task much more important than mine. As Carlisle continued to describe the Duesenberg, Sammy came over to me.

"We're all set, Mr. Robinson. I delivered four trays of puttanesca pizzas to Mr. Salone and his men."

"I know. Thanks, Sammy! You did well!"

"I just did what you and Mrs. Robinson asked."

"Okay. Okay. Now better get over to the other side of the tent and get ready!"

"I'll get over there right away, Mr. Robinson."

"I want to remind everyone that this car is being sold at no reserve!" Carlisle said. "No reserve for the most beautiful car in the world! I have $2,000,000 from Mr. Thomas. Thank you, sir! And now $2,500,000 from you sir, right here in the front row! Now, $3,500,000?" The crowd buzzed and suddenly the bidding came to an abrupt halt. "C'mon now! Where's all the money gone, everyone?" For the first time all day, Carlisle was at a loss for words.

It finally occurred to me. What bidders remained were out of money! They had expended their funds on other cars they had earmarked for purchase. No money was left for Emmanuel!

"Ladies and gentlemen! You are about to witness the buy of the century! Can someone PLEASE give me at least $3,000,000 for this spectacular car?" Carlisle pleaded desperately.

I stretched my arm to the sky. "Yes!" I shouted.

Carlisle examined the audience with his experienced eye. While he understood there was great interest in the Duesenberg, the lack of bidders was discouraging. He realized many bidders had left so he went right to the close.

"Going once . . . going twice . . . last chance!" Carlisle looked over at Salone. He and Riter were still standing near the curtain. Salone shook his head, a no sale signal to Carlisle. The crowd witnessed the headshake, became infuriated, and erupted into a roar.

"Salone!" someone cried out. "You have to sell! It's at no reserve! Sell the car!"

Ada dropped the pizza tray, ran up to the stage, and complained vehemently to the three auction officials seated behind Carlisle. The person seated in the middle was Edward Dean, the other owner of the Noble-Dean Auction Company. Miles Noble was milling quickly through the crowd trying to settle them down.

"Mr. Dean, sir!" Ada said. "My husband is Judge Andrew P. Robinson II. I am sure you realize he is a well-known Supreme

Court Justice from the United States. I want you to know, sir, he will initiate the largest lawsuit this auction house has ever seen if this car is not sold. In fact, he will pursue treble damages, which I am sure will be a knockout punch for the most famous classic car auction house in the world!

"You have a tent full of disgruntled collectors who have witnessed the shenanigans between your auctioneer and Mr. Salone all day long. Make your decision! Will you be selling the Duesenberg to Mr. Cruise, or would you rather face the largest lawsuit for fraud ever presented to an auction company?"

Ada was magnificent! She was right, too. Once the word got out regarding Noble-Dean's price manipulations, collectors would think twice about consigning cars with them. Hundreds of eyes stared silently at the conversation taking place on stage. Ada's stated threat meant the survival of the auction company hung in the balance, and Edward Dean knew it!

Mr. Dean looked over at me. "Do you have anything to say, Mr. Cruise?"

"Only that Mrs. Robinson is absolutely correct!" I answered.

Dean called Carlisle and Salone over to the table.

"What the hell is the problem here?" Salone asked. His rude, condescending attitude sent a negative message to the auction officials.

Dean looked at his paperwork.

"You had a no reserve request on this car. Isn't that correct, Mr. Salone?"

"I had a $30,000,000 reserve. Your auctioneer screwed up!"

"Mr. Salone," Carlisle said. "You never requested a reserve. You were very emphatic about a no reserve sale on the Duesenberg. Mr. Dean, I clearly remember our conversation."

I was proud of Carlisle for not taking the fall for Salone.

"Mr. Carlisle, will you testify to that?" Ada asked as if she were a trial lawyer.

Carlisle looked at Dean timidly.

"Answer her question!" Dean ordered.

"Yes," he said.

"Then *sell* the car to Mr. Cruise!" Dean demanded.

Carlisle walked sheepishly back to the podium. At first he stood frozen like an underling trying to collect himself after an embarrassing encounter with the boss. He picked up the gavel, raising it high up in the air. Venting his frustration, he plunged it onto the podium breaking it into two pieces.

"Sold! Sold! Sold! For the bargain-basement price of $3,000,000! Congratulations, Mr. Cruise, sir! Congratulations, indeed!"

The audience applauded, whistled, and yelled, "Bravo, Mr. Cruise, Bravo!" From the other side of the stage, Salone and Riter began walking toward Ada and me. We braced ourselves. *This would not be good.* I stood erect next to her.

Before they reached us, Salone collapsed to his knees. As we walked toward him, Riter fell against a table and doubled over in pain. Both were clutching their stomachs and moaning, falling to the floor in agony.

I shouted to Tazio. "Get this car into a Genaro trailer NOW! Stay with it! We'll meet you in about fifteen minutes!"

Suddenly, Tommie and Sammy, dressed as medics, were hovering over them. As they attempted to prop them up on their feet, Tommie said, "You fellas are in dire need of medical attention! Let us help you to the first aid trailer!"

Tazio's trailer was parked near the auction tent door. It had been painted white and orange just like an Automedica van. It was outfitted with beds and had all the appropriate medical equipment, including an I/V stand with a package of intravenous medication in the harness. Tommie and Sammy helped Salone and Riter shuffle to the van. Both were in agony and on the verge of panicking.

"Hurry," Tommie said. "We need to get some antibiotics into you fast." Salone's four thugs were on their hands and knees ready to regurgitate. A couple of bystanders helped them up and walked the four men into the Automedica van. We positioned Salone on one of the gurneys inside the trailer; the others we propped against the opposite wall. They were still semiconscious, exactly how Ada described they would be.

"Sammy, put Riter in the back seat of the F150," I said quietly. Tie their hands and feet then confiscate their weapons and place them in the glove compartment inside the truck."

Ada handed Sammy nylon cable ties from her pocket, and then injected Riter with sodium pentothal, saying, "This should keep him on ice until later when he needs to contact his banker and a pay for that beautiful new race car he just purchased."

Waiting there in the darkness with Ada, I could barely see the blue Star of Life emblem affixed to the inside wall. It still reminded me of a crucifix. That's when I saw the black chair against the rear wall of the trailer. The figure sat straight and tall. His outstretched arms rested on the long armrests. His head tilted downward. His face radiated a look of supreme confidence. Francesco was now judge, jury, and executioner.

"Francesco, come over here," I said. "I'll let you do the honors."

Francesco struggled to stand, yet managed to tighten the ties on Salone's wrists so tight he winced. We stood over Salone, staring down at him. His eyes slowly opened, although he remained totally disoriented.

"Hello, Mr. Salone!" Francesco said.

Ada pulled up a small three-wheeled stool so Francesco could be seated.

"Your friends and I—we wanted to wish you Godspeed before we hauled you off to Asinara on the beautiful island of Sardinia. They tell me the food is lousy, but the capers are pretty good, especially the big fat ones like Mrs. Robinson served you."

Ada had removed her wig and wiped off her makeup with a wet cloth. Now, she held up a poison caper the size of an olive.

"We heard you loved puttanesca pizza," Ada said. Salone's eyes opened wider. "We spiced it up with some extra 'flavoring' just for you." Salone was motionless on the gurney, not allowing us the luxury of a reaction. His face was frozen in a disbelieving stare; his knuckles had turned white.

"When you screwed with the Robinson family, you screwed with the wrong people!" I said triumphantly.

We gagged everyone with duct tape and moved them to the center of the floor, securing them with ratchets and tie down straps used to transport cars. Leaving through the rear door, I'll never forget that image of Salone squirming, trying to break free. All five of them crowded together reminded me of a bundle of rubbish placed on the front curb for pickup. I must admit; it was one of the most satisfying sights I had ever seen. We heaved the trailer door upward and slammed down the crossbars. Then we affixed special hockey-puck style padlocks to all three latches. They were tamper and bulletproof. Escape was impossible.

"Hey," Ada said. "Isn't it interesting how an innocent little caper can create such *overwhelming and decisive force?*"

I forced a slight smile. Ada, just remember, we're not out of the woods yet. Riter still has to pay for the Silver Arrow. Any ideas on how to accomplish that?

"Fear works wonders," she said with a straight face. I know you will handle it well, Andy."

TWENTY-FOUR

Crossing
the Tyrrhenian

When we arrived at the west end parking lot, the Duesenberg SJ Emmanuel and the sixteen Villa Christina cars we purchased were already safely secured inside the Genaro World Wide Transport trailers. They would be taken, under armed guard, to Villa Christina this evening. The seven other cars would be delivered to the Palermo Ferry Port, a two-hour drive from Pergusa, and then ferried to the Automobile Terminal at the Port of Naples where they would be shipped back to their owners.

The plan was for Tazio, Sammy, and Tommie to return to the villa with the Villa Christina cars. Ada, Francesco, and I would accompany the on-loan cars in the Genaro trailers to Palermo and then to Naples to arrange shipment. Francesco would turn Salone and his accomplices over to the Naples authorities, who were said to be considerably less corrupted than their Sicilian counterparts. We would leave Palermo at 11:30 p.m. and arrive in Naples the next morning at 10:30 a.m.

Francesco's close friend Primo Genaro, a muscular man over six feet tall with bushy blond hair, was the Genaro World Wide Transport company owner and lead driver. He had a no-nonsense demeanor, leaving no doubt who was in command of the operation. It was also quite obvious how loyal he was to Francesco.

Ada produced the receipt vouchers and gave them to Primo. Auction security people at the exit gate needed to see them to grant the trucks permission to leave. They were also necessary to secure bills of lading at the Palermo Ferry Port. Primo provided us with clear directions to the Via Francesco Crispi in Palermo, the location of the ferry port.

"Primo, we'll meet you at the ferry port at 10:00 p.m.," I said. "In the meantime, you can complete all the paperwork and begin loading the cars on ferry."

"*Perfetto!*" Primo said. "Let's roll!" He jumped up into his cab, and within minutes, the trucks disappeared from the parking lot. One vehicle was remaining.

"Tazio, can you drive that thing?" I asked, pointing to Salone's Prevost Motor coach parked on the grass.

"Mr. Punt, you disappoint me! I thought you knew by now. There's nothing Tazio can't drive!"

"Great! You, Tommie, and Sammy can drive it back to Villa Christina this evening. Tomorrow, deliver it to Hospice Comunita di Catania. Like Carlisle said, 'I'm sure they could use it to make their patients comfortable.'"

"*Si!* You're a good a man, Mr. Punt!"

"You are too, Mr. Tazio. Stay away from those pistachios tonight!"

"No more nuts for me! I just a might down a couple of Negronis though!"

"You earned them! Have one on me, my good friend!"

"Sammy!" I said, as we shook hands. "This is one story your friends back at Johns Hopkins won't believe."

"Yeah, I'm not even sure I believe it, and I was here!"

When Ada and I embraced Tommie, she had tears in her eyes.

"We've come a long way since our day together on the patio when I asked you to locate King Victor's Duesenberg," she said. "You made the impossible happen!"

"Now King Victor's Duesenberg is a permanent part of the Villa Christina collection," Ada said, "the best classic car collection in the world! We'll all celebrate tomorrow night. Have the Negronis and the Zazas ready!"

"Godspeed, Capitano Cruise!" Tazio laughed.

When I got behind the wheel of Tazio's Ford F150, Francesco had his head back against the headrest with his eyes closed. We were all emotionally drained from the intense mental strain of the day. Despite all the stress, Francesco looked content, but Ada was anxious, and I wanted to the get the whole thing over with so we could get back to Fairchester. We'd had enough carpe diem for a lifetime. Still, I had a number of questions for Ada that were tormenting me. Not surprisingly, she had everything all figured out.

"Ada," I asked, "how the hell did you orchestrate our departure from the auction without paying for the cars?"

"I played the Supreme Court Justice card for a few more hands. Mr. Dean turned out to be very accommodating. I made arrangements with him to pay for the Silver Arrow and the Duesenberg SJ Emmanuel within the next twenty-four hours. We now have to 'persuade' Riter to cooperate and wire the money for the Silver Arrow. We need the proceeds to cover the cost of Emmanuel. What's left over can go to the Italian Trade Commission in order to reignite the classic car project."

"What about all the Villa Christina cars? Did our strategy work?"

"Sure did. Once I convinced Mr. Dean the cars were stolen property, and that he committed twenty-three felonies by trying to auction them, we negotiated. I agreed to pay the buyer's premiums on all the cars we purchased if he agreed to give us one week to prove Salone had stolen the cars from Villa Christina. Once Tommie provides the titles from the owners and the trade commission, the fact they were stolen property would be easily proven.

Mr. Dean realized I was negotiating on behalf of a famous United States Supreme Court Justice. He had no trouble complying with my requests. He was also more than willing to provide me with receipt vouchers for all the cars so we could remove them from the grounds."

"Brilliant! So glad my father came through for us!" We both chuckled. "Actually, I do wish he could have been here to witness the execution of our masterful plan. So, Ada, if we're successful getting the $25,000,000 wired, we only have to pay for auction fees on the Villa Christina cars and also pay the $3,000,000 for the Duesenberg SJ Emmanuel. Not at all a bad outcome!"

"That comes out to about $4,000,000," said Ada. "The rest of the money can be used by Tommie to continue to build the Villa Christina collection."

"What about my Silver Arrow replica?"

"It officially now belongs to Salone, so I am sure ESCO will confiscate it along with the rest of his property."

"How 'bout the fifty grand I paid for it?"

"We'll see."

"I hate 'we'll see!'"

☆   ☆   ☆

We arrived at the ferry port in time to watch the jaws of the Principe di Napoli ferry swallow up tractor-trailers, trucks, buses, and cars as if they were Tonka Toys. It was a RORO ferry, one that only rolls its cargo on and off. The ramps were located at the stern. The vessel had a legal capacity of 300 people. It had sleeping quarters, a restaurant with a dance floor, and a band. The entire bottom floor was dedicated to rolling cargo. Primo was directing his trailers onto the ferry ramp as if he had done it a thousand times before.

"Only two more," Primo said. "Then we can drive the pickup and trailer on."

"Francesco," I said. "You've been rather quiet for most of the trip."

"I'm very happy, but very worried, too," he said. "I hope and pray there are enough teeth in ESCO to end this thing once and for all. You don't know, we still have to close down Salone's illegitimate businesses. He's into it all: prostitution, extortion, loan sharking, drugs, and the sale of arms. We believed if his counterfeiting activities couldn't be stopped, it would send Italy's economy into an inflationary spiral that would have international monetary consequences. Additionally, he's funding the Red Brigade in order to overthrow the Italian government. Not only has he been wreaking havoc in Italy, but his criminal activities have also had worldwide consequences. He has to be stopped!"

Once I positioned the pickup and trailer on the stern deck of the ferry, Primo blocked the wheels with heavy-duty yellow wheel chocks. Maxwell Riter was beginning to stir in the back seat. I pulled the blanket off of him.

"Ah . . ." he moaned. "Where . . . where the hell am I?" His eyes were bloodshot, swollen, and barely open. His neat George Hamilton coiffure was completely disheveled. After Ada removed the duct tape, he tried to speak but could only mumble a few incoherent words.

"Let's get him into the sleeper cabin while he's still disoriented," Ada said. Tommie had reserved cabins for Francesco, Ada and me, and one for Riter.

Riter was unsteady and appeared inebriated. "It's the sodium pentothal. It usually takes about seven hours to wear off," she said. "It'll keep him quiet until we can have him transfer some money to pay for his latest acquisition."

After we duck walked him to his assigned sleeper cabin, we placed him on the bed, securing him to the bedposts with more nylon ties from Ada's pocket. I knew she was organized, but for the last two days, she had been operating like a finely tuned Swiss watch, and I was proud of her.

"These ties were used to prevent 'hamburger hands,'" she said. "When my father worked with wires and looped them over his fingers to knot them, he would come home with cut and scarred hands. Someone figured out a better way. There's always a better way for most everything."

"Speaking of hamburgers, I could go for one right now. How about you?"

"Let's get Francesco and find the restaurant."

The Principe di Napoli left the Palermo harbor at midnight. Libertino's, a short-order restaurant, or Bert's as the English-speaking passengers called it, was open all night. We found Francesco on the top deck, gazing out at the sea. During dinner, he seemed preoccupied and lost in his thoughts.

"Please excuse me," he said. "If I don't get some sleep, I'm going to topple right over in my chair."

"Can we help you to your cabin?" Ada asked.

"I can take the elevator, thanks. If possible, you two relax. I'll see you in the morning. Goodnight."

"Goodnight, Francesco," Ada said. Her eyes filled with tears. "Your involvement today was very helpful. You do realize that, don't you?"

"I thought I'd feel more satisfaction than I do. I'm going to bed."

"Funny thing about revenge. Goodnight, Francesco," Ada said.

We both helped him from the booth to his wheelchair. He was unsteady and weary, but smiled gratefully.

"Are you going home *now*?" Francesco taunted.

"Yes," I said smiling. "We will be going home now."

Francesco wheeled his way toward the elevators.

Ada and I shared a bottle of Chianti Classico and the remnants of two greasy hamburgers neither one of us had much desire to finish.

"So, Ada, tell me, what emotions are your feeling right now?"

"Besides being numb, I would have to say, fear. Fear that, once we arrive in Naples, all our efforts will have been in vain. It all depends on whether or not the Naples authorities are clean. This whole thing could backfire with disastrous consequences. What we did seems unreal, like a dream." A long awkward silence ensued. "Let's go for a walk," she finally said.

"It's two in the morning. Shouldn't we get some sleep?"

"I'm too uptight. No way am I going to sleep right now."

We left Bert's and found the elevator. Ada stood close to me. It stopped at the second floor, the door opening onto a narrow platform with railings. The many vehicles on the floor below were crammed tightly together. As soon as we set foot on the platform, Ada hastened her pace toward the stern. She was completely distracted and uninterested in conversation. The railing curved inward as we reached the stern. Tazio's F150 pickup truck and trailer sat in the middle of the last row of vehicles with the trailer facing the stern. Aside from a four-foot-high sliding iron gate, the stern was open to the Tyrrhenian Sea, the body of water separating Sicily from Italy's mainland. It was a wonderful moonlit night. The few clouds were illuminated by the moon's bright glow. A soft breeze chilled the inside of the ferry. I removed my coat and covered Ada.

"It's a blue moon," she said. "The sky is so bright we can see Etna. I read that a blue moon is an optical illusion and the color blue is not what it appears to be. So many things are not what they appear to be."

"Not bad for a history major," I said. "The word 'blue' comes from the Old English word *belewe* meaning a betrayal."

"That's how I feel right now," she said, "like the authorities will betray us and release Salone. He *must* be indicted, tried, and convicted! That's a lot to ask of the Italian judicial system. The system is extremely flawed. You heard what Tazio said, didn't you? About the Corte d'Assise? It's a joke! I did some research on it, too. Only serious murder crimes are tried by the Corte d'Assise. You can be sure Salone's people will terrorize the six laypersons and their families. They'll be scared to death and will *never* prosecute him! I can only imagine what will happen after he's released—to you, me, our families, not to mention all his future victims."

"What about ESCO?"

"I'm sorry. It's nothing more than a masquerade. It's *La Bella Figura*! It's all about looking good. *It's not what it appears to be.*"

Ada moved uneasily back and forth along the railing. Her face revealed all the signs of the heartache she had endured in her childhood. I felt a powerful desire to somehow rid her of her dark memories.

"They never caught the killers who murdered my father. They probably killed hundreds of people afterward and were never prosecuted! That can't happen again, Andy!"

"Ada, it's late. We can discuss this in the morning."

"Let's detach the trailer! It's only a few feet from the end of the ramp. Then it will be all over. No judges. No mistrials. No one gets hurt anymore!" She grabbed my shoulders. With fire in her eyes, she pleaded, "We have to do this!" She ran down the stairway.

Running after her, I shouted, "No, Ada! Stop!" I knew once Ada made up her mind, changing it was next to hopeless.

"Andy! This is perfect! No one's around! C'mon! Slide open the gate at the end of ramp! Help me!" I stood frozen. "Andy!" she screamed again. "Flip the latch holding the trailer to the truck!" She opened the ramp gate. At that moment, my mind was incapable of knowing right from wrong. I couldn't allow Ada to act alone. If she was going down, I would go down with her.

"Move out of way!" I yelled, and then spun the lever to lift the trailer off of the hitch. We could hear groaning from inside the trailer. The mere sound of voices increased our motivation. We pushed. It didn't move.

"The chocks, Ada. Kick the chocks out from under the tires!" She turned and looked at me then slammed her hand on the side of the trailer.

"I can't! I just can't do it!" ripped out of her mouth, as she buried her face in her hands, forcing her to keep her emotions under control.

I ran over to her and placed my arms around her. Her body was shaking uncontrollably.

"It's all right, Ada. Let it go, Sweetheart."

The frustrations and rage she had kept inside her for years finally erupted. She wept releasing a sea of tears. I held her close to me as the moon waned, and she moved her arms around my shoulders and drew me in. She needed me, and it felt so good to be needed by her.

"I want to go home," she said.

I closed the gate and reattached the trailer hitch to the truck. We walked up the stairs and then down the narrow platform to the elevator bank. When we arrived at our sleeper cabin, she was still shaking.

"I'm sorry. I'm just overwhelmed."

After I locked the door, she placed her arms around me and looked deeply into my eyes. Then I kissed her very softly and placed my arms around her waist.

She whispered in my ear, "hurry back."

"Where am I going?"

"Next door. It's about three in the afternoon in the United States. The banks are still open and you need to have our friend Maxwell make that bank transfer!"

"Oh, I almost forgot," I said.

I was up early the following morning, quietly leaving the cabin, allowing Ada to catch up on her sleep. I also wanted some time alone to clear my brain. We'd be arriving in Naples in four hours. I sipped coffee at Bert's and listened to the morning news on the radio. There was a piece about the Pergusa auction. It highlighted Salone's sale of the Duesenberg SJ Emmanuel to Eben Cruise, "a newcomer to the auction scene. He couldn't be reached for comment."

"Good morning," came a voice from across the table.

"Did you sleep well?"

"No," Ada said. "I need to get far away from all this."

"Are you having breakfast?" I asked.

"I'm so out of sorts," she replied. "I just don't think I could keep food down."

"Good morning, Andy and Ada!" Francesco's funk had disappeared as he wheeled in right next to us. "Did you get some rest, Ada?" he asked.

"Not really. It's been difficult."

"I know and I'm sorry," he said. "It will all be over soon. I'm going to the observation deck to get some fresh air." Francesco turned his chair and left.

"What happened with Riter?" Ada asked me.

"He did make the bank wire transfer at around four in the morning. He complained bitterly that he was supposed to be reimbursed by Salone. I told him the two of them could work it out later."

"How did you convince him?" Ada asked.

"Oh, just my powerful persuasive skills," I replied. "You really don't want to know, do you? Riter paid for the Silver Arrow. That's all that matters. I can tell you, the fear of incarceration for life is a powerful motivator."

"I think I'll have some bacon and eggs!" Ada said, with the beginning of what appeared to be a smile. "So, really. What *did* you do with Riter?"

"Oh, he's visiting his business associate in the trailer. They're working things out."

"You know, Ada said, I think I'll have some nice Italian sausage, too!"

We both were considerably more relaxed than the night before.

"*Fatigue makes cowards of us all,*" I said, calling to mind my mother's familiar refrain. "We were really whipped last night, weren't we?"

Ada ignored my question. She finished her breakfast, dabbed her mouth with a napkin, and looked directly at me with one of her no-nonsense expressions.

"I'd like to go to the trailer again," she said.

"No, Ada. Please. We did the right thing last night. Let's not put ourselves in that position again."

"The right thing really gets in the way sometimes, doesn't it?" As before, I was sure I was not going to dissuade her.

"Promise me we'll stay on the upper level?"

"Yes, I promise."

We walked to the elevator and strolled along the platform to the stern, just like the night before. Two or three workers were cleaning the floor and clearing away the debris around the vehicles. Several passengers had gathered around the platform to watch the vehicles unload once we arrived in Naples.

"Look," she said. "There's an open space in the middle of the row. See it?"

"Yeah, it's the row closest to the exit ramp. They must have moved the trailer."

"There's no way the vehicles could be repositioned," she said. "It's way too congested."

"Look! The yellow wheel chocks! Primo is putting them back in his truck!"

"The trailer! It's gone!"

She looked at me with a suspicious eye. "You didn't . . ."

"No, I didn't, Ada! No way!"

My heart pounded. A parade of every emotion I felt during the last few days was marching by me. I looked at Ada.

"I . . . ah . . . think Salone sleeps with the fishes."

Her hands covered her mouth in disbelief. "Andy! Over there!"

We could only see his shoulders and head above the wheelchair, but it was Francesco. He was staring out at the Tyrrhenian Sea, as if he were relaxing somewhere on a distant beach. He rotated his chair to face us. His arms were stretched out on the long armrests and he sat straight and tall without moving. His head tilted slightly downward in a dignified, almost regal pose. He wasn't smiling, yet a look of quiet satisfaction had replaced the defiance in his eyes.

Something was on his lap. At first I couldn't identify it. He wheeled his chair closer to us and parked right below the platform on which we were standing. Then I had a good look. He was cradling the blue Star of Life ceramic emblem from the Automedica trailer as if it were a trophy he had just won from a hard fought contest. For Francesco, it was his symbol of renewal and healing. It still reminded me of a crucifix.

Epilogue

The supercharged power plant on the Mercedes Silver Arrow is like a blast furnace. I'm on the long back straight at the Watkins Glen racetrack in upstate New York on Labor Day Weekend in 1977. As I hit the inner loop at the end of the straight, the de Dion rear end and the tall tires slip a little, but provide enough traction for me to keep the throttle open. Gradually, the wheel spin dies away, and the car straightens and continues to eat up the road. I feel invincible and immensely quick—maybe too quick.

My high-top Simpson racing shoes with added insulation and heavy socks do nothing to protect my feet from being scorched by the firewall behind the pedals. I can hardly see. Oil smears cover my goggles. From my cramped position in the cockpit, the track looks like one big slab of dirty gray asphalt with no curves or guardrails. I tear off my goggles. *I need to get off of the track and get off fast!* I fight with the outer loop at turn five and slam the brake pedal to the floor. Suddenly, I'm airborne—sailing through space with the greatest of ease—I am the proverbial young man on the flying trapeze. However, my flight ends indelicately as I crash land into the outside guardrail at the far corner of the track. I sit there for several minutes, afraid to get out and assess the damage to my cherished

racecar. A few cars speed by and I wave to acknowledge my unin-
jured status.

Tommie and Francesco had the Silver Arrow delivered to our
Fairchester home a few months after our return from Sicily. Once the
Italian authorities discovered Riter's funds were from illegal activities, the bank transaction to purchase the Silver Arrow was rescinded
and ownership was reverted back to me.

After our one-year leave of absence, Ada and I will return to
our teaching positions at Fairchester High School next week. First, I
must test the racing muscle of the Silver Arrow at the Vintage Races
here at the Glen.

A track ambulance pulls up along side of me. Ada, the first one
out, is running toward me. "Andy! You okay?" she yells, "I thought
you were going to somersault and it scared the hell out of me!"

"Yeah, well, I'm okay," I say despondently, as I pull my vinyl
mini-cooler from under the seat. Finding a straw and a thermos of
Gatorade, I remove the cap, and start sipping. I'm glad it's still cold.
"Ada, how does the car look?"

"The car?" she responds. "You're only worried about the car?"

I drag myself from the tight cockpit and wave off the ambulance. "My knees and back are sore as hell," I complain. "I don't
think anything's broken, though." Ada and I walk around the car.
"I'm surprised. Not as bad as I expected. Where *is* that Tazio when
you need him, anyway?"

She shakes her head with a slight smile. I hand the thermos
of Gatorade to her and she takes a sip. "You just dodged a big
bullet. Next time you may not be this lucky. You've got to slow
down!"

"It's like déjà vu!" I say. "For a moment, I thought I was at the
Autodromo di Pergusa . . . like that bastard Salone boxed me in all
over again."

"This is *all* your doing!" she chastised. "There were no other cars within 200 yards of you! You've got no one to blame but yourself! I clocked you at 140 mph on the back straight! That's way too fast!"

"Ada, this thing's a monster! I think it will do 200!"

"You're gonna kill yourself!" she says, "And don't forget: this car isn't insured when it's on the track!"

"Yeah, I know . . . it's just a replica, remember? It *only* has 600 horses." I can see my nonchalance is beginning to annoy Ada. She takes a big swallow of Gatorade.

"Yeah," she says, "and a $50,000 price tag that we cannot afford to lose right now! Maybe we should ship it back to the Villa Christina Museum so that it can be with the Midnight Ghost and all the other cars that were stolen by our friend, Salone. It'll be safe there. You know, Andy, it's the most famous classic car museum in Europe right now."

"I know, but no way are we shipping it back!" We need something for Andrew P. Robinson IV to drive."

Ada shakes her head and closes her eyes, as I prepare myself for her comeback.

"Did it ever occur to you our child might be a girl?"

"She'll still need some 'wheels,' you know!" I laugh.

"You can get that notion out of your mind right now!" she says with absolute clarity. "She'll never be within ten miles of a racecar, if I have anything to say about it!"

"Someday, girls will be racecar drivers too, Ada! You wait and see!" As I turn my attention to my wounded Silver Arrow, I bend down to check the damage to the left front wheel. Suddenly, I feel a wet substance on the back of neck, entering my race suit, and advancing down my back. "Ooh! Ada! No! Ada!" I leap to my feet and arch my shoulders to endure the jolt of frigid Gatorade rolling down my back and into my underwear. Actually, if it wasn't for the stickiness, it felt rather good.

I look at her with a glint of displeasure that only lasts a few seconds. Her hand covers her mouth to conceal her irrepressible laughter. It is vintage Ada and I love her for it. I realize once again how lucky we are to share our lives together. There weren't too many days that passed after we returned from Sicily that we didn't express our gratitude to each other. Carpe diem now has a whole new meaning in the Robinson household. Instead of "seize the day," we prefer "savor the day."

"Can we check out the car now?" I ask.

We examine the front of Silver Arrow. "Looks like we have a broken tie-rod here." I note. "We'll need some bodywork done too—something to do during the winter months. You can help me."

"No! In three months I won't be able to bend over! That would be a great project for you and your dad after he retires next year."

A tow truck arrives to return our Silver Arrow to the paddock area. "You want a lift," the driver asks.

I hesitate to answer and look at Ada. "Nah," she says. "We'll walk."

Hand in hand, we begin the mile trek back to paddock. We hear the cars downshifting through the loops at the end of the back straight. Then they roar past us like ballistic missiles.

"Do you think we'll ever get back to Taormina?" she asks.

"Probably not until we're 'empty nesters'—if ever," I answer. "We're not going to too many exotic places on our teaching salaries and a houseful of children."

"Houseful?" she queries. "There's still some Gatorade left in the thermos!"

I move my arm around her back and squeeze her waist. "Maybe when we retire."

"Let's make that our goal! What do you think?"

"Duly noted," I smile. "Duly noted."

About the Author

Lifetouch Photography

Roger Corea writes about things, people, and places he is passionate about. His first novel, *Scarback: There Is So Much More to Fishing Than Catching Fish*, published in 2014, tells the story of a critical time in the life of a mentally challenged man from the Italian neighborhood of Roger's youth.

Writing is a natural outgrowth of Roger's formal education. He earned a bachelor's degree in English from St. Bonaventure University and completed graduate work in English literature at the University of Rochester. Before entering the business world to work for a large financial services company, Roger taught English literature at Canandaigua Academy and Penfield High School, where he also served as assistant football coach.

Roger lives with his wife, Mary Ann, in Penfield, New York. They have three children and three grandchildren.